BLOOD
TRANCE

BLOOD TRANCE

R. D. Zimmerman

WILLIAM MORROW AND COMPANY, INC.
New York

It is the policy of William Morrow and Company, Inc., and its imprints and affiliates, recognizing the importance of preserving what has been written, to print the books we publish on acid-free paper, and we exert our best efforts to that end.

ISBN 0-688-12139-X (alk. paper)

Printed in the United States of America

BOOK DESIGN BY NICK MAZZELLA

For Lars

ACKNOWLEDGMENTS

I owe a great many thanks to a great many people, in particular to Nanette and The Suspenders (Stephen, Kate, and Mary). Dr. Don Houge offered a great deal of assistance and advice on all matters hypnotic, and his help was invaluable. And a belated, special thanks to Lisa Queen and Leslie Schnur.

BLOOD
TRANCE

Chapter 1

I stood in the entry, right there on the dark slate stones, the gusty May day blowing through the open door behind me, and all I could think of was how could so much blood come from one corpse. When I stepped through the door of Loretta's rambler in suburban Chicago, that was the thing that surprised me the most, the amount of blood from the old woman's body. There was one big shot of it sprayed up and across the yellow and light blue couch, then another big pool spreading across the carpet. That short white carpet that had looked so incredibly perfect just yesterday, but was now being flooded with blood. Was the human body nothing more than a huge, walking vessel of viscous fluid, or were there in fact two bodies? Could Loretta, who'd phoned me not even thirty minutes ago, be dead as well?

I tried to speak, to call out for her, but I couldn't loosen the knotted mass in my throat. I took a deep breath, calmly closed the door behind me, turned back, and made my way to the very edge of the slate. There was a half-wall there, a divider with a built-in trough of plants that separated the entry from the yellow-wallpapered living room, and I leaned against it. Something brushed my arm, and I looked down, saw big, green, heart-shaped leaves stroking me. Wasn't this plant just like the ivy I'd had since college, the one that was now some nineteen years old and had withstood nearly a dozen moves?

I coughed a couple of times, and tried again, "Loretta? Loretta, are you all right? It's me, Alex." Wondering if her younger brother or sister might be here, I called, "Billy? Carol Marie?"

I looked beyond the massacred figure of Loretta's stepmother and I heard movement, quick and faint. Next nothing, then once more something akin to a squirrel hiding in a pile of dry oak leaves and twitching furtively. That could be her, probably was, for Loretta Long, a former patient of my sister, was so horribly agoraphobic that she'd spent twenty years, or so Maddy had told me, hiding from society. Then again, I realized, if that wasn't her in some far corner, if instead Loretta was lying dead somewhere else in this rambler, what I heard could be the murderer, for this was most certainly a fresh kill. Turn around right now, I told myself. Get the hell out of here.

Just past a side chair all done up in blue and yellow floral print, I saw an arm emerge from the hall that led to the three bedrooms. Then a figure, not very tall, rather heavy, hair long and mouseish gray. In a flash, the person streaked past the opening, charging into that very formal dining room. Farther to the left, just past the couch, was another doorway, and that mad figure went whooshing past, disappearing into the kitchen.

"Loretta!" I shouted.

I rushed forward, my feet sinking into the white carpeting, then froze just short of the ever-widening pool of blood. Loretta's stepmother lay right in front of the polished mahogany coffee table that was replete with silver candlestick and crystal ashtray. I'd instantly disliked Helen when I met her this week for the first time, but did she deserve this? Did anyone? I looked at the body, saw what appeared to be three stab wounds—one in the neck, two in the chest—and my stomach rolled like a huge wave ready to burst from my gut.

"I killed her."

Loretta. She was there, emerging from the kitchen doorway, wearing a loose corduroy jumper, a beige one, and a white blouse. Face perhaps once pretty, now heavy and sagging. And pale. Dark eyes that had always looked depressed but never mean. Not until now, anyway. Earlier in the week, when we'd first met, I'd studied her and imagined she'd once had beautiful brunette hair. Now it was mostly gray and haggard-looking. So dry and poorly cut.

She lifted up the knife in her right hand. "I did it with this."

It was a very long piece of cutlery. Blade long and thin and slightly arched, a meat or fish knife. All shiny, too.

"I always hated her," said Loretta, stepping around the edge of the couch and pausing in front of a large print of an English garden.

"Put down the knife."

"So I killed her."

"Put it down, Loretta."

"Why?"

"Because Maddy would want you to."

Invoking the name of my revered sister made Loretta pause, but only momentarily. Then she smiled, rushed forward, and dropped to her knees right next to the coffee table and just across the body from me.

"It doesn't make any difference what Maddy thinks," she said, unable to hide her anger. "If Maddy cared, she wouldn't have left me."

"Loretta, that bus nearly killed her."

"She never even said good-bye."

It was pointless, absurd, to be arguing like this, that corpse between us, the bloom of blood now touching the edge of Loretta's dress. Beige corduroy wicking it up, turning a dark, purplish brown. Loretta dropped the knife into the blood, then leaned forward and pressed both hands fully and flatly into the red stain.

"Loretta, no! Stop it!"

An insane finger painter, she gazed up at me and laughed. God, I had to call the police, get them here at once. I was turning to bolt for the phone, when I noticed her picking up the knife in both her heavily stained hands. I saw the madness carving her eyes deep and dark, pressing her flat mouth wide. My heart clenched, feared the next mad moment.

And then Loretta, a compulsive reader who in the week since I'd met her had always been clutching a book the way a child clutched a security blanket, recited in a surprisingly calm voice:

"Poor hand, why quiver'st thou in this decree?
  Honour thyself to rid me of this shame;
  For if I die, my honour lives in thee,
  But if I live, thou liv'st in my defame."

I knew that tragic drama, that hideous monologue, and I instantly knew Loretta's intentions. For a serious moment I wondered if I should let her succeed.

"Loretta, stop!"

I took one step through the blood, then another, and jumped over the body just as Loretta was lifting that long blade over her own chest. I landed just beyond Helen, my hands swooping down, swinging at Loretta's fists. I hit the knife from her hands, grabbed at her, and pulled her back and away from the body.

"No!" she shrieked. "Let me go!"

She was like a monkey or a cat, some odd creature once domesticated but suddenly turned horribly wild, hands clawing, whipping. I stood above her, she on her knees, and her nails dug into my calf as she scrambled for the bloodied knife that lay by a side table. This person, this thing, was scratching through my jeans, heaving me aside, and I felt myself about to fall. She screamed, voice piercingly high.

And I shouted, "Loretta!"

I pushed against her shoulder, but it had minor effect, and she bulldozed against me, reached desperately through my legs. The knife lay just a yard or so beyond her grip, and I knew she wanted nothing more than to plunge that instrument into her own chest, perhaps slash me in the process. She rammed against my knees, and I lifted my hand, brought it down, smacked her on the cheek. It only enraged her further, and she lunged forward, mouth open, head slightly turned, and chomped down on my calf.

"Jesus!" I yelled as her teeth sunk through my pants and into flesh and muscle.

I tried to jerk away, but couldn't, so firm was her bite. And so I punched her. It was my most immediate reaction. My fist came down, smashing her on the jaw, stunning her at once, causing her mouth to go loose. I shoved her off me, leaned down, hurled her back, and then stepped over and kicked the knife, sending it spinning and streaking across the white carpet and under a chair.

I turned back, and she lay there all crumpled up, knees folded in, head buried in her arms. A discarded human body, rising and falling, pounding with each dry sob.

Finally she moaned, "Oh, God!"

I knelt down to her, reached out, touched her on the back. She didn't react, just went on shaking and sobbing, each breath more stretched with pain than the last. I wanted to apologize for hitting her. I wanted to tell her things would be all right. But I'd had to do the first, and the second would have been a gross lie. Nothing in Loretta's twisted life would ever be the same again.

I glanced back at the butchered body of Helen. What I had to do now was call the police, and I started to rise. Suddenly Loretta was lurching out at me again, this time clutching me around the ankles and embracing me desperately as if I were the Savior Himself.

"I . . . I have to be the bad girl," she sobbed.

I didn't know what to say, what to do. I just stood there, staring down at her brittle hair, her pathetic body.

And Loretta begged, "Please . . . please, just let me be the bad girl."

Chapter 2

"*O*kay, Alex, that's good," called a very distant voice. "*What else can you tell me about that day?*"

Christ, what was that? Who was that?

"*It's me, Maddy.*"

Oh. Oh, yeah. I wasn't down in some rinky-dink Chicago suburb, and I hadn't just walked into the Long home and found that body, all that blood. Nor had Loretta just been clinging to my legs. No, all that had taken place some three weeks ago, and I was just going over it one more time, recounting to Maddy exactly what I'd seen, what had happened. This was a trance, wasn't it? I was under, wasn't I, and wasn't that my sister talking to me from the pitifully conscious and self-conscious world?

"*That's right, Alex. You're in a deep hypnotic trance, and you're an excellent subject. You've gone back through time to that afternoon when you walked in and discovered the body in the living room. Now, is there anything else you'd like to tell me? Anything else you might have noticed that day?*"

God, hadn't we gone over it enough? Hadn't we poked and poked not only at the grisly murder scene but at the many layers of lies Loretta's family had worked so hard to conceal? Yes, I believed in hypnosis, in its remarkable abilities to probe the subconscious and bring to light details and insights previously left unnoticed. But there wasn't, I was sure, anything left to reveal in this trance of blood.

"Just bear with me, Alex. I want to be certain that we haven't missed anything. Now take a deep breath," coached my older sister. *"In . . . out. Deep, deep relaxation."*

I saw myself—dark curly hair, brown eyes, not quite six feet tall and not quite forty—lying there on the recliner next to my sister. I was in that huge attic room of my sister's house, that huge house on her island not far from the coast of Michigan. That's where I was literally, anyway. Hypnotically I was elsewhere. Or at least I was supposed to be. I took a deep breath, exhaled. Back through time, through trance. Go on, Alex, I told myself. Fly back to that Chicago suburb, fly back to that morning when Loretta had emerged from the kitchen, clutching a Chicago-brand stainless-steel knife.

"Breathe in, breathe out . . ."

I inhaled, held it, let out as much air as I could. What had happened? Loretta. Yes, the murder. But we'd been over and over this, both in and out of trance. There was nothing else I knew, nothing left to fish to the surface of consciousness.

"But you just did—the knife."

What did Maddy mean, the knife?

"Chicago Cutlery."

I laughed. It had been a Chicago Cutlery–brand knife, most definitely so because I had several of them and recognized it by its distinctive wooden handle. So what? What good did that do? The police, of course, certainly knew it was Chicago Cutlery, for they'd found it right where I'd kicked it under that chair.

"Yes, but there was something else," nudged my psychic detective. *"You said it was all shiny when you first saw it."*

My mind flipped and my memory skidded back through time as I lay there. When the police had gathered the knife, it had been all covered with blood and Loretta's fingerprints, for she'd dropped it in that pondish stain of blood on the carpet, smeared it around. Prior to that, however, Loretta had raced from the hallway, through the dining room, into the kitchen, and emerged with . . .

"A clean knife."

Exactly. I took a deep breath, plunged myself deeper into hypnosis, into tranquillity, into thought. I felt myself not back in Chicago, yet not there on the recliner at my sister's, either. I was somewhere above and beyond in some sort of dark heaven, in some sort of deep state of concentration where I was smarter, more alert, more capable.

And there was something really weird about all this. I'd arrived and Loretta had raced into the kitchen and come out with a clean knife. Clean because she'd washed it after she'd killed her stepmother? Or clean because that really hadn't been the murder weapon? I sensed the latter was true, for if she'd cleaned the knife just after the murder, why would she soil it again by dropping it into the blood? Why would she do that at all unless that knife hadn't been anything but a clean kitchen tool she'd wanted to make look like the real murder weapon? And if that wasn't the knife that had really killed Helen, what had and where was it?

"Alex, what else was clean?"

I'd already pointed that out in an earlier trance.

"Indulge your big sister."

Not those pale yellow walls. Not the yellow and light blue couch. Definitely not the white carpeting. All of those had blood spread or splattered over them. The only things that I noticed that were clean were the knife and Loretta's beige corduroy jumper that hung loose and formless over her body.

"But why would the dress be clean?"

I didn't know. Of all things, that confused me the most. And what was that business outside with the hose?

"Alex, pull up that image again—go back to that May afternoon, go back to that time when you were standing there and Loretta appeared in the kitchen doorway," she commanded. *"Just imagine that your memory is a piece of videotape that you can rewind and replay. Let me know when you're there."*

It didn't take much. It was just like going through a door, passing into another chamber, passing from the blackness of my trance back to that horrible day. I was either that good or I'd visited the murder scene enough times. For whatever reason, my memory was indeed like a videotape that I could easily access. Yes, I was there, standing by the body.

"Good. Now you heard Loretta and you looked up and she was standing in front of you. Do you have it?"

Yes. The image of Loretta burst in front of me. Pale skin. Gray hair. Chicago Cutlery knife in hand.

"Okay, hold it right there. Pretend it's a photograph that you can hold and study." My sister offered her cue: inhale, deep exhale. *"Tell me, Alex, do you see any blood on her dress?"*

In my mind's eye, I was looking at a photographlike picture of Loretta as she emerged from the kitchen. She'd just blurted her confession, and she was there, knife in hand. Beige corduroy jumper, big and baggy. Loose-fitting. A jumper to hide in, one that didn't reveal a bit of her figure. White blouse, too, with a tall collar. Very clean. Very pressed and white. Sleeves that emerged and went all the way down to her wrists.

That was odd. There was blood splattered on the furniture, on the walls, but nothing on her clothing. I studied Loretta. No. No blood on her whatsoever. A bloody pool of water had been found outside the house, where someone had evidently rinsed off with a hose, but there'd been no soiled blouse or shirt. That didn't make any sense, did it?

"No."

So maybe Maddy was right and the police wrong. In the first week after the murder, I'd gone over my story with the authorities at least four times. Finally, in an attempt to get more, Alfred, the Jamaican man who worked as my sister's male nurse, bodyguard, and chauffeur, had set up a video camera and taped me as Maddy hypnotized and regressed me back to that time. It was all done according to the strict protocol of forensic hypnosis, which required that all of my words and reflections be captured and recorded. That videotape was then delivered to the police where it became a key source of information, because Loretta had barely spoken a word since that night. She was down there in some Cook County jail, eyes open but mouth neither confirming her guilt nor providing information of any sort that might free her. Loretta, practically mute since she'd emerged from the kitchen in her corduroy jumper, clutching that shiny Chicago Cutlery knife and claiming: "I killed her."

Those were her words, no doubt about it, and the police were proceeding as if that were the absolute truth, for they had nothing else to go on, nothing else really to pursue. Which was what irritated Maddy so much, for evidence or not, proof or not, Loretta had been her client once, her subject, down in Chicago. And even though that had been several years ago and Maddy had seen Loretta for only a few months before that ass

of a bus driver had plowed into Maddy, my sister was sure of
Loretta's innocence. Quite positive, as a matter of fact, though
I wasn't sure I agreed with her.

   *"Well, we'll just have to keep at this, Alex, until we unearth the
real truth."*

Chapter 3

Before I'd first been hypnotized years ago by Maddy, my biggest fear was the standard one, that I would fall into a trance and be made to do all sorts of weird things. Like get on a table and take off all my clothes. Or French-kiss a dog. Or reveal secrets, usually the sexual kind, that should always remain hidden. But I'd quickly learned otherwise—that while a skilled hypnotist could lead me into a situation where I might act uninhibited, I would never do anything I really didn't want to.

And I didn't want to be in this trance anymore.

So in my darkness, I stirred and rolled as if I were trying to fight off a dream. I was sick of all the blood. About all that was left was to count the splatter marks and study their directionality, which held no interest or appeal, and so I had to push my way back to the surface. It was as if I knew I was in a dream and if I pushed hard enough, I could get out of it, I could wake myself. I felt myself begin to squirm, then sort of descend, fall out of the dark heaven. Yes, I sensed something beneath me now, the smooth black leather of the recliner. My eyelids fluttered. The darkness was losing to the light. Everything was becoming brighter.

My trance-groggy eyes opened, and I said, "I can't do any more right now."

I pushed myself up, straddling the long black leather recliner, and stared out the French doors in front of me. Out there past the green trees and down the hill stretched the freshwater sea of Lake Michigan, perhaps brown and murky some 350 miles to the south near Chicago and the steel mills of Gary, Indiana, but up here clean and pure. Totally Caribbeanesque in color. Far in the distance I saw white triangles, and knew that I'd rather be sailing on this perfect June day than sitting inside, hypnotically exploring death.

I turned to the recliner that was just a couple of feet to the left of mine, saw my sister, Maddy, lying there in a blue denim shirt and black pants. Wearing sunglasses, too, of course. She always did, day and night, because she'd lost her sight in her teens to congenital eye disease, and her eyes just rolled this way and that, which was a bit disconcerting if you were looking at her. And which was why she hadn't seen the Chicago Transit Authority bus barreling down on her.

Turning her head as if she were looking at me through those large shades, my ever-poised, ever-polished sister, who nevertheless relished Helen Keller jokes, said "I'm sorry to put you through this so many times, Alex. It just doesn't make sense."

"I know."

"But I keep thinking something will turn up."

"I think I've told you everything and then some. After all, hypnosis isn't a real truth serum. I mean, maybe I'm going to start making up stuff."

"Don't be silly."

I got up, started pacing in that ballroomlike attic room with its arched, thirty-foot ceiling. I was Maddy's little brother—younger by some three years—but I was also her new employee, hired to search for and go after things she couldn't. Several months ago I'd quit my exceedingly boring job as a technical writer in Minneapolis and moved to Madeline's island, and this, Loretta's case, was our first real attempt. The idea was that I would explore the outer world and then hypnotically re-create my experiences so that my blind and immobilized sister could see them, perhaps in a way even feel them, and then comment

on it all. Simply, I was to be her outer-world probe, her mesmerized gofer. That was the way she had it figured, anyway.
Maddy, who was undoubtedly the most insightful and intuitive
person I had ever met, and I, who could enter hypnosis in a
matter of seconds and disappear into the ultimate black hole of
trances, the somnambulistic state.

Maddy said, "I'm hungry."

"You're always hungry."

"So?"

"So how do you keep so thin?"

"I roll a lot," she said, referring to her daily wheelchair
treks on the paved paths of her island. "Let's go down for
lunch. I guess this afternoon we're just going to have to start at
the beginning of the week, when you first went to Loretta's."

"Yes, boss lady."

"Maybe we can try to get a clearer idea of who was following you."

"Well, I don't know if there's more to tell you, but if we can
figure that one out, then we should have the whole thing solved.
I'm just assuming that whoever was tailing me was not only the
one who attacked me, but also the same person who killed
Helen."

"Perhaps, but then maybe that's where our thinking's been
wrong," said Maddy. "Would you help me here?"

"Sure."

I tried not to feel sorry for my sister, the double-crip, as I
sometimes called her, but as I saw her grope for the wheelchair
she could not see, it was hard not to. Maddy was both blind and
half-paralyzed—her spine had been snapped and her legs forever stilled by that bus that clipped her—yet I was amazingly
healthy. Why? And when, I often wondered, would I get what
I deserved?

As I went to the leather recliner and helped lift her into
her wheelchair, I again admired her beauty. She had never
seen herself as an adult, so perhaps she still visualized herself as
a cute but gangly, tomboyish girl. All legs and arms, big smile.
And that's what was sad, because my big sister had matured into
a very beautiful woman. Short brown hair, long thin arms and
legs, long trim waist, and of course that long neck. She had a
kind of *Breakfast at Tiffany's* look. Elegantly casual, that was her,

and I knew that if she were both a seeing and walking person, she would have suitors galore. Probably children, too, who'd be totally and disgustingly gorgeous. Instead, however, she'd turned her multimillion-dollar settlement from the bus company into mucho multimillions on the stock market, had bought this decrepit mansion on this private island, then squirreled herself away here.

She reached down and positioned the legs she could not sense, made sure they were in place in her chair, strapped them down with strips of Velcro, then spun herself around. I watched as she felt for the end of the recliner, turned the chair a bit more, then started wheeling herself toward the door. She was that good, that clever, having filled her world full of markers and buoys that I never even noticed.

"I want to go back over who attacked you as well as this Shakespeare stuff. I mean the poem Loretta recited."

"Yeah, yeah, yeah."

I feigned aloofness, my voice light and casual, but actually every bit of my attention was on Maddy, who was wheeling toward a back door. She insisted on doing as much on her own as possible, and I knew she was right in that approach, but half the time it drove me crazy. Like, was she going to miss the door right now and hit the wall? My body tensed. Maddy had a wandlike thing rigged to her wheelchair, a flexible metal pole that hung out in front and worked like a blind person's cane. And yes, she was going to hit the wall, and no, I had to be silent. Shit, I thought, tensing as I slowed to a stop. I didn't say anything because I knew from experience that would piss her off, and instead I watched as she gently glided toward the wall, the wand-thing hit the wood, and Maddy braked. She reached ahead, felt for the corner of the wall, adjusted her course, and wheeled herself on.

I breathed a sigh of relief, moved on through this enormous attic room that was the size of a Viennese ballroom, and passed the huge Tiffany dome that hovered over the main staircase, a huge circular affair. I followed Maddy around and past that, through a back door, and into the rear part of the third floor. When the original owner, a Chicago brewer, had built this twenty-five-room house as his summer retreat, this back part of the attic had been finished off and part of the household staff had lived up here. Now, however, this expansive servants' living room was full of mattresses and trunks of abandoned ball gowns, old bird's-eye maple dressers, wicker cribs, and barrels full of soap flakes. Junk that had been stashed up here over the decades and no one had bothered to remove. I think Maddy liked having all this stuff up here, too. The layers of mustiness had a certain richness to them, something for the nose to mine over and over again. Or maybe it was because it was like an obstacle course that she found amusing to steer through, which she did with great ease.

In any case, while Maddy had made great strides in repairing the rest of the house, she'd left this back part of the attic nearly untouched. And I followed her around a pile of leatherbound photo albums that were covered with a dingy sheet, then down a rear hall, and toward the elevator, an old rope one that she'd had converted to electrical power. Maddy pulled up the lift's two wooden safety gates, boarded, and I stepped onto it.

Closing the gates behind us, I said, "Wasn't this thing used as a broom closet for the last fifty years?"

"Don't worry. I had repairmen all up and down it. It couldn't be safer." She hit the button, and we lurched downward. "Just admire the conveniences of the modern world, Alex. It used to take a manservant to pull this up and down."

"Just like a giant dumbwaiter."

"Exactly." Casually, she added, "Oh, Alex, I forgot to tell you I spoke to my lawyer this morning."

I knew that tone, that high-pitched, cavalier way she just sort of dropped things that I didn't really want to know. What was it now?

"And he said he might really be able to get permission."

As the lift lowered us past the second-floor rear hall, I asked, "Permission for what, Maddy?"

"Of course, the bail is awfully high."

"Oh, shit."

"But that doesn't really matter. It's only money, and I'm sure she won't go anywhere. As a matter of fact, if I remember correctly, I don't think she can swim."

I shook my head as we reached the ground floor with a clank, and said, "I thought I talked you out of that idea."

"Only for about fifteen minutes."

"Why don't you and I go down to Chicago? We could just get on a plane. Wouldn't that be easier? It would certainly be a lot less complicated."

Maddy said, "No, I don't think it would be. You know, the city and everything. It would be so distracting. Here everything's so quiet."

"Well, I still think it's incredibly stupid."

"Oh, Alex, don't be so stuffy. Loosen up, would you?"

I reached for the slatted wooden gates, lifted them both, and replied, "Don't try to derail me, all right? I just think it's stupid. I mean, it sounds like a bad Agatha Christie novel, bringing someone charged with murder not only into your home but onto your island. Watch, there'll probably be a big storm, the power will go out, and we'll all get hacked to pieces."

"Oh, stop it." Maddy shook her head, rolled out of the elevator and into the rear hall. "Loretta didn't kill her stepmother, and you know it."

"I know what I saw, her standing there with that knife, claiming she'd done it. And maybe she did."

I followed after my dear sister, who'd always done everything the way she saw fit. Granted, she was right just about everything—her sage stockbroker, for example, had highly recommended against investing in a certain small medical company, but Maddy went ahead, bought two million shares of Amgen and made a killing—but too often my younger-sibling opinions were requested only if they confirmed Big Sister's beliefs. It was the biggest battle we had—or rather I had, for Maddy saw this issue as my problem alone. So I knew as I trekked after her through the back hall and then the pantry that there'd be no talking her out of this one.

"Okay . . . when's Loretta coming?"

"The judge is signing the papers today."

"What?"

"She'll be here tomorrow afternoon."

Maddy and I had lunch on the many-columned veranda. It was a true veranda, too, not a porch, for it ran halfway down one side of the house, then along the front where we sat, then curled around the other side and ended in a screen porch. At one time these gray planks had been lined with wicker and potted palms, though now only a few rockers were left.

If a house had a personality, I thought, sitting there, rocking, eating a sandwich and staring down at Lake Michigan, this one most assuredly did. Or if this large structure with its white clapboard, green roof, and all these pillars, were a living thing, this one was. And it had nearly died before Maddy bought it and spent well over half a million dollars stabilizing it and bringing it back to life. The family that had built it had peaked in the 1890s, then coasted all the way into the 1970s on old fame and wealth until alcoholism had nearly wiped them out. Now, Maddy had recounted, the last of the heirs were living on the last of the money, scattered across the country, and all were reportedly deep into twelve-step recovery programs. Despite the tragedies that had plagued the family, though, one could sense that this house had always been loved, had always gathered love and held it, and Maddy was the perfect person to now assume ownership. The tragedies of her own life had forced her to retreat here, and she was resuscitating this island estate as the center of her world, one that she could completely control. She knew every corner and board within the house, just about every bush and tree on the island. Sometimes I was sure she'd never leave here again.

We ate turkey sandwiches with garlic mustard and sprouts, cups of chilled vegetable soup, and drank, of course, iced tea with lots of lemons. That was Maddy's beverage of choice, and she was rarely without a glass of it at hand from midmorning until early evening. Maddy carried a cordless phone in a holster on her wheelchair, and it seemed every hour or two she was using it as an intercom to call Solange, her Jamaican housekeeper and companion, for more lemons or ice or tea.

"So tell me about Lucretia," said Maddy, blotting the last of the crumbs from her lips.

"Loretta was obsessed by her story. I think that's the interesting part—that whole week before the murder, Loretta was carrying a copy of Shakespeare's 'The Rape of Lucrece,'" I began, sitting back in the wicker rocker, glancing at Maddy, then out at the lake. "There's something there, though I'm not quite sure what."

"But that's how you knew she intended to kill herself?"

I nodded, which did nothing for the unsighted, then said, "Right. Lucretia was a Roman woman who yielded to rape rather than be killed and framed in an adulterous situation.

The next day, however, she gathered her husband and family and told them what had happened. Even though her family said she was innocent, she protested, and then took a knife and stabbed herself in the heart.

"So along comes Shakespeare who writes this narrative poem about it. Loretta read part of it to me—the same part she recited just before she was about to stab herself. I knew as soon as I heard it that that's what she intended to do."

"Thank God you're quick."

"You know, I have to say that since then I've wondered more than once if Loretta would have been better off succeeding."

"Alex, she's innocent."

"Then why did she say she killed Helen? And why has she barely spoken since?"

"Because she's hiding the truth. When I was still in practice, I saw Loretta only seven or eight times, but we connected in a very real and powerful way. And believe me, the Long family is one sick bunch. Not just Loretta, but Billy and Carol Marie, as well," she said, referring to Loretta's much younger twin brother and sister. "I mean, we have to look at why Billy drank, as well as all the pain Carol Marie felt but tried so hard to mask. Not to mention Helen."

"Yeah, she was a real control queen."

"Absolutely. So you see, there's something very wrong running through the entire family—I think the secrets they kept poisoned them all—but the one thing that's absolutely clear to me about Loretta is her sense of integrity. She's a very honest person, and I don't think she's letting herself really talk now because if she opens her mouth, she knows she'll reveal the truth."

As the cool breeze flowed off the lake and around us, I sat back, knowing that my sister the shrink was probably right on that one. It had been obvious back when I'd walked in on the murder scene that something was quite askew.

"You know what I think?" I said. "I think this whole thing's as twisted, maybe even as sordid, as the story of Lucretia. That's not to say that Loretta didn't kill her stepmother."

"But what about the blood? Why didn't Loretta have any on her clothing?"

"I don't know. Maybe . . . maybe she wasn't wearing anything. Maybe she was completely nude."

"Then what did she do, dash outside and rinse off with the hose?"

"I've heard of weirder."

Off in the distance I saw this huge gray shape dashing from the lawn and into the forest. Then another. I recognized them as Maddy's Irish wolfhounds, Fran and Ollie, the biggest and perhaps unfriendliest dogs I'd ever seen.

"Your dogs are about to devour another rabbit."

"Really? Where?"

"They just dashed into the forest off to the left. You know, they really make me feel like a prisoner here. I can't step out of the house without wondering if I'm going to be attacked."

"Well, they're guard dogs, what do you expect? Besides, all you have to do when you want to go out is get Alfred and he'll pen them up," said Maddy, referring to Solange's husband and Maddy's other employee.

"So much for spontaneity."

Maddy continued, not even noting my sarcasm, "The one thing I keep coming back to is what Loretta said to you at the end."

I'd repeated the line so many times in trance that I now knew it by heart, and I quoted, " 'Please, just let me be the bad girl.' "

"There's something there," mused Maddy. "Something about the family, the way Loretta, Billy, and Carol Marie operated. Something about Loretta's role in the family. She always acted overly responsible or guilty. That's what I wanted to work on in her therapy. She blamed herself for something, but I don't know what."

Referring to another of Maddy's patients I'd seen down in Chicago, I said, "Speaking of basket cases, Ray Preston is about as sick as they come."

She shook her head. "Dear God, I just had to drop so many clients. I didn't have any choice, of course, but I think some of them suffered worse than me. Poor Ray, for one."

I backtracked, started thinking about the letter that had initiated my going to Chicago in the first place, and said, "Maddy, do you still have the letter from Loretta? Can I see it again?"

"Sure."

My sister reached into a pouch on the side of her wheel-chair, felt through several files, then pulled one out. She opened it, touched the first sheet of paper, another smaller one, then came to an envelope, which she withdrew.

"Here."

About ten days before the murder, Maddy had received the letter by express mail; she'd received notification of it from the mainland and Alfred had made a special trip by boat to go in and retrieve it. Maddy had listened with great concern as I read it the first time; not more than five minutes later she was asking me to pack my bags and be on my way to Loretta's.

"Read it again, would you?" she asked.

I cleared my throat and began.

Dear Dr. Phillips:
    I tried to make everything good but instead I
made everything bad. Now I'm really in trouble and I
need your help—it truly is a matter of life and death.
                                    Your patient,
                                    Loretta

"It seemed rather dramatic at the time," I commented. "But I guess it wasn't."

"No, apparently not. Hearing it now makes me think that if Loretta wasn't thinking of murdering her stepmother, then she knew someone was and she perhaps wanted help in stopping it."

"Or . . . or Loretta herself was somehow threatened." I paused on the idea. "Maddy, you don't think Loretta could have killed Helen in self-defense, do you?"

My sister disappeared into her black world, and I knew she was running various scenarios through her mind and imagination in an attempt to sift out the truth. While she could garner incredible insights from a person's tones and inflections, particularly mine, I could discern nearly as much from the way she tightened her eyebrows or wrinkled her forehead or bit her lip. Now the top of her face was stretched high and tight. She had also clenched her left hand and was biting on her thumbnail. Okay, so what was her great idea now?

"That could be, Alex. I don't know. We'll have to look at

that angle." She turned to me, her face bright. "But I think the thing we have to concentrate on first is who tried to kill you."

I knew what she meant. Another trance. Probably right from the beginning, too. I wasn't much up for it, but what choice did I have? If Loretta was really going to be arriving tomorrow, then we had very little time.

I said, "How soon do we get started?"

Chapter 4

Hypnotic age regression was one of the most powerful and draining things I'd ever experienced. Several months ago, Maddy had put me in a deep trance, then led me back through my life until I'd reached age ten, and around me appeared my gangly, thirteen-year-old sister, my father, my mother. At first they were faint, ghostly figures from a distant time, but then my memory and my mind collaborated like two mad charlatans, and before me stood the three most important people of my life, completely real and three-dimensional, living and breathing. It was too much. Immediately I started bawling, losing it like I hadn't since I was a kid. We were all out on the porch of our house in Glenview, our pleasant Chicago suburb, and we were this pleasant, at times even wonderful, family. I looked at my hands, my arms, and they were small. I was small. I was a kid again. It was as if I'd aged like a tree, a ring for each year, and I'd returned to one of those inner rings, and it was all there—Mom, Dad, Maddy, and me—as if I hadn't lost that time or any of us, but merely been around the corner, or rather at the outer edge of all those rings. And it was great. No, incredible. Dad was gazing at me, smiling, then running one hand over his not-yet-gray hair, and Mom—

no, Mommy, that's who she was—was so pretty and young and that laugh of hers so big and full of fun. My teenaged sister eyed me, looked at me, giggled. Oh, what great times those were.

So why, the hypnotist voice of the adult Maddy had called from outside that scene, was I so upset? If I was back then and it was wonderful, why was I sobbing so? I caught my breath, replied that the answer to that was simple: Even though I was back then with all my family, I somehow knew the future. Yes, that's right, Maddy had explained, you've returned to the past with your adult knowledge and insights. Which was precisely why I was so upset, I told my controller of the trance. I couldn't stop crying because there was nothing but pain ahead. This wasn't going to be the happy family forever and ever. The dad would be killed in a plane that fell out of the sky. The mom would lose her mind yet live on. And the sister . . .

I now sat on the beach in front of Maddy's house, the waves rolling against the fine sand. I took a deep breath, stared out over the ripples of water. After lunch Maddy had gone out on one of the paved paths that criss-crossed this island, her little wand scraping the ground in front of her as she wheeled her way toward good health. I, on the other hand, had come down here, seeking solace or clarity or, if I was lucky, both. Maddy and I had decided to take a break from each other, a little breather before this afternoon's long regression.

That was right. A breather. I was emptying myself, that was what I was doing. Trying to prep myself to channel what had happened a few weeks ago. I was to be little more than a medium, and my head had to be clean and clear, so I lay back, stretched out on the sand, breathed in the cool air, tried to let myself go. But couldn't. Why? Because age regressions scared me. All of the past just came hurtling at you so hard and so fast, overwhelming you, even smothering you. At least that's how it had felt when Maddy had regressed me to age ten. So was that why I was fearful of this afternoon's regression back to Loretta and Chicago? Had I been resistant all along, and had that kept me from revealing or discovering what I might have missed the first time? Quite possibly so.

It was true that when my old girlfriend, Toni, had been killed last year, I'd eagerly regressed to a time when she still

lived. I'd wanted her back, though, wanted to find the truth of
her murder as well as of our relationship. Loretta's case, of
course, was different. Not as personal, not as close, so did that
possibly mean I'd been holding back out of laziness? No, there
was something else.

I stretched out, rested my hands on the sand, listened to
the water crash, puffed out my lungs, and told myself to relax,
relax, relax. I sensed the sand molding to the contour of my
back, closed my eyes, and felt the warm rays of sunshine spread
across my face, bleed into my skin like butter into hot corn.
Hypnosis drew its power, I had come to believe, because it
opened a more direct line of communication between the conscious and the subconscious, those two parts of a person that
were usually at battle with one another. And even though I
wasn't in trance, I took a deep breath, called inward, tried to
reach that deep inner part with which I had recently been so
much in touch.

I asked: Why? Why am I resisting? Is it all the channeling,
the energy it takes?

That distant part that lurked in the damp darkness of my
soul was silent, not a peep.

Talk to me, I silently called. Tell me why I'm holding back,
what I'm afraid of.

I wanted to hear a clear answer, a simple explanation. Instead I heard a rumbling, a sound that was rolling from a
distant corner of my mind. It was a voice, I realized, echoing
within me, bouncing around somewhere far inside. I strained
to decipher the words, to make sense of it all. I couldn't, for it
was nothing but jumbled syllables, until suddenly the words
burst around a final corner like a sound hitting the last of the
canyon walls, and I clearly and unmistakably heard two words:
It's yours.

My eyes snapped open and my hands clawed into the sandy
beach.

Rather shaken, about twenty minutes later I made my way
back up the hill and to the house, entering the front door,
which was on the west side. I didn't pass through the large
entry hall, through the billiard room and back toward the elevator, but rather started for the steps, grabbing on to the
thick oak banister and glancing up as I climbed. The staircase

was circular and open in the middle, a twenty-foot-wide shaft that rose through the entire house and was capped with an authentic Tiffany dome that had been transported all the way here by boat after the 1893 Chicago World's Fair. The ceilings of the house stretched a generous fourteen feet high, and I was already huffing by the time I'd made it to the second-floor landing. The half-dozen main bedrooms stretched off from here, and I caught a glimpse of Solange working in one of them.

"Great lunch," I called. "Thanks."

Dust cloth in hand, the black woman turned and smiled out the door. "You're welcome."

A woman of few words, Solange had a regal, very proud stature, and she continued her light cleaning, wiping an old mahogany carved bed. Both she and her husband were always working, proving themselves of use—even though a cleaning crew came once a week from the mainland to tackle such a large house, Solange always did as much as she could—but I think it was Maddy who was more dependent upon them.

The staircase from the second to the third floor grew narrower, the banister a tad shaky. Glancing down, I hugged the wall and wondered if Maddy had had the structural integrity of this checked. The carved wood around the dome above was cracked; how much water damage had been done before Maddy had spent $75,000 on roof repair? At the small third-floor landing just beneath the dome, the floor sloped; the next time I'd definitely be taking the rear staircase because a fall from here would mean certain death. I passed a huge radiator, next a large light bulb that looked as if it hadn't been changed since the 1890s, and then I pushed through a wooden door and burst into Maddy's trance room, that huge attic room. My sister was already there, sprawled out on her recliner, hands meditatively folded over her stomach. A vision of mesmerized peacefulness.

"You look like a swami," I said as I caught my breath.

"Shh."

I crossed the room, aware that I was interrupting Maddy in the middle of a trance. And glad that I was. I stepped over to the open French doors that led out onto the small balcony, then turned and sat down on the edge of my recliner, which lay parallel to my sister's.

"Maybe you should wear beads and turbans," I said, staring at her. "You could start a sect out here on the island."

Maddy reached out and swatted, hit nothing, tried again, then struck my knee on the third try. "Alex, I was under!"

Of course she'd been, and knowing that Maddy frequently used hypnosis to see things and walk places she could no longer go, I asked, "Where were you?"

"None of your business."

"Oh, one of those. I hope he was good-looking."

"Stop it, would you?"

I stretched out on my recliner, fidgeted, shifted, tried to find some sort of comfort. But my back was tight and I couldn't decide if I wanted my hands by my sides, on my stomach, or placed on my chest. Shit. I took a deep breath, spit it out.

The Great Seer lying next to me asked, "What is it?"

"I can't get comfortable."

"I can tell that much by the way you're squirming."

Perhaps it was my belt pushing into the small of my back. I reached down and pulled up my jeans. That hardly helped, though, and I suddenly understood the princess's obsession with the pea.

"Alex, are you upset about something?"

"Maybe there's something wrong with this cushion. Something's digging into my back. Or maybe I've got some sand in my back pocket."

"No, I mean, is there something else?"

"I don't know. I don't really feel like doing this. I'm not in the mood for hypnosis right now. It won't work. Let's try later."

"Tell me what's really the matter, Alex." Maddy offered a deep breath and exhale, her version of relaxation à la subliminal persuasion. "There's something bothering you, isn't there? What is it?"

"Well, when I was down on the beach I had this odd sensation. I don't know, maybe it's the water here. Maybe it's Shirley MacLaine. Maybe she's influencing us all. I mean, it was weird. I was lying on the sand and I heard this odd voice inside me."

"What did it say?"

"Oh, Maddy, I don't know. It said . . . it said . . ." I stammered in embarrassment. "It said: 'It's yours.' " I shook my head. "Am I going nuts? I mean, what the hell does that mean? 'It's yours.' "

My sage sister quickly observed, "The subconscious is both very wise and fearful."

"I just have this sense that there's something more I know about Loretta. Something I haven't realized yet and something someone would kill to keep secret."

"I know."

I clenched my fists, stared up at the wood ceiling high above. Did she always have to be right?

"What else?" she asked.

"I'm afraid. That was an awful week. I was attacked, you know. Nearly killed. It wasn't big fun."

"I know, and I'm so sorry. I didn't know things would turn so badly." My dear Maddy let my confession hang there for a long moment before saying, "Just lie back."

"I am lying back."

"Then just get comfortable."

"I can't. I don't know if this is going to work."

"Let's just try. Breathe in . . . out. In . . . out. Don't worry, Alex. Just let yourself start a nice, deep trance. There's no danger here today."

"But there will be tomorrow," I quipped, "when Loretta arrives. Do you think we can handle it?"

"In . . . out."

I took a deep breath, nudged aside my resistance, and let her take over, let her lead into and up to the great plane, the vast blackness of hypnosis. The other world. The inner world. That's what we were supposed to be doing here and now this afternoon, and so I closed my eyes. Let my body take in a large amount of air, held it, let it go, and the air trickled over my lips long and slowly. Relax.

"Maddy, this is important this afternoon. I know that. I know I need to let go of my defenses and go deeper. Maybe that's been our mistake; maybe I just haven't been going deep enough. Can you do a long induction for me? I think that's what I need."

"Of course I can."

"I mean, none of this quickie stuff, right?"

"Just get comfortable, Alex. Breathe in . . . and out. In . . . and out."

Without even thinking, my breathing began to pattern Maddy's. I was like a trained dog. I just did it automatically, not questioning, not knowing why, but not caring either. In . . . and out. I lay there with my eyes shut, the rhythm of my body taking its cues from my sister, and I thought, I love hypnosis. I love letting go. And it struck me that this was why it was working between us. Maddy loved control, while I loved giving over. Was I sick?

"Maddy, do we like this too much?"

"Just relax and clear your mind."

I did as she commanded, following the orders of my gurulike sister. Suddenly I sensed previously unnoticed clots of tension in my forehead, in my neck. They were there, all tied up, but the very act of noticing them caused them to begin to melt.

"Okay, Alex," began my sister. "You're going to enter a deep state of hypnosis. You want to and you can. It's just a matter of sitting back and relaxing. If you do that, if you calm your mind, a door will open and you'll be able to step through and into that world. There's nothing to worry about, Alex. I'm here. No matter how far away you go, I'll be right here by your side, and whenever you want, I'll bring you back."

Her great disclaimer, I thought. She'd be right with me. How godly of her.

"Good. Now, you've been resisting a bit because you are afraid."

Yes, I was, but knowing Maddy sensed this somehow comforted me and that in turn enabled me to go deeper.

I said, "After what I went through and what happened to Helen, wouldn't you be a little nervous, too?"

"Absolutely, but you're no longer in Chicago. You're here at my house. It's safe now." Gently, Maddy said, "Alex, I want you to go into a trance and use your imaginal unconscious to try to describe the person who tried to kill you."

"But I didn't see much, hardly anything."

"You saw something, though. You know how a police artist conjures up a sketch of a suspect?"

Eyebrow here, nose there. I'd witnessed the process on

television, had seen a number of crime-alert posters in my old neighborhood.

"Sure."

"What I want you to do is stretch that concept a little further. I want you to slip into a deep trance, but instead of doing a sketch, something that's flat and one-dimensional, I want you to conjure up a three-dimensional image."

"Are you kidding?"

"Not at all. You know something about that person. You saw something. It's time to acknowledge that."

"I am the camera?"

"Exactly. You've just got to let yourself see what you know." Greasing my mind with propaganda, Maddy added, "Alex, you're one of the best hypnotic subjects I've ever seen."

My big sister's praise flattered me, but should I let it? Was this simply more of her subtle manipulation, her way of getting what she wanted?

"Are you just saying that to promote a good trance, or do you really think so?"

"It's the truth, Alex."

"Promise?"

"Absolutely."

Good. I always wanted to excel at something. Who would have guessed it would be hypnosis; who would have known my mind would have run freest and wildest in such an odd state?

"So I'm going to count to three."

Just the thought of it pushed all the buttons, sent me rushing ahead of her. I let go and opened my veins, my being, to a flood of tranquillity, which came madly rushing in.

"One, roll up your eyes and take a deep breath." My dear sister paused, then preached the litany of the trance, commanding: "Hold it. Now two, keep your eyes up and slowly close your eyelids. Concentrate on the two separate acts. Eyes up, lids slowly, slowly closing. Okay, let them close. And three . . . relax your eyes and exhale."

It was the same method I used in self-hypnosis, but for some reason Maddy could do it so much better, just as I could make a perfectly decent ham sandwich, but my mother had been able to take the same ingredients and make the perfect one. So now Maddy said three, and it was like a trapdoor opened beneath me and I went tumbling down, tumbling in. Lead on, O Wise One, I thought. It was like I was a scuba diver, swimming through my mind, and most of the time I was up above on the surface. But then I could don hypnosis and dive below, and what was down there in the depths was incredible. Or was I rising off the recliner, ascending into the dark universe?

"With each beat of your heart, Alex, you fall deeper into hypnosis. You turn around, and there is an escalator. Which way is it going, up or down?"

Maddy knew me, realized that some days I liked to ride up an escalator, getting lighter and lighter, and sometimes I liked to go deeper and deeper, my body growing heavier and heavier.

"It's going down," I said, clearly seeing the silvery steps and the moving black handle.

"Good. Now step forward, Alex. Step onto that escalator. I'm going to count from one down to ten, and when I reach ten, you'll be at the bottom of the escalator and you'll be in an extremely deep trance. One."

Yeah, yeah, yeah. I was going to have to tell her to come up with a new one. The escalator bit was getting old. Nevertheless, I stepped onto it, held on to its rail, and let it carry me down.

"Two. It's a relief to let go, to let yourself be carried deeper and deeper. And you can let go. As the steps move downward, you feel an amazing sense of calm sweep through your body. Three."

I just stood there, riding down into the black depths of hypnosis. And she was right; it was a relief to let go, be carried away. Warm waves of relaxation came billowing up from below, blowing over me, wrapping around, beckoning, pulling me downward.

"Four. You're moving deeper with great ease, Alex, and your body is growing heavier with each moment."

My sister went on, sliding past the numbers five, six, seven. And I went deeper, just standing there on the escalator of my imagination and riding into what seemed a black hole.

Behind me a faint voice called, "Eight."

I turned around as I descended. Looked up. My Maddy was still up there, droning on, her voice growing fainter and fainter as she massaged my mind, my arms, and my legs with her words. She told me how my entire body was overcome with relaxation, how my mind was open, my body light. And she was right on all that. I was drugged by her chant.

"Nine. You feel so relaxed and your body seems so heavy because you're almost there. You can see it, feel it. You've almost reached the bottom. And ten . . ."

The escalator suddenly came to an abrupt halt. Everything was quiet. No hum of machinery, no drone of my sister. I looked around. Oh, I was at the bottom. End of journey. Where was I? The escalator had indeed carried me very deep, and I was in some sort of buried cavern. No, I was down in some dark room, and I stepped off the last stair of the escalator. A ripple of puzzling thoughts ran through my mind—where was I, what was I doing down here, what was I supposed to be looking for? And just as quickly I knew; oh, yes, I was supposed to be looking for a face: nose here, eyes there, hair of that shade.

The light was extremely faint, and I could see nothing except a door with a black handle. I stared at it, knew that the truth was behind there. If I went through, my imaginal whatever-it-was might very well show me that face I was searching for. I just had to open the door. But could I? Should I? I had an uneasy feeling, a queasy sense that while I might see something important inside, there was danger as well. Yes, perhaps even someone waiting to do me harm. Still, I had to go in there, so I crossed the dark space and went up to the door, put my hand on the handle, and twisted it. The door was supposed to be locked, wasn't it? Sure it was, but instead it was open. I pulled the door, and it gave easily. A flash of fear ripped up my spine. Turn away, Alex. Don't do this. Don't go in there. Get out of here. Yes, I had to leave, shouldn't, couldn't do this because whoever had attacked and nearly snuffed out my life was in there.

But then a phone in that room began to ring. I paused. Should I get it?

"Go ahead, Alex, answer it."

Chapter 5

Some big sister, some protector, I thought, my hand still on that black doorknob as the phone continued its ringing plea. Maddy had said she was going to watch out for me, and here she was encouraging me—no, egging me on—wanting me to enter that room so that I might see a face and learn a secret. I was now certain, however, that I shouldn't enter this next chamber because I knew someone was in there, waiting for me. Someone who'd once come after me. Oh, Christ, was this real or a dream or something else altogether?

"If this is the way to what you've repressed, what difference does it make?" called a voice all the way from the top of the escalator. *"We'll sort out what it means later."*

Listening to the phone scream and scream again, I supposed there was no difference. Yet I sensed there was great danger in learning that truth, just as there'd been danger when I'd been followed that week prior to Helen's murder. And—

The telephone continued its biting ring. I didn't hesitate a moment longer. I had to answer it, so I swung open the door, half expecting some sort of mad person to leap out at me. Instead, this next room was smaller, and right in the middle of the room, some twenty feet ahead of me, stood a small table. On that table sat the ringing phone, a big old black one. I charged in, rushing to the phone, rushing to pick it up, because I had to answer it. That was it. The phone would give me answers, so I had to hurry. There could be a person on the other end of that line wanting and needing to tell me something, and when I had that bit of information, the entire murder might make sense. I broke into a run, extended my right hand. I had to get there, answer it, and I was getting closer and closer. In one swoop, my hand reached down and scooped the receiver out of its cradle.

"Hello?" I shouted. "Hello? Who is it? Who's there?"

At first there was nothing, only a faint crackling over the line, but then a strange voice uttered that phrase, saying, "It's yours."

The next instant the line went dead, totally and absolutely. No static or anything.

"Hello?" I hollered. "What do you—"

I heard quick steps behind me, but before I could turn around something was thrown over my head, then jerked back. I gasped as a cord was abruptly pulled against my throat, digging in, cutting off all my air. Jesus, someone was strangling me. I understood right then that death was to be mine, but I didn't want it and I dropped the phone, and my fingers clawed at my neck, trying desperately to pull the cord away. Whoever was behind me, however, was so strong, so powerful. As hard as I could, I jabbed my elbow back, hit a stomach, sent the person reeling backward and away. All at once the cord around my neck went flaccid.

Gasping for air, I spun around. A large figure stood there, arms, legs, and face completely wrapped mummylike in dingy, white gauze. Oh, Jesus, this was exactly what I'd feared had been lurking in this room, but what was this? Fantasy or reality?

Grabbing a large knife from the floor, the odd being said, "There are things you mustn't find out, things I won't let you find out."

As I stared at this unknown person, I realized I'd been absolutely right, that the reason I hadn't discovered any real truths or answers in Loretta's case was because deep within my subconscious I knew it was too dangerous for me to recall the real facts. I had simply blocked myself from finding the truth in order to protect myself. But were those fears legitimate or imaginary? Could there be real danger at this point in going back and unearthing the truth?

"Yes, possibly so, but again, even if those fears are only imaginary, it's important to confront them. Don't worry, I'll be with you as you let things unfold. You don't have to decide at this time what's real and what's not."

The rational part of me, the conscious side, knew, however, that an irrational paranoia was substantially different from someone actually threatening to do physical harm. For instance, if Loretta hadn't killed Helen, then whoever had would be more than willing to come after me now. That was a very real possibility, something far worse than this shrouded thing here in this room. In any case, where did I go from here? I eyed the door behind me, which was still ajar. I could make a dash for it and fly out and back up that staircase, back up and out of this trance. A retreat to safety. Or I could take a stand.

"That's right. You've come here for a purpose. You need to uncover this person's true identity."

I had to discern the color of hair, the shape of brow, and to the cloaked thing I said, "I must find out who you are."

Whether it was male or female, I couldn't tell, and it laughed a worn rasp, said, "I won't let you."

"Do you mean you'll stop me out of concern for my well-being?"

It shook its head. "No, I mean I'll kill you in order to keep my identity hidden."

This was too weird, too dreamlike, yet too real to be a dream or even a nightmare, and the thing raised one of its arms and a huge gust of wind came out, swirling and blowing all around me. All at once the door behind me blew shut, slamming with a loud bang, and the thing started coming forward. Knife in hand, it raised its arm. Oh, my God. I stepped back, realized there was no way out. Shit, this was way too much like a Bergman film for me.

I hit the wall behind me, my back flat against it. There was nothing to do but run. Where, though? I dashed to the right. As soon as I did so, the thing let out this hideous shriek, came charging forward, and the knife came slashing through the air, certain to plunge deep into my heart. I ducked, spun behind this thing, this person or whatever it really was. I grabbed onto an arm, my fingers sinking through layers and layers to that mealy gauze, and twisted it back and around. The thing screamed like a baboon, heaved itself back, and I lost my grip and was hurled aside.

It turned, raised the knife, laughed, and said, "There's no escaping me."

I started backing toward the door. Perhaps it wasn't locked. Perhaps I could get out of here. I made a dash, racing for the door, grabbing on to the black handle, twisting, pulling. It was no use, though. It was bolt-tight. I turned, saw the thing stomping toward me, ready to slash and gouge me, stab me over and over and over. Oh, Jesus, this wasn't my own fear now stalking me. I realized this was the mysterious killer, the very one who'd murdered Helen, the one who'd plunged that knife into her so very many times. Pressing myself against the locked door, I realized I was cornered, that I was next. How could I escape? What about my Sorceress of the Trance? Where was my Higher Power when I needed her?

Suddenly there was pounding. Someone was banging on the door, hitting it forcefully. Oh, no. Was that another one of these things coming at me from behind?

"No. Just stand aside, Alex."

I moved to the side as the pounding grew louder and stronger, and I glanced into the room, saw that creature continue to stalk me, knife again raised. Hurry, Maddy, I thought. There are only seconds, moments. It was now only some ten feet away, moving in on me, one slow step after another. I had dodged it once, could I again? The thing was so incredibly strong. I had felt its strength, its raw power. There was no way I could battle it.

All of a sudden there was a huge explosion. Splinters of piercing wood shot everywhere, and I covered my face, my body. I heard the creature cry out, saw that it had been stabbed with a multitude of wooden shards. The center of the door had been blown open as if blasted by some huge gun. Light was pouring through from the other side.

And a voice said, *"Hurry, Alex!"*

I leapt forward, scrambled to squeeze through the blown-apart door.

"No!" shouted the creature, lunging after me.

I had one foot through the opening, and was soon halfway through the gash, pushing madly to get to the other side. My fingers clawed at the spikes of wood, pushed them aside. I looked over my shoulder, saw this hideous person racing closer and closer. In desperation I pulled myself through until my pant leg got hung up on a spear of wood. I reached down, ripped my pants free. And the thing was diving forward, making a last attempt to grab me by the ankle, smiling because it knew it was going to succeed. In one last effort, I jerked myself free and then fell through the door, tumbling down on the floor on the other side.

I sat there, my breath coming in terrified gasps. The person cloaked in gauze was too big; it couldn't get through the hole in the door and chase after me. It struggled and pushed, then realized it was futile and stood there staring at me. I was safe, I realized, and I pushed myself up, came to my feet.

My hypnotic chauffeur said, *"Take a good look at that thing, Alex. The face beneath the gauze is what you need to visualize. This is what you're up against. Do you want to continue?"*

To my left I heard the escalator click on, and saw that the stairs were moving upward, that if I stepped on I would now be carried up and out of this trance. That was the easy way out, the return to the so-called real world. But did I actually have a choice? Not really. If I ignored that creature back there, if I retreated from this trance, I'd never discover the truth and that thing would never be purged from me. The fear, real or imaginary, would always be lurking within the shadows of my subconscious. I would carry it with me for the rest of my life. I had to go on.

Magically, another door appeared. I knew what was behind that one. Loretta. Her story. The murder of Helen. It was all back there waiting to be revisited.

"That's right."

Impulsively, I went over and reached for the knob of this other door, knowing I had to enter and not come out until I had the truth. My fingers twisted the handle and began to pull.

"No!" ordered the creature behind me, standing in the doorway. "If you go through that door, I'll pursue you. I'll come after you, I'll kill you."

I hesitated, wondered if I should abandon this trance, return to it another time when I was perhaps stronger, more cunning. That would be the wise thing, but just then I heard the scream of a woman. It rose from the other side of this door, called to the heavens in pain. I knew that voice; I knew who was in trouble and who needed help. Loretta.

And I quickly threw open the door.

Chapter 6

I rushed through this next passage, there was a bright flash, and immediately I was standing alongside an open car door. I turned, glanced into the empty auto, and wondered where in the hell I was and what this was all about. Not quite sure what to do, I scanned the deserted street. Holy shit. I'd stepped through a wall or a dream or some such thing and had come out on the other side.

"That's right, Alex. You've passed from a scene where your fears took shape to a scene where your memory is replaying something that actually happened. Would you like a break or would you like to press on?"

I glanced into the dark sky above. Oh, yes. My sister had followed me here, and she was up in the heavens, observing and noting, even guiding my every movement. How typical.

I had no choice but to go on, however. So okay, it was night. That much was obvious, for the sky was filled with dots of stars. I turned back to the car, bent over and looked inside, and noted a large manila envelope on the passenger seat. Maddy had given me that just before I'd left the island, asking me to hand-deliver it to Ray Preston, a former client of hers. I shut the door of the red car, which was all too familiar. Oh, I thought. That was it. That made sense. I'd just flown into Chicago, this was a rental car, and I'd just pulled up to a single-level suburban home. I glanced at the white house with the red-brick chimney and remembered who lived there. Oh, God. That was where the murder took place.

"Where it will *take place. You're not there yet."*

What?

"You're at the beginning, Alex. Helen won't be killed for a few more days, remember? That scream you heard is your link to that time. Let it take you back there, let it transport you and pull you back . . . and back . . . and back. Be there totally and completely. Hear that voice . . . now."

A scream? Where? My eyes quickly shifted, glancing from one house to the next. Was someone in trouble? I'd heard something, hadn't I? Yes, moments ago, just as I was climbing out of the rental car, I'd heard this plea, this siren of fear. But from where? I turned around, looked into a park that was thick with trees. Had it come from there?

Almost in response to my question, a woman's voice rose from the forest and into the dark night, screaming, "No!"

I looked from side to side, checked all the houses. This nice, supposedly safe suburb was locked tight, everyone sealed away for the night and plugged into their TVs. Oh, shit. Some woman was being attacked in the park and no one had heard the trouble but me. I had no choice. There was nothing else to be done.

Without a further thought, I charged across the street and into this park that wasn't a simple park with a basketball court, wading pool, or anything so planned, but a nature reserve that was thick with trees and bushes, darkness and stealth. I hurried between two large evergreen trees, their branches dense and scratchy, and up to an oak tree, then froze. There was nothing but blackness before me, an endless sea of it, and I recalled that, yes, this was how that awful week had started. What an ominous beginning. But if I pushed on, kept all this going, and relived that week again, how would it be different, what would I see that I hadn't before?

"Your fear, Alex. If you can look at it clearly, give it a face and identify it, then I think we'll know who murdered Helen. To do that, though, you must reexamine each and every detail."

Yes, my fear. It was here, pounding in my chest, and right out there, too, in these woods, threatening, wanting to do harm. This time I had to concentrate on it, hunt it out. I understood that what I'd been afraid of that week and ever since had been unclear in my mind. A figure that I could not honestly see or picture.

"As if cloaked in gauze?"

Exactly. So what I had to do was use every bit of power hypnosis brought to me, use its ability to focus free of distraction to peel off that disguise, expose that person. I heard steps charging across the forest floor. Whoever was to kill Helen could well be out there, pounding through the night. I had to find it, confront it, strip it of mystery.

Somewhere in the woods, a vulgar voice laughed and called out an oddly familiar threat, "I won't let you get away!"

A woman's voice replied, "Please, no!" And then she called, "Help! Someone help me!"

I was running again. Pushing forward. Smashing a branch down, plunging deeper into the woods.

And I called, "Where are you?"

From the left, the woman answered, "Over here! There's someone after—"

She broke off in a scream that scraped my ears. I turned, rushed toward her plea. Running over the forest floor, I swerved in and out of trees, stumbled over branches. I heard steps from over there, off to the left, and I veered over, stopped and hung on to the base of a tree, my fingers grasping thick hunks of bark. All at once there were steps in front of me, charging close by. Next I heard someone behind. I spun around, studied the blackened woods. At first there was nothing, only the dead of the night, but then I noticed something, a shape, a figure that bloomed in the darkness. Gradually it took form, and I realized it was a person, of course. My heart began to pound as I noted the shape, the light-brown coloring of the clothes. Oh, God. I moved a half step back, took shelter behind the tree, for this was it, that thing, that person concealed in layers of material that had so recently confronted me in a room in a different plane of this life.

Suddenly I sensed something else, heard another person running. Deep short breaths and heavy footsteps filled my ears. I spun around and a figure swooped out of the night, bolted right toward me. Lots of hair, a pale, pale face. Horrified eyes, all large and desperate. The terror came exploding out of her, bulleted itself directly at me.

"*It was her?*"

Yes. That was when I first saw her. Long, dull gray hair, full, flat face. I didn't know it then, back when it was really happening, because we had yet to meet. And so this person, this woman, well, she didn't know what to think when she first saw me. I edged out from the tree for I understood it was she who had screamed, who was being pursued, but when she saw me standing right before her in the dark, she skidded to a desperate halt.

And begged, "No!"

I didn't know what to say, how to react, so I just pushed my hand through the air, reached out for her. She started shaking her head and inching backward, the fear boiling in her, overflowing from her trembling lips, her shaking hands. Obviously, she thought I meant her harm, that I was reaching out to take her and beat her, perhaps rape her, too. For a very odd and quiet moment, the two of us stood in silence, the night dulling our vision, our senses. I could barely make out her eyes shifting from side to side, searching and hunting for escape. And then in an instant, that was exactly what she did, turned and tore back into the darkness.

"No, stop!" I called. "Wait, I don't want to—"

But it was too late. I started to run after her but then she screamed, only ran faster, and the next minute she was gone, gobbled up again by the blackness. It was hopeless—worse yet, stupid—to pursue her, so I slowed, then stopped, and stood in the middle of these dark woods, wondering what to do, how to proceed. Should I rush after her anyway and try to help her, to convince her that I meant no harm? Or should I leave her, so petrified, so in danger out here, and call the police? I could dash to my car, honk my horn, shout for help. Which, I realized with a dull sense of hopelessness, was exactly what I should have done in the first place. And which I should do now, but I scanned the woods, and it struck me that I was all twisted around, that I had no idea where the street was. Oh, shit. I could set out in any one direction and I'd certainly hit a street in this suburb, but who knew how far I'd have to go, how long that would take.

She started screaming again, that woman who'd dashed away from me, and my decision was made. There was no time to seek out help beyond the confines of this park, and reflexively I was flying through the woods, following those screams that with each second were more and more sobs of desperation. And I understood. This woman was no longer running. She had been caught and someone was beating her. I heard the thuds, her moans and cries.

As I clawed through the darkness, used her pleas like radar to direct me, I shouted, "Leave her alone! Stop!"

My voice sparked hope in her, and she begged, "Help me, please!"

There, off to the left. Her voice was clear, and I dashed through an opening, a small clearing of sorts with a picnic bench, and then back into the woods. I needed power, though. Power much larger than I to battle the attacker who might be armed.

So I insinuated great authority, calling in my biggest, deepest voice, "Police! Get down on the ground with your hands behind your head!"

I scooped up a large branch, which wasn't much but at least something. The woman's cries soon became less desperate, less pained, and I followed her voice, hoping that her attacker had fled. I came around a large bush, and there she was, this woman with the grayish hair, lying on the path. She eyed me, quickly pulled her arms over her chest, and I stopped, careful to keep my distance.

"No, it's all right," I said, laying down the branch. "I won't hurt you. I came to help."

She raised one of her hands to her mouth, then swiped at her eyes.

"Are you all right?" I asked. "You're not cut or anything, are you?"

She shook her head. I moved no closer, instead bending down a bit. What in the hell did we do now? How did we get out of these woods and back to some sort of safety?

"My name's Alex, and I—"

In the pale light I saw her eyes suddenly grow wide again and burst with fear. She raised a hand, then stabbed a finger through the air, pointing over my shoulder. I spun around just in time to see the blur of a person come charging up behind me. Oh, Jesus. Against the dark backdrop of the forest I saw this shape—

"Dressed in what?"

Tan. All tan clothing.

"Male or female?"

As I knelt on the forest floor, I could clearly see that it was a woman. Short gray hair. Aged face, lined with wrinkles and a chin that was quivering. Thin body. And tan dress. Hers was a face of death, and she meant to kill me. That much was not only clear in those deep, demented eyes, but also in the way she held that knife. She was clutching it high overhead and she meant to plunge it as deeply as possible into me. Dear God. No wonder the woman I'd first heard screaming was so terrified. This attacker was as determined as she was apparently vicious.

"I'll kill you!" the woman screeched, slashing the air with her knife.

What had I walked into? What was this all about? I'd assumed that the first woman, the one now behind me on the path, was being attacked by a man, perhaps a rapist. But I was wrong, and as quickly as I could, I grabbed the branch and swung it out at this assailant, kept her at bay. She halted, and I kept prodding, poking at her with the wood. I was certainly stronger than she was, for I had to be at least twenty years younger, but her knife was long and undoubtedly sharp.

The older woman jumped forward, again slashed the knife at me but missed by feet, and said, "Why are you doing this? Leave us alone!" At the woman behind me whom I'd come to rescue, she shouted, "Loretta, get up! Run!"

"What?" I muttered, knowing that in this small neighborhood there could be only one. Over my shoulder, I shouted, "You're Loretta? I'm Alex, Maddy's brother."

Behind me I heard a distinct gasp of realization. All at once the woman I'd been sent to visit scrambled off the forest floor and hurried up behind me.

"No, no, don't hurt him!"

So there I was between the two of them. Loretta behind me and—

"It's all right, Helen!" desperately continued Loretta. "He wasn't trying to hurt me."

Oh, my God. This older woman now in front of me, the very one who'd wanted so desperately to slash me to pieces, was Helen, Loretta's stepmother. Maddy had mentioned her, told me to take special note of her because in therapy Loretta had revealed the black side of Helen. The very side I was now witnessing.

Helen slowly lowered her knife, tried to catch her breath, and said, "What do you mean? What are you saying?"

"It's not him. It's not! He's . . . he's from Dr. Phillips. She sent him to visit me."

So it was obvious this older woman hadn't attacked Loretta, either. Or was it? This couldn't be some sort of trick, could it? After all, not only had the figure I'd seen chasing Loretta through the forest been wearing the same color clothing, I'd witnessed the same sort of savagery in the two.

"Well, what's he doing out here?" demanded Helen. "If it wasn't him, then was it—"

"Oh, I don't . . ." Loretta started to talk, stopped, then stammered, "I . . . I don't . . . don't know."

"I just got out of my car," I offered, "when I heard a scream. It was obvious someone needed help."

As we stood there in the darkness, Helen eyed me, shook her head slightly, then said, "Just what the world needs, another do-gooder." Still clutching the knife, she turned. "I guess we'd better get back to the house."

"Yes, come on," said Loretta, hurrying after her step-mother. "Let's get out of here. You won't go right away, will you? You'll have some coffee, won't you, Alex?"

"What?" I replied, unable to hide my confusion. "Sure, I guess."

As the three of us started down the path and out of those dark woods, I glanced past Loretta. Helen was moving swiftly along, and I stared at that knife she held so tightly. That knife.

"What about it?"

I'd seen it before. How was that possible, though, when I'd only just arrived and had never seen Loretta or Helen before?

"Be clear on this, Alex. You've come back to the past with knowl-edge of the future. Had you really seen the knife before, or is it one you would see again?"

Yes, again. I would see it again because it was that long-bladed knife, the one with the wooden handle, that Loretta would soon claim she used to kill Helen. The one supposedly used to pierce and puncture Helen's body over and over again. Oh, my God. Helen was carrying it now, in complete control of it, and all I wanted to do was rush up, twist that knife out of Helen's hand, and hurl it far away.

"But you've come back to observe and study the past in order to glean new truths from it."

So it wasn't something I could alter?

"Would that you could."

Amen.

Chapter 7

Sitting at the dinette table in Loretta's bright kitchen, I kept staring at that long knife with the arched blade and handle of good, solid wood that Helen had wanted so recently and so desperately to plunge into me. The knife lay on the speckled white Formica, and Loretta kept pushing it around, scooting it this way and that, as she pulled the coffee maker away from the wall, next reached for a ceramic canister of coffee lined up against the wall.

If Helen wasn't going to ask, which she hadn't, I certainly would. "Are you sure you're all right, Loretta?"

"What? Oh, yes."

"Don't you think we should call the police and report it?"

Seated on the vinyl chair next to me, Helen quickly interjected, "Report what? That my daughter went into the park after dark when she knows it's dangerous? Dear Lord, if you only knew how many times I've told her not to go into those blessed woods at night."

Rather in shock at her response, I stared at her. Ten, perhaps fifteen years older than Loretta, Helen Long was a fairly tall woman, her grayish hair freshly coifed, and her attractive face crisscrossed with numerous fine, shallow wrinkles. But she wasn't attractive, not really. There was something much too tight about her small mouth, something much too angry in those eyes that lurked behind the gold-framed glasses.

I said, "My God, she was attacked."

"By whom? I didn't see anyone, did you?"

"Well—"

Helen looked right at me, and I fell silent. I'd seen someone rushing through the forest, most definitely so. That could have been Helen, I supposed, in her tan dress, but . . . but what was going on here? Helen should be pumping Loretta with questions; she should be trying to piece together what happened out there.

"No," continued Helen, "this is nothing, really. Just a little scare."

Someone being attacked in the park labeled as nothing? Something was being left unsaid, an entire dynamic left ignored, and it struck me that, of course, Loretta could have fabricated the whole thing. No, that couldn't be, either. I'd seen the fury in Helen's eyes. The danger had been real to her as well.

I asked, "But, Loretta, you saw someone, didn't you? Someone attacked you, right? A man?"

Searching for guidance, Loretta stared at her stepmother. She started to speak, then stopped. I didn't like this, for I'd heard the screams, seen the terror in Loretta's eyes. All of it had been so real.

Finally she muttered, "I . . . I don't know. It . . . it was so dark."

Helen leaned close to me, nearly whispered, "Please." Meaning, of course, please don't press this. And then she turned to Loretta, and asked, "Is that decaf?"

"Ah, no," replied Loretta, pausing.

So what did this all mean, that there really hadn't been anyone out there and that Loretta was way more psychotic than I'd been led to believe? That could mean, of course, that this had happened before, might even be a regular occurrence. If that were the case, though, why had Helen been chasing through the woods with that goddamned knife and why had she been so absolutely ready to stab it into me? I wondered if there was a neighborhood thug, and I was about to ask, but it was clear I wasn't going to get any answers, at least not right now. Loretta was obviously the weaker, the more timid of the two, and I'd try to pry it from her later.

"Well, maybe your friend here doesn't drink real coffee at night," Helen chided. "You know, Loretta, that's awfully thoughtless of you. Not everyone's like you, not everyone can drink a pot of regular coffee just before going to bed and fall right to sleep." Helen reached over to the counter, lightly brushed the knife aside. "The decaf's in the other canister. That one."

"Oh."

Right from the start I disliked Helen, and not just because she'd recently come flying at me in the woods, ready to attack and kill me. Or because I wasn't getting any sort of straight answer. Or because of the sparse, rather unfavorable report Maddy had given of the woman, either. I just didn't care for the way she had led us back to the house in silence, then ordered us into the kitchen for an enforced, or rather patrolled, cup of coffee. And I didn't care for the way she directed her step-daughter around as if Loretta were her own personal maid.

Loretta looked at me, eyes open and innocent, and asked, "What would you prefer, Alex, decaffeinated coffee or regular?"

I wanted to counter Helen and cast my allegiance with Loretta. It was late, though, and the last thing I wanted was to be lying in the dark in some musty motel room, my eyes wide open as my heart pumped away.

"Actually, I'd like decaf," I replied.

"You see?" said Helen. "You see, Loretta? You have to think of others. You always have to ask."

"Yes, Helen."

"Alex, take it slowly here and focus clearly on this and this alone. What was Loretta's reaction?"

I looked at Loretta, studied her, and watched as her hands curled into tight fists. Tension, that was it. A lot of it. She glared at her stepmother for just an instant, and that's when I saw it.

"Saw what?"

All the hatred. It came beaming out of Loretta's eyes, all hot, wanting to cut into the other woman, slice her as if with an invisible knife. You couldn't miss it, so blatant, brazenly exhibited for just a moment before Loretta quickly moved on, her fingers clawing open the canister of decaf.

"But I bet you'd like it strong," said Loretta. "I remember your sister. She drank her coffee very, very strong. It was so black you couldn't even see the side of the cup showing through."

"Yes," I said, "that's the way I like it, too."

It was all rather surreal, and I glanced at Helen, who was looking away, lost in thought or disinterest. I wanted to punch her, of course, for the problem was already clear. Perhaps Helen wasn't the source of the severe, even debilitating, lack of self-worth that had caused Loretta to seek my sister's professional help several years ago, but she certainly was doing nothing to improve it.

As I sat there watching Loretta so carefully measure the coffee and pour the water into the machine, as I noticed how Helen was observing Loretta's every move, I realized how little Maddy had really told me about this family. And just then I had this thud of a realization, the sinking kind, as if I'd been tricked yet again. How typical. My sister had done it once more. She'd sent me first into a situation, then later into a trance, without telling me all she knew. In her sessions with my sister, Loretta had most certainly alluded to, if not outright told Maddy about, the dynamics going on now between Loretta and Helen. How could she not? And I guessed there was more, too, for it was completely obvious that this sick household had been infested by contempt and hate.

I felt myself pausing, then splitting in two. One part of me magically floated out of the scene, right out of that kitchen in suburban Chicago. There was someone watching over all this, someone who could answer these questions, I knew, but I got nothing in response, which pissed me off. I needed an answer. Had to have one in order to move on. If I got nothing from way up above, from my regal sister who was now impersonating some form of higher power, then I was going to jump ship and completely abandon this flight of a trance.

"All right, yes. I knew there were problems between Loretta and Helen. And, yes, you're right. Loretta hated her."

Just as quickly as the answer came, so did an intuitive realization. I understood now. This was why Loretta had come to see my sister. Loretta had sought out the help of a therapist not because she felt herself to be worthless or was afraid to leave the house but because deep inside, hidden from everyone, she was such an angry person, someone so full of rage that she was afraid she was going to explode.

Oh, shit. I gazed back into my trance, looked down on myself sitting in that kitchen, watched as Loretta carefully handed me a cup of hot, black coffee, then served her step-mother as if this was some sort of test she was terrified of flunking—don't spill, Loretta!—and I understood. Loretta had sought out professional help in large part because of her boil-ing hatred of her stepmother.

"Correct again."

And Loretta had talked about her anger and maybe even about wanting to hurt Helen. She had, hadn't she?

"Yes. We'd just gotten into that in our last session. We'd been using hypnosis almost from the start, but when I put her under in that last session, there was a personality split of sorts. The good Loretta, the one who'd been struggling to do everything right, was pushed aside by the bad Loretta, a little girl full of rage who wanted nothing more than to scream and to—"

Kill Helen.

"Unfortunately, yes."

How, with a knife?

"Yes."

Oh, Jesus. I understood now why Maddy had taken Lor-etta's note so seriously, why she'd been so eager for me to pack my bags and head down to Chicago. Maddy had been afraid that the note was a sign, a forewarning, that Loretta was in-tending to kill Helen, so she'd sent me off, hoping that a har-binger from her would stop it. If so, though, why hadn't my sister said anything directly, given me clear directions?

"I should have. That was my error."

A mistake that had cost Helen her life? Oh, my God. That was why Maddy was so interested in this, even obsessed by Loretta, because if she proved Loretta innocent, Maddy would also prove herself guiltless. That was it, why Maddy was willing to do anything, even bring Loretta to the island.

"Your coffee's getting cold."

I knew I was being manipulated but I also knew it was unimportant. An issue for later. Suddenly the two parts of me were fused back together, and I looked down, wrapped my hands around a mug that was warm and steaming.

A distant voice chanted and commanded, *"Take a sip, feel it pull you back to that moment, that time. Swallow the coffee and taste it again. Was it indeed strong?"*

Without thinking, I lifted the mug to my lips, took a long sip, felt the bitterness dark and heavy in my mouth. And when I raised my eyes, there they were, those two women, stepdaughter and stepmother who were almost close enough in age to be sisters, staring at me.

"This is good, Loretta," I said. "Nice and strong."

"You don't want any milk or sugar?"

I shook my head.

"I know that's the way your sister liked it, nice and black," she repeated.

Loretta's tired eyes suddenly grew wide as if she'd forgotten something. Not saying a word, she dashed out of the kitchen and into the living room. As I heard her fumbling for something in the other room, I glanced back at Helen, who looked at me and shook her head. Seconds later, Loretta was back, clutching three photographs mounted in acrylic frames. She hurried over to the table, eagerly holding one of the pictures out to me.

"See, I have a sister, too," said Loretta, proudly. "That's Carol Marie. She owns a store in the mall. She's very clever like Daddy. Good in business. Isn't she pretty?"

It looked like a high school picture, makeup just so, hair all done up, but she was attractive, and I said, "Yes, she's very pretty."

"And this one's my brother, Billy. He was a good student. Top grades. And such a beautiful writer. He writes wonderful poetry." Loretta smiled. "Billy and Carol Marie are twins; did you know that?"

"Yes." Studying the second picture, I saw a young man, light-brown hair, thick mustache, a handsome guy, and I asked, "Are they younger?"

"Oh, yes. Lots younger. I'm the big sister." Loretta fell into some sort of sad thought and glanced away. "Our mama died just after they were born."

"I'm sorry." I motioned to the third photograph. "And who's that?"

The smile bloomed again. "That was our daddy."

"My husband," muttered Helen.

As if her stepmother weren't even there, Loretta said to
me, "Helen was his second wife. After our mother died, Daddy
married Helen. That's when we moved up here, up to this
suburb. We used to live in the city. Before that Helen was
Daddy's—"

"Loretta, please!" interrupted Helen. She looked at me.
"John died five years ago from a stroke. We all miss him."

"Yes, we do," agreed Loretta, looking down at the table
top. "I miss him lots."

Helen took a sip of coffee, then moved the conversation
away from her family, saying, "So you're the brother of the
famous Maddy."

I nodded. To me my sister was just my sister, quirky and
wonderful, not someone famous, just someone with a myriad of
traits that often drove me crazy. Maybe I still harbored anger at
her for the times she beat me up as a kid or tricked me; maybe
I just knew all of that was part of her as well. Whatever, through
the eyes of others like Loretta, I was now beginning to understand that Maddy had a gift. An ability to touch people in a
profound and simple way. It was the gift of trauma, I knew.
Inside that shell of misfortune created by her blindness and
hardened still further by her paralysis lay a brilliant pearl,
which Maddy had claimed and made good use of.

"I wear it with a joy many cannot understand."

To Helen, I said, "Maddy left her practice quite quickly, as
you must know."

Loretta interjected, "The bus."

I nodded. "And ever since then she's felt bad about leaving
her clients in the lurch, so to speak. She just wanted me to look
in on a few of them and say hello."

"How nice," said Helen, a smile noticeably absent from her
face. "Well, you can tell her that everyone's fine here."

Loretta quickly asked, "Oh, yes, but why don't you come
back tomorrow, Alex? Why don't you come back and tell me all
about Maddy—I mean Dr. Phillips."

"Loretta," said her stepmother, "I don't think that would
be a good idea. I really don't want you getting upset. We've had
enough commotion around here for a while. Besides, I'm sure
that Alex has many other things to do."

Loretta pursed her lips, folded her hands, then said, "I'd like him to come back."

"It's really no problem. I'd enjoy it," I said, challenging Helen with a strong look. "I have plenty of time."

"Oh, good!" said Loretta, a large smile on her face. "That would be wonderful—I like visitors. Come back tomorrow, about eleven? I'll make something cold to drink and we'll sit outside and talk, all right?"

"Absolutely."

It was two against one here, and Helen clamped her thin lips together, said nothing. Finally she sipped at her coffee.

And finally she said, "Well, obviously my advice here doesn't count. Do as you two please. Now, if you'll excuse us, Alex. It's been a rather long day."

In other words, get the hell out. I looked at Loretta, studied her face, hoped she had the strength to battle Helen after I left. But did she?

I took a last sip of coffee, started to rise, and invoked my sister yet again, saying, "Tomorrow, Loretta, you have to tell me what's new in your life. Maddy specifically wants to know how you're doing."

"Oh, yes. Oh, good." Loretta started to get up, too. "I'll walk you to your car." She paused, defiantly added, "I'll be right back, Helen."

As the two of us left the bright kitchen and crossed onto the white carpeting of the living room, Helen called after us, saying, "Just stay away from that goddamned park."

For all the order of the living room with its perfect floor covering, prim yellow-and-blue-upholstered furniture, and knickknacks so perfectly placed, I detested it. As we passed through it, another image kept seeping into my mind, one of chaos and violence. What I now saw here was artificially created, I knew. A desired perfection, one that would be wiped away in, I sensed, a horrible death. By the time we reached the front door I was shuddering with visions of the future. I moved past them, and Loretta and I stepped outside and into the cool night air, then proceeded to my small rental car parked by the curb.

As we strolled down the drive to the street, in a low voice I said, "Loretta, Maddy got your letter and she's quite worried."

In a display of trust that I didn't expect so quickly, Loretta slipped her hand through my arm, and replied, "I'm afraid, too."

"Of what?"

Loretta looked back at the house, and I followed her paranoia, glancing back as well. Helen stood in the living-room window, arms folded across her stomach and staring after us.

Loretta continued, whispering, "I don't know—things. I'll tell you tomorrow."

Loretta was even more pale, her hair even more straight and flat in the dark. I saw the fear in her eyes as she kept glancing back at her stepmother so distinctly framed in the picture window.

"Loretta, just tell me this," I said. "Was there someone out there in the park chasing you tonight?"

"Yes."

"Do you know who it was?"

She nodded.

"Who?"

And she replied. "The man who hates my family."

With that she leaned forward, wrapped her arms around me, and kissed me firmly on the cheek. I stood there, taken aback, then watched as Loretta rushed back down the drive and inside the rambler.

Chapter 8

I liked nothing of what I'd seen tonight and didn't know what to make of any of it. Maddy had sent me to see one of her former patients who she feared was plotting to kill her own stepmother or perhaps take her own life, and I'd just seen justification for either or both. As I drove away from Loretta's, however, I knew it wasn't so simple, particularly in light of that business in the park. For a moment I'd been almost ready to believe there hadn't been anyone out in the woods pursuing Loretta, that perhaps it had all been a creation of Loretta's pitiful mind. But Loretta herself had just countered it all, said there had been someone after her. Someone with a good amount of ill will toward her family. And I had to believe that Helen knew there'd been danger as well, for she'd been there, hatred in her eyes, ready to slash.

I didn't like this, not much at all. I turned off their street, taking a right around the far edge of the park. My motel, where I'd already checked in, was some fifteen minutes away, just the other side of highway 294, but I had no real desire to return there and drop myself in front of CNN or MTV. It wasn't even ten. Certainly there was a restaurant somewhere out here, one of the chains, that was still open. It was just a matter of finding my way out of this soft tangle of streets, this 1950s creation of winding roads, lanes, and culs-de-sac. But where was I? This area was a blur of suburbs, endless spacious homes surrounded by endless trees, and I wasn't even sure which suburb I was now in. Whether Loretta lived in Wheeling or Mt. Prospect, a finger of Arlington Heights or perhaps even in Deerfield, I couldn't guess.

It was so quiet as I drove, the night so empty and dark, that I noticed the other car, the one that appeared behind me about a block from Loretta's, almost at once. I didn't think at first that it was following me; that idea didn't even occur to me. I noticed the powerful headlights, the beams reflecting off my rearview mirror and cutting into my eyes, but I didn't give it much thought.

"Was this the first time he came after you?"

Yes. But even though I had no idea of the danger, I felt panicky. I'm not sure why, but I did. After the incident in the park and the odd conversations with Helen and Loretta, everything seemed off-color.

"Off-color like the car following you, which was . . ."

I glanced in my mirror, saw the other vehicle pass beneath a streetlight. Funny brown. An off-brown, something that was once a chocolaty color but was now more washed out.

"Hold that image. Look at it," directed my other-world boss. *"So it was an old car?"*

Sure, old car, old color, paint faded. Big grill. Lots of chrome. I guessed it to be a Ford, something that had seen many miles and much use.

"Good. Go on."

To test my fear, I turned left at the next corner and accelerated. For a few seconds the street behind me was dark and quiet, and I thought I was all wrong, just being paranoid, but then that same large automobile came screeching around the corner and racing in my trail. Reflexively, I sped up, tried to keep a lead. I checked the mirror, saw the car still gaining on me, and turned left, my tires crying as I whipped around. It was a short street, and at the very next corner there was a clump of birches, a fire hydrant, bushes and so on, and I steered right, turning past them. I kept my speed up, charging on. I kept checking the rearview mirror, too, hoping whoever it was wasn't really following me, but those bright beams came out of the night, lunging out, catching me in their light. This couldn't be,

I wondered, a couple of doped-up high school kids, out for a night of suburban terrorism, could it? No, that'd be ridiculous. So why would anyone follow me?

"Because not only had you just rescued Loretta in the park, she'd just kissed you. Obviously he understood you were very close or somehow very sp cial to her."

Whatever this was, it was ridiculous, and when I came to a stop sign, I decided to play along no more. I pulled to a complete halt. I wasn't going to give in, I wasn't going to play this game, and I turned around in my seat and stared out the rear window. I had a temporary macho idea that I should jump out of the car, stand firm, demand to know what this was about. But reason as well as any number of weird stories, most of them involving Los Angeles, kept me in my car, and I stared back at the old Ford that was barreling down on me. Shit. It was doing just that, barreling, racing faster and faster. In one instant I wondered, This guy isn't going to hit me, is he? And in the next moment I knew he was. As the other car zeroed in on me, I could hear the roar of his engine filling the night.

I spun back in my seat, rammed my right foot forward, stood on the gas and stared in the mirror. I knew at once there was no way I was going to make it, that there were only seconds before he rammed me, but there wasn't even that much time. I was probably going only ten or fifteen when there was an enormous crash and I was jolted and hurled forward. My head snapped back against the headrest, and my ears rang with the sound of crashing metal and breaking glass. As my body was thrown against the seat, the steering wheel jumped out of my hands. The next instant it seemed like I was flying upward, that I would smash against the ceiling of the car, but then the seatbelt locked, digging into my gut, holding me down. I lunged out for the steering wheel, grabbed it, and tried to keep some sort of control as the surge of the larger auto, its thrust, hurled me forward. Up ahead I saw a parked car, knew that I was about to be rammed directly into it, and wrestled the wheel to the left. I smashed my foot on the gas pedal, and there was the shrill tearing of metal as I somehow broke loose and pulled away.

Not letting up on the gas, I started swerving, right to left, left to right. I didn't know how else to avoid that thing, that huge mechanical monster of a car lunging at my rear, trying to ram me again. I didn't move quite fast enough, and my car was clipped on the left taillight. My auto shook and jolted like a bumper car. I twisted the steering wheel in the opposite direction, and sped ahead. I looked down at the dash, saw that we were now roaring at almost sixty down this sleepy street. Like two warring birds, we swooped from side to side as we zoomed around a long curve in the road. I didn't know what I was going to do, how I was going to escape this thing. If he succeeded in crashing me into a tree or parked car, then what? Would he jump out and shoot me?

"But it was a man?"

Yes. I glanced in the mirror, saw a guy behind the other wheel. There wasn't much light, just some from his dash, so I couldn't make out much. Only short hair. And a coat.

"A tan coat?"

I couldn't tell, not really. But this could have been the figure I'd seen chasing after Loretta in the park. The guy that had been after her and whom Helen wanted to kill.

"Hold the image, Alex. What else can you see? Describe him."

Something across the top of his mouth. A shadow or maybe a mustache. That was about all I could discern. It was just happening so ridiculously quickly. My eyes flicked back ahead, studying the road, hoping for a way to safety, when I saw it. Light. A lot of it about a block ahead. There was a main thoroughfare up there, I remembered. At least four lanes. If I could make it that far, perhaps there'd be a way of losing my tail in the traffic. Maybe there'd even be a cop.

All of a sudden there was another great whack of metal against metal, and almost instantly my car was flying into someone's front yard. I saw a mailbox, heard a large thud as I plowed it over. And then a tree. I hung on to the wheel, turned back to the road, plowed through the grass, and swooped through a web of heavy branches. Almost as quickly, my rental car bounded back onto pavement, and I was streaking off again.

I glanced back in my mirror, saw the car with its big lights. I expected it to charge after me, but it didn't. I sped on as fast as I could, yet the other car began to fall back. I didn't stop. Didn't dare. Yet as I sped to the main road up ahead, as I passed under the bright lights and off toward my motel, I couldn't help but wonder. Why was he now letting me get away?

Chapter 9

That question kept echoing in my mind, even an hour later after I'd eaten and retreated to my motel room, where I took a shower. Wearing a T-shirt and underwear, I lay down on my bed, a full-sized thing with an orange bedspread, and stared up at the bumpy, sprayed-plaster ceiling. I'd deal with the ruined rental car tomorrow, but what had all that been about? Had someone just tried to scare me away, or had that guy really meant to kill me?

The big question, though, was whether or not this recent attack was somehow connected to the matter-of-life-and-death note Loretta had written to my sister. My first inclination was to say that, sure, it had to be. Then again, I sensed that although there was a variety of things going on here, they might not all be interconnected.

I rolled over and checked my watch, which sat on the fake-wood bedside table. As soon as I saw that table, the phone, the bedside light switch, I was struck with a powerful sense of déjà vu. This room with its two identical beds covered with identical orange spreads, the two armchairs covered with green fabric and small table in between, as well as the television that sat upon the three-drawer dresser, were all so amazingly familiar.

"That's because you've returned to all this in hypnotic trance, Alex."

No, all this was familiar because we'd become such a bland country. I knew this room not because I'd stayed in specifically this number before but because it resembled just about every other motel across the country. In the name of buy-all, have-all corporate efficiency, everything had become the same. The only difference in rooms across the country was whether or not the remote control had been ripped off or whether you got free shampoo or simply a free shoeshine towelette. It was amazing to—

I dropped my digression when I noticed that it was after eleven and that it wasn't too late to call my sister, who regularly stayed up until one or two. After this first contact with Loretta, I wanted to talk to Maddy, for I had questions, things I needed to find out, ideas to test.

I leaned over to the phone, dialed, and she picked up on the first ring.

"Hi," I said, "it's me."

Her voice now humming not through trance but over the telephone lines, Maddy asked, "How's Chicago?"

"Actually, I don't know. I flew into O'Hare, then came up here, wherever here is. I think I'm just a little north of Glenview."

"Our old home territory. If you get a chance, you should go check out our old house. I wonder what it looks like."

"Yeah, I wonder," I echoed, though I didn't have much interest in finding out.

A wave of sad memories threatened to wash over me, and it struck me that my relationship with Maddy was an incestuous one, not in terms of sex, of course, but definitely in terms of emotions. We were bound together in tragedy, stitched tightly together with a thread of painful memories. A normal brother and sister grew up, went their own ways, and developed their own lives. But we'd been hit with so much crap—Dad's sudden death, Mother's Alzheimer's, Maddy's impairments—that it was hard to move on. It was all so hard to understand, and that confusion kept us glued together. As I sat there in my motel room, telephone to my ear, I wondered if I'd done the wrong thing in going to work for Maddy, if I hadn't taken the job for all the wrong reasons. Now that I was away from her and her island, it was clear that I'd taken the job not simply because I was bored with technical writing but because of my desire to be closer to my sister.

"Alex," called my ever-perceptive sis, "are you all right?"

"Yeah, I'm fine. It's just been a long evening."

"What happened?"

I went through the whole thing, getting out of my car, hearing the scream. All that business in the woods. Then the odd conversation back at the house. And, of course, being followed and rammed.

"Shit, Maddy, you should see my rental car. It's all beat to hell."

"If they give you any trouble at the rental agency, just tell them I'll pay for the whole thing. The important thing is that you're all right. You are, aren't you?"

"Not a scratch."

"Well, just be careful, Alex. I had no idea things would get this rough. Take care of yourself—you're the only brother I have."

"Yes, boss." I started twiddling the phone cord around my finger. "What do you know about Loretta's younger twin brother and sister?"

"Not much, really. Billy and Carol Marie are something like twelve years younger than Loretta, I think. Their mother died quite soon after giving birth to them."

"Was it complications from the birth or something else?"

"God, I never even thought that it might be anything but natural," said Maddy over the line. "I hope it was, anyway. I do know that her death was extremely difficult for Loretta. If I remember correctly, it was about then that she started having trouble. Going out and all, I mean. Somehow Loretta managed to make it to high school and even graduate, but ever since she's pretty much stayed at home."

Recalling what Loretta had started to say about Helen, I asked, "What did Helen do before she married Loretta's father? Did she work for him or something?"

"She was their cleaning lady."

"No shit."

"And they were married pretty soon after Loretta's mother's death. Like a couple of months after, I think, when Billy and Carol Marie were obviously still infants."

"That would be about when the family moved out of the city and up here," I speculated. "But if Loretta's mother didn't die of anything natural, you can guess who'd be number-one suspect."

"If that's the case," mused Maddy, "I wonder if Loretta saw something. Maybe that's what all this is about."

"Whatever, Helen must have done a hell of a job cleaning house," I said, recalling that the house was spotless now as well. "Either that, or Loretta's father thought it'd be cheaper to marry her than pay for a full-time live-in."

"How cynical of you, Alex."

"You haven't met her. I just can't imagine anyone falling in love with Helen. She wasn't what you'd call a warm and fuzzy personality."

"No, perhaps not. But outwardly, at least, she did do an okay job of raising those kids. Loretta said Helen always made their breakfasts, packed their school lunches, and cooked a hot dinner." Maddy asked. "So what do you have planned for tomorrow?"

"I'm getting together with Loretta sometime. Before that, though, I have to go to the car-rental place and see what kind of trouble they're going to give me. If there's enough time afterward, I thought I'd take that envelope up to Ray Preston."

"Oh, good. And you'll give it to him personally?"

"As promised." I thought of our childhood days in these environs, and said, "You know, when this is all over, you should come down here."

"That'd be fun, but—"

"Oh, come on, Maddy, you can't hide away on that island forever. We could stay downtown, eat at all the best restaurants, see a show. It'd be a blast. How long have you been up there without leaving? Over a year now, isn't it?"

"Well . . ." My sister's voice trailed off. "We'll see. It's just so hard for me; you've no idea."

"Maddy, you could hire a private jet—you've done that before—to bring you right to Meigs Field downtown. It couldn't be easier. I'd meet you."

"But then I'd be at the mercy of someone else."

"Just me."

"But I couldn't push myself, you know," she said, referring to her wheelchair. "I wouldn't know where things are."

"Just think about it, would you?"

"I will, I promise."

From her tone, however, I already knew that while she might think about it, she'd already decided against it. I shook my head as I sat there on the bed. No one was more stubborn than Maddy.

"There's one thing you never told me," I said, knowing it best to move on. "Why did Loretta come to see you? I mean, how did she find you? She was way out in the 'burbs and you were downtown." I paused, got no answer, "Maddy? Maddy, are you still there?"

After a long moment, her voice faint and oddly shaken, she said, "Yeah, I'm here."

"Are you all right?" Clearly she wasn't. "Did I say something?"

"It's just the idea of Chicago." As if she were crying, she paused, then cleared her throat. "It's just so . . . so . . ."

"Painful?"

"Exactly. I don't know if I'll ever come back, Alex."

"Oh."

I understood, or thought I did. The city of Maddy's birth was also where she'd lost her sight and lost her mobility. Thinking about it, if I were she, I don't think I'd want to visit the vortex of tragedy, either.

"Listen," I said, "it's late. I'm sorry, I didn't mean to upset you. Let's just talk tomorrow."

"Yeah." She sniffled. "I love you."

"Likewise."

I hung up, hoped Maddy was okay, wondered if she'd put on a video and listen to a movie, forget about it all.

"I think I cried myself to sleep," called my familial seer.

The next instant I felt terribly and thoroughly numb with exhaustion. I rubbed my face, went to the bathroom and flicked off the light, then returned and flopped down on the bed. I barely remembered collapsing and pulling the sheets over myself.

"Right. You slept very well, very soundly. Then the next morning you woke up refreshed. And then?"

Chapter 10

My second rental car was red, too. It was the first thing I attended to the following morning, and they were none too pleased at the car agency when I drove in and told them how I'd been chased and rammed by some hood, probably a gang member. I walked around the car with the manager, a balding guy with a walrus mustache and a gut to match, and we inspected the battered rear end, the dents and dings on the side. As he muttered and groaned, I pulled out some clumps of dirt and grass that were wedged up in the wheel well.

"This must be from when I was forced up into that yard," I said, holding the grass up as evidence.

The manager paused at one dent, felt it with his fingertips, then stared at me, shook his head, and groaned a polite, "Shit." He studied the indentation, then looked back at me with a skeptical eye. "What'd the police say?"

"Nothing. I haven't reported this." I saw him nervously pull on his big mustache, and I added the lone word, "Yet."

"Shit."

Fortunately I had played my credit cards correctly, having charged the rental on the one that would give me the most insurance, so every bit of damage was covered. Nevertheless, when I inquired about renting another car, the manager shook his head, tugged quickly on his mustache, chuckled a high, cynical laugh, and told me that wouldn't be possible until after I'd talked with the police. I immediately imagined the hours that would consume, and I began scheming another course. In the end, after a number of phone calls to corporate headquarters and insurance agents, I got my car, albeit reluctantly, having guaranteed the auto by charging the entire value of it on Maddy's credit card. The whole process took almost two hours, and I was sure it would have taken all day had I not had a multimillionaire sister to lube the way.

Of course, somewhere along the way, somewhere in there with all the other calls, I phoned Loretta to postpone our meeting, a shift of plans she didn't care for at all.

"Why?" she'd asked, voice deep and curt. "Is there something the matter?"

She sounded hurt, as if she were taking it personally, as if she were worried that overnight I decided I didn't like her. I reassured her that I wanted to come over, that something unforeseeable had come up. She wanted to know what that unforeseeable thing was, and the best lie I could come up with was closest to the truth.

"Car trouble."

I don't know why I didn't want to tell her about being chased last night, but instinctively I knew it was best not to talk about it, at least not yet. I didn't want to fuel an already anxious person who herself had been attacked in the woods the previous night. And in any case, she understood the idea of car trouble, the possibility of that, and when I told her I had to return my rental car and get another, she then assertively said she'd be waiting for me about noon.

"It shouldn't take you so very long to return a car," she chided me. "All you have to do is drive in and drive out."

I said I thought it might take longer and that I'd see her at one. She offered a gruff okay to that, then hung up.

As it turned out, I had over an hour to spare, which left me with more than enough time to make it up to Ray Preston's place of business, a small dry cleaner's he owned. I checked the address on the envelope and headed off in rental car number two for Northfield, a small, rather sleepy burg that fell in the shadows of the more prominent and wealthy Winnetka. I cut across a string of towns and took Edens Expressway up there but in the gridlock that was tightening boalike around Chicago and its endless suburbs, the trip took almost forty-five minutes. By then I was sure that it would have been lots cheaper and faster for Maddy to have sent the envelope by express mail.

Gold Medal Cleaners was easy to find, a nice gold store-front at one end of a short strip mall. As I pulled up and shut off my car, I looked up at the store's large, plate-glass window, saw a notice about a special on shirts, hung not boxed, and a neon sign that glowed: ALL CLEANING DONE ON PREMISES. Inside I spotted a woman customer, a couple of young girls behind the counter, and a man standing by one of those long racks, the mechanical kind that revolves. My eyes met the man's, held for just a moment longer than was customary, and I saw his brow quickly go up as if in recognition.

Taking the envelope from the seat beside me, I climbed out of my car and went in, passing the woman customer, who was now exiting with her plastic-sheathed clothing. A bright-faced, attractive girl greeted me from behind the counter, her brown hair pulled back in a tight ponytail, her teeth clean and white.

"Hi, what can I help you with?" she called. "Do you have anything to pick up?"

"No, but is Ray Preston here?" I said, then lifted up the envelope. "I have something to give him."

"Mr. Preston? Oh, sure. He was just up here. Wait a minute, I'll go get him."

While she disappeared into the back, a girl with red hair appeared, smiled at me, and started pinning numbers to clothes and then stuffing them in a nylon bag. I stood there, dumbly staring first at the rack of clothes, then turning and studying a gum dispenser by the front door.

A moment later, the brown-haired girl returned, saying, "Mr. Preston's on the phone. If you want to leave the envelope, I'll make sure he gets it."

Maddy's request flashed to mind. Make sure he gets it, she implored. Hand-deliver it to him, face to face. Just make sure you see him, she had said. It wasn't like this was a secret doc-ument or anything. It was something much simpler; the reason Maddy had wanted me to see him, shake his hand, perhaps have a short conversation, was I knew, that Ray had been one of her clients. And once I returned to Maddy's island, I was sure I would be thoroughly grilled, for first and foremost and forever and ever, my sister was a shrink. One who had been worried about the clients, some more than others, she had abandoned. So I knew I had to see him personally and I knew that invoking my sister's name would gain me an audience. It always had everywhere else.

"Actually, would you tell him that Dr. Phillips's brother is here?" I said to the young woman. "Tell him I'd like to see him and that I'll wait. I'm not in a hurry."

She disappeared, but I didn't have to wait long, for she reappeared with Ray in tow. He emerged from the jungle of dry cleaning, a deeply puzzled expression on his face.

I took the initiative, extending my hand, and saying, "Hi, I'm Alex Phillips, Maddy's brother."

"How did he look?"

He was very nicely though simply dressed, cotton khaki pants that were freshly pressed and a blue oxford cotton shirt that was distinctly and crisply starched. He had short brown hair, nicely trimmed, neatly combed. His mustache, not particularly thick by any means, was a little lighter in color. And his skin was pale. That was what I noted. It was like he was indoors all the time, like he never left his business. He had a big, white, boyish face, nice-looking, with the lines of middle age just beginning to appear.

"So he looked healthy?"

Yes, that was what he looked like, a big boy, face clean and body a tad plump. There was a hint of a shadow beneath his eyes, but no real circles, nothing that indicated poor health.

He looked at me in disbelief, then hesitantly reached over the counter and shook my hand. "Dr. Phillips's brother, really?"

"Yes, really," I replied. "I was coming down to Chicago and Maddy asked me to deliver this to you."

He studied me as if I'd been sent by a ghost from his past, as if I were a messenger from someone sacred, thought to be long lost, and said, "No wonder you kind of look familiar. I saw you drive up—that was you in the red car, wasn't it?—and for a second I thought I knew you. You kind of look like your sister."

I shrugged. While the resemblance between Maddy and me was slim, it was there. The same sort of eyes and nose, the shape of it all, the angles in the center of the face.

"Not many people pick up on that. You have a good eye." I held up the envelope and said, "Maddy asked me to give you this."

"Oh." He glanced at the package, then suggested, "Why don't we step outside?"

Ray Preston led the way out of his small but apparently prosperous shop, around the edge of the building, and down the alley. He stopped after a few feet, took a single cigarette from his shirt pocket, a butane lighter from his pants, and lit up. I looked at the ground, saw lots of butts mixed in with the gravel. So this was the break area. How attractive.

He asked, "How is she?"

"Fine. Keeping busy. She bought a big old house on an island and I think the repairs will keep her occupied for the next ten years."

"But, I mean, the accident. I heard she couldn't . . ."

"That's right. She's paralyzed from the waist down, but she's just as active as ever."

He turned away, a calm rather mild-spoken person, and shook his head. When he looked back at me, however, his white face was flushed red with fury, his blue eyes wide. He looked like an angry sportsman, someone who'd lost not just unjustly, but horribly, and who was now brimming with rage, someone looking for a target, any target.

"Goddamned drunk drivers! That's what hit her, wasn't it? Some guy who was drunk?"

I nodded, rather spooked and not understanding where his anger was coming from. "A bus clipped her—the driver was drunk. He'd already been warned two or three times."

"Jesus fucking Christ!" he cursed.

He took a long drag on his cigarette, sucking on it deeply as if it were a joint and he was trying to get every bit out of it and into him. All that heat and smoke. What was it fuel for? What was boiling inside him? He shook his head, cursed some more, and walked away from me. I understood now why Maddy wanted me to deliver the envelope. She wanted to see if he was stable and calm. I'd have to report that he definitely wasn't, not from what I was seeing in this brief encounter.

Then he turned back to me and in one simple sentence it all made sense.

"That's what got my little girl—a drunk driver."

Oh, I thought. That was what was causing his eyes to redden, his voice to choke with grief. And that was undoubtedly why he'd ended up seeing my sister, the shrink.

"I'm sorry," I said. "I didn't know."

"Yeah, some fucker ran a stop sign and broadsided my car. It was about a year after my wife and I were divorced, and I had my daughter, Lisa, for a few days. She was only six, and we were hit right out here," he said pointing to the street. "Right on her side."

She was probably killed instantly. Or maybe she died in her father's arms. Or perhaps Ray Preston's wife was there, too. I sensed there was a gory end to the story, one I didn't want to hear, for all of a sudden I was flooded with my own memories, those of Maddy's accident. The initial phone call at work. How long it had taken me to get to the airport. How sweet and smiley the stupid flight attendants were when all I felt like was smacking them and everybody else who looked happy. And then the days of waiting. Would she survive? Would she be able to talk? Walk?

I wanted to get out of this territory and off this subject, so I stretched out my hand, held the envelope toward him, and said, "Here. Maddy asked me to give this to you. I think it's something that you left in her office and that got mixed up with her things. She said she's sorry she didn't get it back to you sooner."

His brow pinched up in a puzzled expression, and it was quite obvious he couldn't imagine what his former therapist would be sending him after all this time. Perching his cigarette between his lips, Ray Preston accepted the parcel and started opening it at once. I was about to turn away, to beat a retreat to my car, but I couldn't hide my curiosity. What could Maddy possibly have sent? I moved closer as he ripped off the end of the envelope, as he dug in one hand and pulled out a letter.

Ray read it aloud. "Dear Ray, You left this in my office that day, but unfortunately I was never able to enjoy it. Sorry it's taken me so long to get this back to you—it was mixed up with my things. I hope you are well, and do call if I can ever be of help. Fondly, Dr. Phillips."

It was all clear to Ray; he knew what was in the envelope, and he looked up at me, mumbled, "Oh, God. Your . . . your sister. She was so good. I mean, sometimes I forgot she was blind. I wasn't thinking one day and I took this in to show her."

He pulled out a color photo of a beautiful child, a little girl with light brown hair, bangs, round face. She wore a little white dress, had dimples, a cherubic smile. Oh, shit, I thought, Maddy had never been able to enjoy the picture because she'd never seen it, hadn't been able to.

Ray took a deep breath, bit down on it, tried not to cry, muttered, "Oh, God."

"I'm sorry. I . . . I . . ."

I was speechless, that was what I was. Why did Maddy do this, have me deliver this photo? Was she that thoughtless? No, not at all. Not really. She was extremely cunning, however, and Maddy had certainly calculated that if I, a mere messenger from his former shrink, couldn't stir up any kind of raw emotion, then the picture of the dead girl most certainly would. And if it did—and it most definitely had—that fact could be construed to show how much Ray still needed his therapist. And that in turn reflected quite poorly upon my sister's ego and her need to feel indispensable and important.

Disturbed by Maddy's motivations, embarrassed by the situation I was now in, I muttered a quick farewell and left Ray Preston red-eyed and clutching the photo and memories of his little girl.

Chapter 11

"Then when Lucretia resists," Loretta recounted to me as we sat in her backyard, "this Roman soldier, Sextus Tarquinius, draws his sword and tells Lucretia that if she does not sleep with him, he will kill her and his own slave, place their bodies side by side, and tell everyone that they'd been caught in the act of adultery."

"How awful," I replied.

I wasn't sure why Loretta was telling me the story of the rape of Lucretia, but there was obviously something of importance, a truth of some sort, in the story, for I could see the passion in Loretta's eyes. Ever since I'd arrived at her house that cloudy afternoon, Loretta had been clutching a volume of Shakespeare that contained the narrative poem of Lucretia's sad fate. Loretta had been holding it against her breast when she greeted me at the door, and she never put it down as she made us both a glass of iced tea, led me past the scorning Helen, across the patio, and to a far corner of the yard. As I sat there on the coarse crabgrass, I stared at Loretta, tried to comprehend what this was all about. This wasn't happenstance, her telling me all this, particularly in the absence of Helen.

"So rather than have everyone think she's been dishonorable, Lucretia lets Sextus take her. You know, they did it."

81

Loretta looked at me, her eyes wide, wanting to make sure I understood that fornication had taken place. "But that's not the end of it. Lucretia's a very, very honest, even righteous person. So the next day, she gathers her family and tells them what happened, telling them that her body but not her heart had been taken. And then Lucretia pulls out this long, arching knife, saying . . ."

At this, Loretta cracked the Shakespeare volume and read,

"Poor hand, why quiver'st thou in this decree?
  Honour thyself to rid me of this shame;
  For if I die, my honour lives in thee,
  But if I live, thou liv'st in my defame."

Loretta dropped the book in her lap, threw back her head of thick graying hair, slammed a fist against her chest, and said, "And then poor Lucretia plunges the knife into her chest and kills herself on the spot."

It was all very dramatic. This story, the way Loretta was recounting it and beating her own chest. I studied that pale face that suddenly didn't seem so pale, for it was flushing with color and passion, and I admired how her eyes were coming alive with animation. Loretta, I thought, would have made an excellent English lit teacher, one who could have imparted her love of the word to her students. I couldn't help but wonder, however, how the theme of this poem was supposed to enlighten me or what the story itself was foreshadowing.

I glanced back at the house, and just as quickly as I saw Helen's thin figure staring out one of the rear windows, she disappeared. I knew Helen didn't like my being here and that it infuriated her that Loretta had led me out of the house and to the farthest edge of the property.

"That's a very moving story, Loretta," I said. "You tell it quite well. You must have studied it a great deal."

"I have," she said quite proudly. "There's a library not far from here, and I've read everything they have on Lucretia. They even ordered some books from another library for me."

"How nice."

"Yes, I love to read. I read all the time."

"To escape?" I asked.

"Yes, to learn about distant places."

I tried to pose a leading Maddyesque question, and I said, "Are there things you want to escape from?"

She smiled, frowned, and then her mouth fell flat. "Well, sure."

"Like what?"

I watched Loretta's eyes as they hit upon the yard, the house next door, a large oak tree, and then circled around and came back to her own home. She stared for a long time at the low white structure, the simple but empty patio in back, and then her eyes fell to the grass in front of her and she pulled at a blade of grass.

"I don't know, all this."

My first thought, of course, was that Loretta had been raped. She so clearly identified with Lucretia, sympathized with her plight and dilemma, I couldn't help but wonder if she'd been similarly violated. If that were the case, was Loretta planning a course of action similar to her tragic Roman heroine's? Was her letter to Maddy nothing more than a veiled plea for help?

I cleared my throat, said, "My sister, Maddy—"

Loretta instantly brightened, looked up, blurted, "Yes, Maddy. She's your sister. How is she? Is she all right?"

"She's okay. She asked me to apologize for having left so abruptly. You know there was a terrible accident and that she was in the hospital. You know that she didn't want to leave you, don't you?" I asked, directly and forcefully delivering one of Maddy's main messages to her former client.

"Yes, she was hit by a drunk bus driver."

"Right, and she lost the use of her legs. She's doing all right, though, and she wanted me to say hello and ask how you are."

"Me? Oh, I'm fine."

Loretta paused in thought, and looking at her I felt a bit of pity, I supposed, but also a great deal of affection. I liked her simplicity. Perhaps it was that she never strayed more than a few blocks from this house, for it was clear that she was not caught up in the complications of modern society. No, she seemed not at all affected by computers or global communications, not even by the myriad of input and stimulation brought right into the house by cable television. Definitely a misfit in terms of today's world. I imagined her in a long white dress on some English country estate and knew that if she'd been born a hundred or two hundred years ago, she could have lived her entire life on such a place and fit in quite perfectly. No one would have given a thought to her not leaving the grounds.

Loretta smiled. "I like Maddy. She's so pretty and nice. She was so nice to me."

"Good." Then I gently said, "She got your letter."

"Oh?"

"And she's worried about you."

"Oh."

Loretta said nothing, just started pulling on another blade of grass. I'd been in therapy, knew the trick of silence, how shrinks used it to try to get you to play the next card. But Loretta was quite the expert poker player. She volunteered nothing further.

I prodded. "Maddy said it was all right for you to talk to me. She wants you to talk to me because she's worried about you."

Loretta looked across the expanse of grass, brushed several strands of her long straight hair out of her eyes, but still said nothing, holding on to her silence and privacy. Of course, I couldn't expect Loretta to talk to me as openly as she had with Maddy, but I'd still hoped invoking my sister's name would grant me a certain amount of access. I supposed it had, actually, for I was out here in her yard, just the two of us, but I could now see Loretta pulling back, even starting to shut down. I pulled out my last and best effort.

Before I lost her completely, I said, "Loretta, in your letter you said you needed help and that it was a matter of life and death. What's the matter? Are you in danger?"

She shrugged, drew in a deep, long breath, opened just a bit, and hesitantly said, "We . . . we did something bad."

"Who?"

"My family."

"What happened?"

"Something . . . something bad," she repeated.

"What can Maddy do to help you?" I asked.

"Nothing. I shouldn't have written her. I'm sorry. Tell her that, would you? It's too late."

"No, I'm sure it's not, Loretta. Just tell me what happened, and I'll do what I can. Maddy will help, too."

"No, she can't. Neither of you can. It's hopeless." She looked down, shook her head. "We deserve to die."

Oh, God. Oh, Jesus, I thought. It flashed before me: Loretta is going to kill herself, stab herself just like Lucretia. I could see the desperation, the despair, in her eyes. What should I do, could I do? Intervene, blow the whole thing up by talking to Helen?

"Don't panic, Alex. Loretta and I were talking about this very thing when she was in therapy. Something quite traumatic happened in her family, and this is her great secret. It was the focus of our work together. She was getting ready to divulge it when I had my accident. That's why my leaving was so hard on her—she trusted me and then I abandoned her. Find the key to this secret, though, and you'll unlock her mystery. That's what you have to do, Alex, find that key."

I slowed my thoughts, tried to make a little more sense out of this, because somewhere inside me I knew that exposing Loretta's words, fears, and even threats to Helen or others would be the worst possible course of action. I had some time, I sensed. This had been brewing for a while. There was no immediate emergency. I ran my hand over the grass, took a swig of iced tea, tried to plot my next move.

"This is good tea," I said, trying to defuse things a bit. "Maddy would love it. She drinks this stuff by the gallon."

She smiled. "I know. That's why I made it for you. In honor of your sister."

I didn't ask how Loretta knew what Maddy liked to drink, but I suspected that she knew a lot about my sister. Like everyone in therapy, I was sure Loretta had noticed every detail about her therapist—from her shoes to her blouses to the framed prints on her walls—and gathered all these bits and pieces and tried to form an image of what that person was like in real life beyond the office.

I switched tactics, asked, "How's your brother, Billy?"

She opened her mouth, almost said something, then glared at me as if I'd almost succeeded in tricking her. Instead, she looked away and shrugged her shoulders.

"I don't know."

But she'd been about to say fine, hadn't she? Hadn't I seen the beginning of that word perched on her lips?

"Why don't you know?" I asked, following Maddy's suggestion to push her on this one. "Don't you see him?"

"No, Billy's gone."

"Gone or disappeared?"

She stared at me distrustfully. "Both. He ran away. Why are you asking about him?"

"Because I'd like to talk to him, if you wouldn't mind. Do you know where he is?"

"No," she quickly replied.

She looked away, stared off into yard after yard of grass Pinched her lips tightly together. I felt as if I could read her thoughts, that she was wondering just what kind of huckster I was.

"You don't know or you don't want to say?" I asked. "Which is it, Loretta?"

She wouldn't budge, which I took to mean she didn't want to say. I'd pushed too hard, perhaps too fast, however, and I could see her pale face redden with anger. I'd asked too many questions, cornered her even, and it was obvious she was going to give me nothing further.

Still, I nudged a little more, asking, "What about Carol Marie? How's she?"

"Fine."

"Did you say she owns a store?"

"Yes."

"Here or downtown or—"

"Here, right here. At the mall." She eyed me suspiciously. "Are you really Maddy's brother? You don't look that much alike, really. Her hair's short and straight. Yours is curly. And she has a ballerina's body, real long, not broad like yours."

"Well, I'm really her brother." I added, "She's almost three years older than me and she's my only sister."

Loretta moved her head slightly to the side and eyed me with such great scrutiny and suspicion that I thought she was going to ask me to prove my sibling bond to Maddy.

Instead, Loretta asked, "Are you a shrink, too?"

"No."

"Well, that's good, because if you were, you wouldn't be a very good one."

I deflected the criticism, adopted her bluntness, and calmly laid it out for her, saying, "You wrote a letter to Maddy, which worried her a great deal because she cares for you. She knows you have a problem with Helen, and Maddy knows something's wrong in your family, that something happened, and she wants to help. She couldn't come to Chicago to see you in person, so that's why she sent me." I paused, hoped this would work. "So what would you like me to do, stay here for a few more days, or leave and report to Maddy that there's nothing we can do?"

A glimmer of a grin quivered across Loretta's lips. She gazed down at her right hand, traced a vein on the back of it with her left index finger. Then she started picking at her fingernail.

"I was wrong to doubt you. I'm sorry. Just then, just the way you said all that, you sounded exactly like Maddy, like Dr. Phillips. Gentle but no monkey business. Very matter-of-fact, you know?"

I didn't let up, pressing, "The choice is yours, Loretta. What should I do?"

She lifted her glass to her mouth, took a long swallow of iced tea. Her eyes looked everywhere—grass, sky, tree, hand. And finally, directly at me.

"Carol Marie's store is called CM Fashions. It's at the Glendale Mall. Go talk to her. Talk to Carol Marie and ask her about Billy. Ask her why Billy had to run away."

Chapter 12

I left Loretta sitting in the yard. She said nothing further, just turned and stared off into a neighbor's yard, and so I got up and walked toward the house, empty glass in hand. As I approached the rambler I saw the back door, the one that led off the kitchen, swing open and there was Helen behind the dark screen, just the image of her. Tall, well-preserved, cropped gray hair, attractive. And dying, I was sure, to know what Loretta and I had talked about.

I reached the patio, spotted the path that led around the house, and recognized my route of escape. I set the glass on a round metal table, then veered off to the right.

"Thanks for the tea," I called to Helen as I walked toward the rear of the garage.

She stepped halfway out the door, one foot in, one foot out, hand still on the tiny knob—such a midwesternly pose, I thought—and called after me, "Is . . . is everything all right?"

"I think so."

Not satisfied, she pressed. "If something were wrong, you'd tell me, wouldn't you? I know the children aren't that fond of me, but I promised their father I'd look after them, and I've done the best I could. And I do care what happens to them, I really do. So you'd tell me if there were anything I needed to know, wouldn't you?"

"Sure."

It was the first hint of softness that I'd seen, and I wondered if I shouldn't just go in and talk with her. Part of me hesitated, though. Maybe we'd talk later, but not now, not yet.

So I lifted my hand and said, "I'll be in touch."

I glanced back at Loretta, who was flat on her back on the grass and staring up at the sky. What was at issue between these two women? What kept Loretta leashed to a house inhabited by a stepmother she clearly didn't like?

As I backed out of Loretta's driveway and made my way along the edge of the park, I gazed off into the thick woods. That was connected to Loretta's family somehow, all that business in the park last night. I knew that now; it hadn't been a random attack out there. No, I sensed it and was quite certain it all tied into whatever Loretta's family had done, whatever had happened, whatever they wouldn't tell me. I sensed that Helen had come slashing out of the night not simply in defense of the screaming Loretta but also to protect something else, which had to be that secret, the familial one.

"Yes, that's quite possibly true," called a voice with more perspective than I had. *"Now I want you to shift a bit, move your thoughts elsewhere. I want you to think carefully: When you were driving then, as you were heading to the mall, did you notice if anyone was following you?"*

I had to be chased and my car slammed into only once; I wasn't eager for it to happen a second time. I wasn't that dumb, and I wasn't more than a house or two away from Loretta's that afternoon when I checked my rearview mirror the first time. I saw some car, a blue thing, way back there, and was relieved when it pulled into another driveway. No other vehicles appeared, but I kept my attention on the street behind. Too much attention, really, because I missed a stop sign at the first corner and nearly broadsided someone. I slammed on my brakes, skidded to a quick, short stop.

"Watch it, jerkface!" shouted some young guy in a convertible.

I waved my apologies, turned right, accelerated, and hurried on, relieved that no one was after me a second time.

"What then?"

The Glendale Mall, a huge, sprawling affair built in the middle of nowhere, was close to my motel, and I'd passed it earlier that morning. It was only a few miles, five at most, and I'd be there in ten, fifteen minutes. Then I'd look up Carol Marie, who I hoped would fill in some of the blanks. It all seemed simple.

Once I reached that main road, I was no longer concerned with the idea of someone tailing me. It no longer seemed a possibility. Besides, it was broad daylight, the traffic was light, and I just disappeared into conjecture, tried to figure out what this was all about, why Loretta was sending me to Carol Marie's store.

"Now Alex . . ." beckoned my faraway trance coach, who then breathed in, breathed out. *"Just picture that you're mesmerized by the hum of the wheels, transfixed by the white stripe on the road. Don't worry—you can still drive. In fact, your driving skills are better than ever. Much more sharp and reactive. There's no worry about how you're going to reach your destination. Another part of your brain has clicked on and is directing you there."*

Everything seemed to disappear from around me. I spaced out, let my body be carried along by the car that seemed to be magically driving itself. My mind seemed to detach itself, turn into something else. A gust of wind. A soaring bird. All my thoughts flew upward. High. Way high. Rushing through the wind.

"That's right, Alex. There're two parts of you. The conscious part of you that stays switched on and takes care of all the mechanics of operating the car."

Switched on autopilot, I thought. Highway hypnosis. Virtually every single person had been similarly mesmerized by the road.

"Exactly. And the other part is the subconscious part of you that disappears and flies away. Now, can you tell me what that soaring, birdlike part of you notices?"

Cars, concrete. I was flying somewhere above my own rental car—the second one—and down below me I saw machines on wheels that rushed down bands of concrete.

"But you see more, don't you? Of course you do. You see much more. It's all recorded somewhere in your mind, so just let the film

replay. See it again. As the conscious part of your being drives the car down the road, there's another part of you that's thinking and noticing lots of things. Things that you saw once and never gave a second thought to, such as . . ."

The lady with the two shrieking kids in the backseat. She was turned, looking right at them, and screaming. Jesus Christ, I thought, keep your eyes on the road. And the flower truck. A big purple thing with a flower tied to its side mirror. There was a man driving that. A big fat man with a cigarette.

"Anything behind you?"

Two motorcycles at a big intersection about a half mile from Loretta's. A man and a woman on these monster choppers. Some fun that must have been. And a semitrailer plastered with an enormous picture of a boy and a girl drinking milk. Lots of cars coming down a road on my right. I could have come that way, I realized. I remembered looking at the map, and that other road was another route from Loretta's.

"What color cars do you see coming from that direction?"

Red. Black. Yellow. Maybe blue. I really didn't notice. There were just a bunch of them.

"So you turn and which of these cars continues after you?"

Ah . . .

"While the conscious part of you is driving, Alex, the subconscious part is busy flying around and taking in all sorts of things. Things that you might not be aware of."

I couldn't tell. Didn't know.

"Watch this film a second time, Alex. Look at it carefully. What do you see?"

Nothing that I could remember. Perhaps a green sedan. Maybe it was a truck.

"Get completely involved, Alex. Let the fragments of memory flow together. Was there a big brown car behind you like the one that rammed you the previous night? Did a big brown car pull out from the other road? Could he have gone the other way and caught up with you at that intersection?"

I was being asked for something I didn't know. Stop it, I wanted to yell out. You're focusing me too much. Hypnosis could do only so much, and it certainly couldn't perform miracles. Hell if I knew if there was a car like that big old brown thing behind me. I'd checked near Loretta's. I was as careful as I thought I needed to be. Other than that, I didn't notice a blessed thing. Nothing!

"Okay, just relax. Just take a deep breath. Hold it, then let it slip out . . ."

Chapter 13

I didn't like this. Didn't care for the way things were going. As I was driving, an uneasy sense of paranoia began to filter through my head and contaminate my thoughts. I feared another attack like the one last night. I feared—rather knew—that I'd entered someone's territory, and that that person would attempt to kill me. An odd image filled me as I crossed a highway and drove into the huge parking lot of the Glendale Mall. It was sketchy. Quite vague, actually. But the memory of that guy in the car last night, combined with some fearful vision of a person cloaked in gauze and pungent with violence, made me shiver.

"Yes, you are in danger, and, yes, someone will make another • *attempt on your life. But not yet. Not till the evening. Just stay with that moment, that afternoon. You are driving into the mall and it's' cloudy and—"*

No, the sun broke through the clouds, brightening and warming the June afternoon. As I drove on, I checked the sky, noticed how it was clearing, and I disregarded the thought of someone tailing me. I continued on, followed a tangle of roads and loops until I arrived at a large building that looked like a huge, fancy bomb shelter with skylights. I steered off to one side where I saw a bank of black glass doors, above which was posted MALL ENTRANCE.

The interior was as generic as the entryway. Plunging inside, I gravitated toward the stereotypical central courtyard, resplendent with a massive fountain, of course, and some very non-midwestern palm trees. I looked around and realized I could be anywhere in the United States. In an odd way, I had instant orientation, for there really wasn't much difference from the last ten malls I'd visited, and I knew that there'd be a map by the money machine I spotted.

Though CM Fashions was one of the few non-national stores in the mall, I found it by one of the chain bookstores, the one with all the orange shelving and fluorescent lights. Carol Marie's store was bright as well, with white walls, strips of clean, smooth pine for shelves, and racks full of pastel clothing. A lot of cotton, I thought, and then realized that was their specialty, clothes of natural fabrics. There were two women working in the store, one in her early twenties with frizzed blond hair, who was folding clothing, and another woman, early thirties, who was going through some papers behind the cash register.

As I approached the counter, I could see the woman's resemblance to Loretta. Same oval face, same tall forehead. The general characteristics were similar between the two sisters, but this woman was not just ten or fifteen years younger, she was also quite attractive. It was as if someone had taken the plain, dowdy Loretta and softened her eyes, heightened her cheekbones, made her nose a bit more petite and her hair rich and brown. Yes, this is exactly what Loretta would look like if she hadn't collapsed inwardly. Furthermore, in Carol Marie I instantly recognized a person who both internally and externally was not gray and pale and withdrawn, but someone who was lively and social, someone with vibrancy.

I stepped up, but before I could say anything, the woman I was sure was Loretta's younger sister looked up, put on a pleasant though slightly forced smile, and said, "You must be Alex Phillips."

I couldn't hide my shock. "How did you know? Did Loretta tell you she'd sent me over?"

"No. Helen just called and told me you were coming."

"Oh," I replied, a stunned, stupid smile on my face.

Scratch anything positive I might have started thinking about Helen. What a bitch. That confirmed it. How had Helen gotten that out of Loretta, with ease or had she threatened her stepdaughter, somehow forced her to reveal where I'd been headed and with whom I hoped to talk? And if Helen had found out that much, she could have found out everything we talked about. As I stood there, my mind whizzing ahead, I had to wonder if that meant that Helen knew everything about my being here, specifically that Maddy had sent me down here because of Loretta's desperate note.

"Why don't we go in the back room?" To her employee, Carol Marie called, "Beth, I'll be in back. Let me know if you need help."

"Gotcha," the young woman replied.

I followed Carol Marie, who wore white pants and a pink cotton sweater, past the dressing rooms and then through a small door and into a rear room that was packed with clothes and boxes and paper. There were several racks crammed with clothes, and in one corner there were a couple of chairs and a small table with a coffee maker.

"Want some?" Carol Marie asked, pointing to the brown liquid that looked as if it had been on slow-cook since morning.

"I'll pass, thanks." The way Carol Marie just said something rather surprised me, and I asked "You call your mother by her first name?"

"What, Helen?" Carol Marie sat down, poured herself some coffee and added a couple of packets of sweetener. "No, she's my stepmother. She raised me and Billy, my twin brother, or she did the best she could anyway, which wasn't all that great. But, no, she's not my real mom. No way, thank God. She used to be our cleaning lady. My real mother died a week after I was born." She laughed nervously. "So what can I do for you? Please, have a seat."

Interesting. Carol Marie and her brother had never known their real mother, so for all intents and purposes Helen would have or could have easily filled that role. Helen, after all, had been in their lives since they were born and had married their father when they weren't even six months old, yet Carol Marie made her relationship with her stepmother perfectly clear. Definitely distanced.

As I sat down in one of the folding chairs, I said, "My sister, Dr. Madeline Phillips, used to be Loretta's therapist, but then—"

Carol Marie, now seated across the table, stirred her coffee, then leaned forward, eyes wide. "That's right. That terrible accident. God, Loretta found out about that and cried for weeks." A sense of morbid curiosity—the one I'd seen all too often when the subject of my sister came up—crossed her face, and she asked, "Is she all right now? I heard she was paralyzed. How awful."

"She's doing fine. Actually, she's worried about your sister. That's why I'm here."

"Loretta? She always has everyone worried. Bless her heart, she was the best big sister Billy and I could have had—she was more like a real mother to us than Helen—but something happened. She just never moved on, grew up. She's just stayed stuck in that stupid house, even though she and Helen hate each other."

"They do?" I probed.

"Oh, God, yes. They always have. I think Loretta never left, if you want to get right down to it, because she thought she needed to protect our dad from Helen. And maybe she did. I'll tell you one thing, the two of them are going to go to battle over the house. Loretta says that the house was never supposed to be sold, that it's supposed to be coming to us kids, but Helen says it's hers to do with as she pleases."

"I'm not sure I understand."

Carol Marie shook her head. "Helen's planning to sell the house. She wants to get rid of it and move to Florida. None of us would mind seeing her go, but the problem is Loretta. It would mean throwing her out on the street."

"Yeah, it would."

"And there's no way in hell Daddy would have wanted that to happen. Confidentially, I've met with the lawyer to see if there's something we can do, if there's not some little clause in our father's will or something so that Loretta at least has a roof over her head." Carol Marie sipped her coffee, rolled her eyes. "Oh, family. What did Loretta do, write your sister?"

I didn't know what to divulge, how much, how little, and in any case I was dumbfounded that Carol Marie had asked. If that much was obvious to Carol Marie, had Maddy and I merely been duped?

"She did, didn't she?" pushed Carol Marie, a sly grin on her face. "Oh, God, and she probably sounded all dramatic and worried and scared."

"Actually, that's exactly right. She wrote a rather desperate letter to Maddy."

"Oh, God, I'm sorry. When Loretta gets upset about something, she starts shooting off letters left and right, and I tell you this house thing has got her twisted in knots. It should, of course. It's a really big problem, especially for her."

"Absolutely." I asked, "So it's your opinion that Maddy shouldn't worry?"

"No, she shouldn't. Anyway, there's really nothing she can do. It's the house that Loretta's upset about, and all of that could soon be in the hands of the lawyers."

I glanced away, stared at a stack of boxes, and thought back to the brief letter that Loretta had written to Maddy. Loretta had said it was a matter of life and death, which could revolve simply around her fear of being forced out of her home. And for her that would in fact be a very grave threat.

I turned back to Carol Marie and asked the question with which Loretta had armed me. "What about your brother, Bill? Loretta said I should ask you about him."

It was as if I'd slapped her. All the energy fell from Carol Marie's face, and it was her turn to disappear into distant thought.

Faintly, she said, "Well, there's . . . there's not much to tell." Carol Marie looked at me with a sad smile, said, "Billy's a hopeless alcoholic and he disappeared about three years ago. No one's heard from him since."

"Really?"

"Yeah, we all thought maybe he was dead, but about a year and half ago I saw a show on the homeless. You know, on TV. And there he was, my very own twin brother, sleeping on a subway platform in New York. I can only say it's a good thing our dad was already dead, because if he'd seen that, it would've killed him for sure."

"It must have been a shock."

Across the small table I studied this woman who appeared

at first glance the most well adjusted of the three children in her family. Attractive, well dressed, the owner of a successful store—I wondered how she'd survived. What she'd been up against. I could see some corner of sadness, a gray area of pain, and I wanted to know why this woman had succeeded in life and why Loretta and apparently Billy hadn't. Then again, I noticed that Carol Marie wasn't wearing a wedding ring, which meant none of the three siblings had chosen the traditional 2.2 kids route. Quite possibly they'd all shunned the suburban family ideal, and quite possibly this family line could die out. What I wanted to find out was what was keeping it from thriving.

That head of blond, frizzy hair poked into the back room, and Carol Marie's employee called, "Help, we just got swamped!"

Carol Marie took a big slug of coffee and bounced back, energy and excitement masking the pain I'd briefly seen.

As she started to get up, she said, "Owning your own business is so much work, I can't believe it. I'm supposed to be doing bookwork this afternoon, and instead my other employee called in sick and I have to be in the store until closing tonight."

We made small talk. As we moved from the rear to the front of the store, we wrapped things up, with Carol Marie promising that she would talk with Loretta and assuring me I didn't have to worry.

"Thanks so much to you and your sister," said Carol Marie. "We'll let you know if Loretta needs any help." With that she turned to several women, and enthusiastically offered, "And how can I help you ladies?"

I drifted out of the store, Carol Marie's words bouncing around in my head. I could see all that she'd said, buy it all, but there were some holes; that was all too obvious. Something had shattered this family, and I wanted to know what. And, damn it, I thought, cursing myself, I forgot to mention the incident in the park. I wanted to find out if Carol Marie would have any reaction to hearing Loretta had been chased and Helen had come to the rescue with a knife. Or what if anything she'd say about my being chased and my car rammed last night.

I stopped, looked back into the store. Someone else was just wandering into CM Fashions, and Carol Marie and her assistant were more busy than ever. I really needed to ask her about the park, what she thought might have happened. I sensed she would say she knew nothing, but it was the quality of her reaction that I needed to witness. Now, however, was obviously not the time.

So I resolved to get a cup of coffee and stop back in ten or fifteen minutes. Immediately my eyes lifted upward, scanned the second floor for the ubiquitous food court, and spotted a couple of bright umbrellas off to one side. I started for the escalator, wondering why anyone would come to an enclosed mall and sit under an umbrella. Were you supposed to pretend that you were really outside, perhaps at some fashionable outdoor café on the Champs Élysées? The snobbish part of me wondered if the masses had grown that dumb, if they could so easily be fooled. Evidently so.

I bought a cup of coffee at a frozen-yogurt stand, shied away from the umbrellas, and sat down on a bench overlooking the first floor and the courtyard. Down below there were a fair number of people, primarily mothers with children in tow and groups of giggly teenagers out for some after-school activity. As I was gazing downward, however, I sensed someone behind me, got that uneasy feeling of eyes upon my back. I turned, scanned the food-court area, but saw just a couple of tables of people. Then I gazed up the corridor, eyed an older couple walking along, a single man, but nothing more, not really. It was strange, though. I just couldn't shake off this sense of being observed.

"Because you probably were. You just have to assume that he was out there."

Malls had always made me uneasy with their artificial environments and their processed air, the sterility of it all. I just didn't like sitting there, so I quickly finished my coffee, started down the escalator. As I rode down, one hand on the moving black handrail, I looked across the courtyard and toward CM Fashions, hoping that it would be less busy by now. And apparently it was, because from my vista I saw Carol Marie emerging from her store. Great, I thought, my eyes trained on her. I'd catch her, ask a couple of more questions, and be on my way.

Carol Marie didn't go far, just down about a hundred feet and toward the money machine. I could see her the entire time, and wondered at first if she was going for some extra cash. But then I watched her as she reached into her pocket and pulled out a coin and went up not to the money machine but to a nearby carousel of phones. Immediately my curiosity was aroused—to say nothing of my suspicions. Certainly CM Fashions had a phone, undoubtedly one with several lines. So why would she, the owner of the store, be stepping out to make a call? Even if it was private, she could have just closed off the back room. Unless . . . unless what?

Had I walked right over when I reached the bottom, I would have been fairly obvious. Carol Marie probably would have seen me. Instead I made my way up against a row of stores, moving by a hat boutique, a shoe store, a venerated men's clothing store with a window of khaki pants and button-down shirts. By nature I wasn't a paranoid or suspicious person, but none of this was making sense. I knew as I neared the phones that I hadn't been given the bottom scoop on Loretta and her family. And I guessed I wouldn't get it no matter how many questions I asked or how direct I was. Instead I'd have to connive.

The phone carousel was a solid post about six feet tall with a half dozen phones blossoming around it. Each phone had a slight partition shielding it from the next, and when I went to the phone opposite the one Carol Marie was using, I could hear virtually nothing. I stepped back, gazed beneath the phones, saw Carol Marie's white slacks and white shoes. From the way her shoes were pointing, it was obvious she was half facing the central courtyard. I moved the other way, started approaching her from behind, and stopped at the next phone. I could hear only a bit more. Only a nondescript mumbling. Everything else was blotted out by the fuzzy roar of the fountain.

I didn't have much of a choice. I could always claim coincidence, and so I slipped up to the phone right next to Carol Marie, held my head low, and positioned my back to her. My face was shielded by the partition, and I leaned back a tad. I could hear her then, voice low and extremely agitated.

"Jesus Christ, I have no idea how much she told him," said the anxious Carol Marie. "No. No, I can't. I have to work until closing." Then she listened, said nothing until finally, "Okay, I'll see you then. I agree. We can't stop now; we've got to go through with it. But if that stupid bitch told him about Ray Preston, things could get really messed up."

Chapter 14

"Jesus Christ, Maddy," I said, pacing the big third-floor ballroom of my sister's house. "I still can't believe you didn't tell me."

"Well, I didn't know, not really."

"You mean to tell me you didn't know that Ray Preston was somehow connected to Loretta's family?"

"Alex, please."

"Cut the bullshit, would you?"

Reexperiencing it all in trance made me upset all over again. I couldn't remember when I'd last been so mad at my sister, and my fury had burst my trance like a needle popping a balloon. In one explosive moment my trance to the past was destroyed and I was back on the island, confronting not Loretta's sister but my own. And wondering who of all of them I could trust: Loretta, Carol Marie, or my sanctimonious Maddy.

I walked not toward the balcony but toward the far wall where three tall leaded windows overlooked the side yard. Leaning against the glass, I peered down some sixty feet to the lawn below, shook my head. Then I spun around and stared at my darling sis, who was lying way across the room, some thirty feet from me, so meditative, so Gandhi-like, on her black leather recliner. Her arms were at her sides, as still as her paralyzed legs, and with those sunglasses on I couldn't tell if her sightless eyes were open or closed. That didn't make any difference really, but I just wanted to know where she was—still focused on me at the mall with Carol Marie, or here, now, and paying the real me her complete attention.

"Maddy, do you hear me?" I loudly called across the towering room. "I can't fucking believe you did that to me."

"Alex, calm down. You're getting way too emotional about this," she said in a soft, rather distant voice.

"That's fine for you to say, you weren't stuck in the middle of it all and no one tried to kill you. No one lied to you, either."

"For God's sake, I wasn't lying to you."

"Well, if you didn't lie to me, then it was one hell of a sin of omission!"

With one finger, she pushed her glasses up her nose, rolled her head calmly toward me. I was sure that lots of her clients had gotten mad at her in therapy, that she'd pushed them until they'd furiously broken through some psychological barrier, which undoubtedly had been Maddy's long-sought goal for them. But this wasn't therapy and I wasn't her client. I was her younger brother and it pissed the hell out of me to see how much in stride she was taking my anger.

"Alex," she said, condescendingly, "haven't you heard of such a thing as client confidentiality?"

"My, what a convenient excuse."

"Alex, Ray Preston was a client of mine. I can't divulge what he told me in our sessions. I'm not only ethically obliged to maintain his privacy, I'm legally bound as well."

"I'm glad you can so rationally legitimize deceit, Maddy. I'm glad you think it's all right to send your brother so blindly into a dangerous situation without telling him what to watch out for." I snidely said, "You're like all shrinks, you know how to analyze clients, people that you're careful to keep at arm's length, but you don't know how to care for those close to you, your very own family."

That did it. With both arms, she shoved herself upright, wiggled deeper into the seat of the recliner, and I could plainly see that if she hadn't been paralyzed she would have either run over and slapped me or gotten up and kicked a chair or a wall.

"Stop it, Alex!" she shouted. "Don't talk like that! You know how much you mean to me. You're the only brother I have, for God's sake. I'd never knowingly put you in danger. My God, you're the only family I have left. I didn't know there was anything dangerous when I sent you down to Chicago. All I had was that letter from Loretta, who'd been very unstable the last time I'd seen her. When I read the letter I thought she was contemplating suicide and that it was a plea for help. That was why I sent you down there. I just wanted you to check it out, to talk to her. I thought at worst we'd have to intervene, maybe send her to a hospital, but, Alex, no, I didn't, I really didn't think any of this would happen. I swear to God!"

It was my turn to be calm, and I stood across the room, arms folded across my stomach and quite pleased with myself. I stared at the large Tiffany dome, the large expanse of stained glass that capped the fifty-foot-tall stairwell, the backside of which rose into this attic space like the dome of a mosque. And, yes, I was pleased. Or rather, relieved. I guess I'd just wanted to make her as mad as I was, and her distress was all it took to blot out my fury. Barely breathing and silently standing there, I studied the stained-glass dome, then my sister, and wondered where we could go from here.

"Alex?" she called, turning her head and sightlessly scanning the room. "Where are you? You didn't leave, did you? Alex?"

"I'm right here."

Still propping herself forward, she turned in my direction and said, "Please believe me. I honestly didn't expect anything like what happened. I had no idea anyone would be killed, least of all Helen. I just thought Loretta was in danger."

"From whom?"

"Herself."

"Are you sure it wasn't from Ray Preston?"

"Alex, Loretta had talked about suicide before and I was afraid this time she might really try."

I knew my sister, not only from our childhood days when she felt glee at mercilessly tricking me in any number of pranks, but particularly after what we'd been through when Toni, my old girlfriend of college days, was killed. I'd always, and often stupidly, trusted Maddy, and I'd learned the hard way to raise a flag of caution in questionable matters. As always, I had to remind myself that there was as much information in what Maddy didn't say as in what she did. So actually I was already assuming there was more to come. It was just a matter of asking for the details, then double-checking to make sure I got all of them, which was going to take some digging, no matter how direct I was.

I strolled across the room and toward the French doors that opened onto the balcony and the vast view of Lake Michigan. I moved slowly, though, one cautious step at a time as if I were pondering a crucial move in a serious game of chess. My main question was, of course, who was the pawn?

"You didn't answer me before, Maddy, and you're not answering me now. Did you know Ray Preston might know Loretta or someone in her family?"

"Alex . . ."

"Screw client confidentiality, Maddy. We're talking about murder. You knew, didn't you?"

She meekly replied, "Yes. Both Ray and Loretta were my clients, so, yes, I was aware that Ray had some dealings with Loretta's family."

"What kind of dealings?"

"I don't know."

"Maddy!"

"No, I don't, not really."

Like a lawyer finding a chink in the armor of a witness, I stopped just short of the French doors, turned toward her, and rather dramatically said, "Not really?"

Maddy lowered herself back onto the recliner, placed one hand on her forehead. She was silent, but she knew she'd been caught or cornered. She started to say something, stopped, then began her confession.

My often-too-clever-for-her-own-good sister said, "I started seeing Ray after his little girl was killed, and that's what I was working on with him."

"What do you mean?"

"His pain, his grief. He had a tremendous amount of anger over her death and he didn't know what to do with it, where to go with it. That's what we were working on. I was trying to help him deal with his grief in a healthy, sane way."

"I don't get it," I commented, moving up to the doors and peering out. "How does that hook in with Loretta and her family?"

"I'm not really sure. He never mentioned them, not at all. That's why all of this is so confusing."

Two separate people, not related, both seeing my sister. How had Maddy made the connection between the two of them? Had Maddy been more than her amazingly insightful self? Had she been psychic?

I asked, "If he didn't say anything, then how did you figure out there was any sort of contact or association between the two of them?"

Behind me I heard nothing. I waited, let the seconds drag into pained silence. And then asked the obvious.

"It was Loretta, wasn't it?"

When there was still no reply, I glanced back, saw Maddy apparently in deep thought and slowly nodding her head. Her face was flat, expressionless, her eyes hidden behind her glasses. A mournful face—that was it. So what was it that was making her so sad?

Finally she said, "Yes."

"Well, what did she say?"

"Nothing, really. She only alluded to something." Maddy lifted her shoulders, then slowly lowered them. "Loretta just showed up at my office one day and demanded to see me. I had clients all day, booked solid. The receptionist told her I had no time, but Loretta insisted on waiting, said she'd wait until the very end of the day. When I was told about her, I was concerned, of course, that it was someone at suicide risk, so I briefly saw her between patients. That's how I first made the connection between Loretta and Ray Preston."

"What do you mean?"

"Well, I asked her how she found me, why she decided to come to me. And she said she'd heard about me from Ray Preston, whom I'd actually seen that morning. In the course of this first and rather short conversation, I ascertained that Loretta was not an immediate threat to herself, but I did note how nervous and agitated she was. I had an opening the following day and asked her to come back. She did, and I saw her for a full hour, and it was only then that I realized how difficult it was for her to come into the city. Not just physically but emotionally, you know, because of her agoraphobia. She didn't drive and she was afraid of the bus, so she took a cab the entire way.

In fact, she paid for the cab to wait then and every other time she came to see me. She was afraid of not being able to find a way home." Maddy drifted away in thought, then added, "I saw her for only two months, and that was the principal focus of our work, her fear of being out in public."

"But what about Ray? What else did she say about him? She must have said something, didn't she?"

"No, not specifically anyway, and that's what was so confusing. In our last session, it came up that Loretta felt her family had done something very bad. She said someone had been hurt. She revealed this to me in a very slow, calculating way. Like she was testing me. Like she knew I knew the person whom she was talking about. Of course I didn't, not absolutely so, but the only person we knew in common was Ray Preston. All this came up at the end of the session, but I clearly got the impression that Ray was the one she was talking about."

"What did she say specifically?"

"Nothing more than that, that her family had done something very bad and someone had been hurt." Maddy started biting the tip of one of her fingernails, then said, "We ran out of time, unfortunately, but I was planning to make that the focus of our next session because suddenly everything was clear. You know, sometimes it takes awhile to get to the heart of the matter, to peel away the layers that a client has used to disguise an issue. And in a flash I suddenly understood the crux of why she had come to see me."

"Which was?"

"Well, it wasn't about leaving the house or being fearful of crowds. Yes, that was a problem, but she didn't want to deal with that, she wasn't prepared to. It wasn't why she'd gathered her energies and courage and come all the way downtown to see me specifically. No, it was about this something that her family had done. She had to tell someone, it was burning inside her, and somehow she had decided that the someone she was going to tell was me."

It didn't take a genius to understand why Maddy had progressed no further in untangling Loretta's riddle. Sometime between that session and Loretta's next scheduled appointment, Maddy had been struck by that bus, which had automatically curtailed her practice and sent her clients scurrying to a smattering of other therapists. All her clients but one.

"Loretta didn't see anyone else after that, did she?"

"No. Afterward, a few weeks after the accident, that is, I found out that one of my associates had contacted her and encouraged Loretta to come in, but she wouldn't. Loretta just kept saying I was the only one she could talk to and that now she'd never talk to anyone else."

How pitiful, I thought. A grown woman who was afraid to venture farther than her neighborhood library finally did just that. She reached out for perhaps the first time in her life, found someone to trust with a long-buried secret. But then that someone was literally plowed over by the harsh city. Poor Loretta, I thought. It was no wonder she refused to come out a second time.

But it didn't take a genius or a shrink or a psychic to deduce how Loretta and her family might be tied to Ray Preston. If, as Loretta had said, her family had truly done something bad, there was only one horrible thing that had happened in Ray Preston's life.

"So you assumed," I postulated, "that someone, although you didn't specifically know who, in Loretta's family, was responsible for the car accident that killed Ray Preston's daughter, Lisa."

"Of course I did."

Which wasn't so very far off. In the week that I had been down in Chicago prior to Helen's death, I'd learned that and much more.

I turned to my sister, said, "So you were aware of Ray's anger?"

"Of course."

"And when you received Loretta's letter and learned she was potentially in danger, you—"

"I assumed either she was contemplating suicide or someone was indeed threatening her."

"Someone like Ray Preston."

"Exactly."

"Which is why you sent me to see him—to see if he'd gone off the deep end."

"Correct again." Maddy slipped off her sunglasses, laid them in her lap, and began massaging her pale and naked eyes. "I didn't think Ray was a violent man, but I wanted you to go see him just to check it out."

"I wish you'd told me all this. It would have made things a little bit easier and a whole lot clearer."

Plus a lot less crude. I'd felt like such a thug handing over that picture of Ray Preston's little girl. But it had worked. When he'd broken down upon seeing the photo, it had broadcast to me loud and clear that he was still in deep pain, a message that I could easily relay to Maddy.

"I would have mentioned it," said Maddy, "but once again it was the issue of confidentiality. How much of what I was told in the privacy of my office could I in turn tell you? And, anyway, it was just a wild guess that he might be the reason Loretta had written to me."

A wild guess that now, in retrospect, was pretty damn accurate.

Maddy asked, "So does all that make a bit more sense?"

"Sure."

"Are you ready to get back to it? Can we go on?"

"Yeah."

I guess I understood why Maddy had done what she had. Or at least she had me believing her rationalization. And like Pavlov's dog, I began to relax. I knew what was ahead. I sensed myself breathing in and out in longer, deeper breaths as I turned from the French doors and started for the recliner. Just the sight of the comfortable slope of leather, the knowledge that within a few moments I'd be slipping back into trance, sent an addictive sense of eagerness up my spine. I didn't want Chicago, necessarily, but I always wanted the rush of mesmerized tranquillity.

Maddy sensed me crawling onto the recliner, said, "That's it, Alex. Get comfortable."

I would and I did, stretching out, placing my hands first by my sides, then mummylike over my chest. I rolled my neck from side to side, heard it crack slightly. Took another breath.

"You obviously know what this means," I said, as I beckoned my body to relax, relax, relax.

"In . . . out." She said, "Of course I do."

"And now I understand why you doubt Loretta's story so much, why you don't believe she killed her stepmother."

"Roll your eyes up, Alex: One."

As I followed her command, I said, "Doesn't it mean both

you and I know something the police don't even have an idea of?"

"Yes. Now while still looking up, slowly lower your lids. And: Two."

"But isn't withholding information illegal, Maddy? Shouldn't you have told them?"

"Told them what, that I had a devastated client who might have known Loretta? Should I have sicced the police and all their detectives on that ruined man?" She was breathing loudly and clearly like a yoga master imparting a great lesson to a student. "Besides, I can't tell them. I have an obligation to maintain."

As I hovered on the edge of trance, teetered right there as if ready to plunge into some black bottomless pit, I understood why Maddy had pulled me into all this and why she was now pushing me on. She might not be able to tell the police that Ray Preston should be considered a prime suspect in the death of Helen, but I most certainly could.

Maddy called to me as I stood on the brink, saying, "Now, relax your eyes, and—"

"Wait," I demanded. "Suppose it was Ray who killed Helen. If it was, then why in hell would Loretta try to cover for him? Why would she try to take the blame for killing her own step-mother?"

"That's for you to find out," she replied from a distance. And then in a simple few words, my sister blew me away, flicked me off that cliff and back into the abyss, just by saying, "And: Three."

Chapter 15

I was swept away, carried off on some magic carpet, and I tumbled back into suburbia, which now more than ever was my kind of nightmare. Suddenly I found myself by a fountain in a mall, and I glanced around. Where the hell was I? I'd seen dozens of malls, this one just as bland as all the others, and I couldn't figure out what I was doing there until I glanced around, first saw a standing carousel of phones and then a store called CM Fashions. Of course.

I glanced at my watch, saw that it wasn't quite six in the evening. Only minutes ago I'd overheard Loretta's sister, Carol Marie, making plans. And if I'd understood correctly, Carol Marie would be at her store at least until nine-thirty when the mall shut down for the night. I had no idea what would transpire after that, but I had every intention of finding out. In fact, I didn't think I had any other choice.

I took my chances and left for a while, exiting the mall and crossing the freeway to a chain restaurant, where I experienced another powerful, albeit false, sense of déjà vu simply because I'd eaten in the identical restaurant in, if I remembered correctly, Florida. Or was it Nebraska? I checked out the soaring ceiling, the yellow booths, the plastic-coated menus. The layouts of both restaurants were identical and I was quite certain that in the other restaurant I was seated at the same table, one in the corner that overlooked the parking lot.

I stretched my time at the restaurant, ordered a seafood salad, and spent the next hour eating as slowly as I could and reading each and every page of the *Chicago Tribune*. Shortly after seven, I drove back to the mall, tried to guess where management would ask workers to park, assumed it would be the rear, and pulled into a spot that I hoped wouldn't be too far from Carol Marie's car.

She could have changed her plans. She could have cut out early. As I dove back into the mall, those and more worries began to cloud my thinking. I feared that I'd done it all wrong, that I shouldn't have left the mall at all, but in the end I had nothing to be concerned about. I circled the fountain, peered across the jets of water, and spied CM Fashions. Carole Marie was in there, now the only one working. It was almost seven-thirty.

Trying to kill time, I visited a few stores, pretended to be interested in their merchandise. I was careful, however, to check back every ten minutes or so, ascertaining that Carol Marie was indeed still there, and as it approached nine, I found a bench up on the second floor and sat down. From up there I had a clear view all the way across the courtyard and into CM Fashions, yet I was far enough away to be confident that even if Carol Marie noticed someone sitting up there, she wouldn't be able to recognize me.

It turned out to be a good thing that I'd taken up an observation post, too, because Carol Marie closed up shop early. I watched as two women drifted out of the store about ten after nine; before anyone else could enter, Carol Marie came out and pulled a grilled gate across the front of the store. Less than two minutes later she reappeared, a blue purse over her shoulder, and locked up.

I didn't expect her to get out of there quite that quickly, and I had to bolt from my position, take the escalator two steps at a time, and then hustle down one of the long, tunnellike corridors. Carol Marie had just reached the exit when I spotted her, and I slowed, pleased that I'd been right, that she had evidently parked behind the mall. Once she was outside, I hurried to the doors and spied her as she walked off to the right, her stride direct and brisk.

My car was parked to the left, in an area marked with a lime-green monkey bolted to a post, and I wasted no time dashing to it, bringing the engine to a solid rev, and then swinging around, up one lane, then back down another. I entered a zone identified by a red zebra, and a large light from atop a huge pole flooded everything with an odd tone. I peered down the row of angle-parked cars, saw nothing, no movement of any kind. Just bumper after bumper after bumper.

Way up ahead I saw something bob. A coifed head of hair. Someone moving quickly through the vast sea of automobiles. I hung on to the steering wheel, pulled myself upward. Yes. It was Carol Marie, making her way past the zebra zone, past the pelican zone, across one of the mall's winding inner roads, and to the most distant parking area, which was undoubtedly for employees. Then she stopped, turned slightly. I assumed she was unlocking a car door, and just as quickly as I saw her, she disappeared.

I pressed on the gas, went racing up the aisle. At the end I turned right, and looking across a small berm of dirt and the inner drive, I noted the white taillights of a car as it backed out of its spot. A small blue car. Nothing fancy. In fact, much less than fancy. It was an old car, quite battered with dents and huge blistering scabs of rust. The driver turned the vehicle straight at me, headlights ablaze, and I got a clear view of the driver's seat. Oh, shit. My heart pinched up. There were two people in the front seat, both young and laughing, probably just off from work, but neither one of them was Carol Marie.

I searched all directions, spotted a car approaching me as it wound down the drive and toward the main road. It was a white auto, a Ford Taurus, and as it quickly cruised past I spotted Carol Marie in the driver's seat. I couldn't help but panic. She was going one way, I the other. Plus I was still in the parking lot, while she was over there, across the small earthen berm and on the mall's drive. Shit. I rammed the car in reverse, backed up and around, then sped past the mass of parked cars. I looked to my right. Carol Marie was turning toward the main road.

There wasn't enough time for me to leisurely follow the exit signs that would eventually lead me out of here. I'd have to go another hundred yards or so to do that. Instead, I turned sharply to the right, hit the curb, then pressed on the gas as my rental car heaved itself up and onto the small berm, squashing several bushes in its path. On the other side I dropped onto the pavement with a clunk and steered around the drive and toward the main road. Carol Marie was there, stopped at a light and just three cars ahead of me. I took a deep breath, told myself to chill out.

From then on it was easy. Following someone who didn't suspect or even consider the possibility of being tailed made it simple. Still, as Carol Marie passed down the broad, four-lane road and off into the night, I was careful to keep my distance. I tried to keep at least two or three cars between us, which didn't prove to be that difficult, and I switched on the radio, squirmed in my seat until I was comfortable. This, I sensed, was going to be a rather long ride.

And it was. From the Glendale Mall, Carol Marie cut over about a quarter of a mile to the freeway, which she turned onto, heading south on 294. She swerved quickly across the bands of concrete, settling on the farthest and fastest lane, and I knew then that we'd be going into the city. I steered over, stayed behind a van that was in a parallel lane, cranked up the radio still louder, and kept a close eye on her.

A few minutes later the monotony of the suburbs began to melt away. The highway snaked around, we cut onto 90, which resurfaced as the Kennedy Expressway, and soon the lights of the Loop, pushing into the navy blue sky with its glistening towers, rose like Oz in the night. A city at night, sparkling like this, was one of the few, perhaps the only, man-made thing that I thought was truly a marvel, a thing of inspiring beauty. As the freeway curled through the neighborhoods of brick apartment buildings and old, grimy factories, the skyline beckoned like a dream, a piece of utopia right here on earth.

We didn't make it that far, however. Just past Irving Park, Carol Marie signaled and began to cross to the next lane. She hesitated there, then moved over to the next. And then the next, until she was speeding down the far right lane, ready to exit. I thought she might turn off at Belmont, but she sped past that. Then I assumed she might exit on Diversey. Two cars behind her, I gripped the wheel tightly, ready to swerve off. She similarly bypassed Diversey, though, hurrying on until she finally exited on Fullerton.

Still careful to keep my distance, I followed her, and pulled

off with a single car between the two of us. At the bottom of the
ramp, she turned left, passing under the freeway, and I wondered if we'd be heading all the way over to the lake. Perhaps
Carol Marie was to meet someone in the tony Lincoln Park
neighborhood. But who, someone of power and wealth? And
what for? I tried to pull this together, to imagine what it could
all be about. I suspected but wasn't sure.

"So even before you got there, you thought it might be him?"

There was only one person so darkly cloaked. It couldn't
have been anyone else, really, given what I'd overheard Carol
Marie say on the telephone.

"Did you notice at all that you were followed? Did you think it a
possibility?"

All my attention was ahead, focused on Carol Marie, as I
tailed her down Fullerton. I didn't notice anything else, didn't
even think that anyone else would be interested in Carol Marie's
evening trip into the city. I just kept my eyes straight ahead,
trying to see what she was doing, where she was going. And
about a mile, maybe less, after the freeway, I saw her blinker go
on. She was turning right at the next street, turning past an old
car wash with a huge octopus—buckets and sponges hanging
from its tentacles—atop the roof. I glanced around the neighborhood. The Octopus Car Wash had long ago gone bust, had
obviously not been used in years, and the other small buildings
and warehouses in the area appeared similarly neglected.

When Carol Marie rounded the corner, I slowed, pulled
over on Fullerton. I couldn't just continue right behind her.
The street she was turning onto was small, not much more than
an alley. I let her disappear from sight, then pressed on the gas
and slowly moved on. When I steered around the corner,
though, her car was gone. The white Taurus had disappeared.
I could see a block or two ahead, but there was nothing, only a
couple of old parked cars. It was just a street of abandoned
warehouses, buildings left by companies that had fled to distant
industrial parks.

On my left stood an old brick building, a one-story structure with a few punched-out windows and graffiti sprayed all
up and down. Nothing there. Just a locked building, no parking
area. I looked to the right. At the rear of the Octopus Car Wash
I saw something move. Not much. Just the last of a tall wooden

gate being slid shut. I drove past, continued on another hundred feet or so, and parked. I got out, locked my car.

A van and a couple of other autos passed me as I walked through the dark and up to the rear of the car wash's large lot. I came to a chain-link fence that had big sheets of plywood bolted to it. I peered through a crack, and in the dim light glowing from the alley, I saw the white Taurus now parked behind the car wash, right behind the garage door that had once opened and sucked dirty cars in. At first I didn't see Carol Marie, but then I heard the rustling of keys, the clicking of heels on concrete. I followed the sounds to the faint image of Carol Marie standing in a shadow and unlocking a door. The next instant she disappeared, stepping into the main building of the car wash.

I scurried around the side, found that the gate Carol Marie had driven through was unlocked. I scooted the gate back a bit, eyed the car, then slipped through the crack and darted in. The giant octopus towered over the building, over me. I made my way past a giant tentacle that curled down the side of the building and came to a filthy window, the glass thick with grime and its ledge covered with pigeon shit. As if Carol Marie had been gobbled up by the building, there was no sign of her, no lights, no sounds from within.

I couldn't resist. Moving up to the door Carol Marie had slipped through, I took the handle, pulled it, and stepped into a dank and black space. A bit of light dribbled in from the glass garage doors, and ahead of me I saw huge brushes, rollers, great tubes that had once carried hot air, and endless pipes and hoses that twisted like the car wash's namesake. I scanned the area, saw nothing moving, heard nothing fidgeting. If there was an office here, I thought, Carol Marie must have disappeared into some cloistered managerial space.

I heard a foot scrape along concrete, nice and long and slow. But it wasn't from somewhere inside. I turned. Through the window I'd tried to peer through moments ago, I now saw a figure, the features indiscernible. It was obvious, though, that it wasn't a woman. No, it was a man, big and thick, of that there was no mistake.

Great. I was caught somewhere between the unseen Carol Marie and some thug who was slowly making his way toward the door. At first I assumed this guy was here to meet Carol Marie, but his movements were so slow, so tentative. I saw his shadow pass the grimy windows, saw him stop and listen and try to ascertain who and where, what and when. It all looked so familiar, not unlike my spying actions. So was this guy looking for Carol Marie, too? Had he been waiting here, expecting her to enter the abandoned car wash, or could he have followed her as I had? If that was the case, of course, it meant he knew I was here also. My heart began to beat wildly.

"Why? Because Carol Marie knew by then that you had followed her? Is this when they were waiting for you behind the door?"

I nearly panicked in fear of violent things to come, and my mind, fearful of what Loretta's sister could be involved in, scattered in search of understanding. To whom had she been speaking on the phone and exactly what couldn't they stop? Loretta's letter came immediately to mind, and I realized that Loretta might not be contemplating suicide but someone else might be plotting murder. Then I took a long jump in an entirely different direction, leaping to what everyone thinks of in relation to modern American crime: drugs. The cotton clothes Carol Marie so nicely imported could be brought into the country sewn full of pouches of heroin or cocaine. Nothing these days was impossible, and perhaps nowhere could be better for dealing than the suburbs where deceit and mistrust flowed so freely yet were so well concealed.

There was no time for such wild speculation, though, and I reached out, felt a pipe that ran from floor to ceiling. I stepped along, for the figure behind me had reached the door, was now pulling it cautiously open. I saw the round shapes of a couple of barrels next to a closed door. I had no choice but to hide behind the barrels; there was nowhere else to take shelter. My best hope was that Carol Marie wasn't expecting this man, because he'd most certainly seen me enter the building. If they were together, though, I could only imagine the two of them rooting me out and what would ensue, particularly if either one of them carried a gun.

As my feet slid over the gritty concrete flooring, I searched for but still saw no sign of Carol Marie. I stepped over a bar along the floor, recognized it as a pipe used to keep a car moving straight through the car wash. I stopped at a column lined up and down with water jets, scanned farther ahead and saw two more doors, and wondered where the hell Carol Marie could have gone. Glancing back I could no longer discern the man. I thought I heard a faint noise, the near silent sound of a step, but I couldn't be sure. As quickly and quietly as I could, I moved over to the two barrels that sat near the wall, and then I knelt down and cowered into the dark behind them.

Peering out, I more clearly saw the figure now creeping into the car wash. Not too tall, not too heavy, the clothing plain and undistinguished. I felt a strong sense of familiarity, but couldn't make out any of the features, the face entirely wrapped in darkness. He moved into a small triangle of light that beamed in from outside, leaned against a pipe; I saw a pale brown shirt, the material thin. And then I spotted a raised hand holding a small black gun.

It all happened much too quickly after that. Things occurred so swiftly that I barely had time to react. Off to my left something creaked. I turned, noticed the door immediately to my left was slightly ajar. There was no light, only blackness, but hadn't it been closed only seconds ago? Then only inches to my right I heard something scratching and moving. Oh, Christ. Oh, shit. I saw a long, low thing. Pointy nose. Long skinny tail. I'd cornered a rat.

Still hunched over behind one of the barrels, I inched out. I scanned the faint light for the man with the gun, could see nothing besides the wilted brushes and hoses of the car wash. What should I do? Could I do? Stay half hidden in this rat-infested corner? Make a break for the door?

Hanging on to the top of the metal barrel with one hand, I scooted farther around. Then suddenly from behind me I sensed a whoosh of cool, damp air. I started to turn around. It was too late. The door behind me had opened. There were two dark, towering figures. They came rushing out, came charging right at me. The first was larger, holding something high in the air. It looked like a baseball bat. And that's what it felt like when it whipped through the air right at me and into me, smashing me on the back of the head. I had tried to turn away and duck, to shield myself with my hands. But it was too late. My head reverberated with a giant, dull thunk, and then I fell forward.

The last thing I heard as I collapsed on the cold concrete was a gunshot and a long frightened scream.

Chapter 16

I didn't know how long I'd been out, half an hour at least. Maybe not quite. And when I woke up, I was lying face forward on the ground, my head turned to the side, one cheek pressed against the cold concrete floor. Instinctively, I started to push myself upward, and as I did a huge wave of pain pounded my head and nearly flattened me again. Oh, shit. I brushed the dirt from my face, pinched my eyes shut, carefully touched the back of my head, and winced in pain.

Only the faintest light was seeping from outside, and I looked around, certain that I would see another body or two lying around somewhere, but there was nothing. No voices, either. Only complete silence and no lights. I reached up, felt for the top of the metal drum, and pulled myself to my feet. Still rubbing my head, I scanned the area. The door right behind me, where the two had come hurtling out, was now open. I stepped into the middle of the line where cars and soap had once so freely mingled, and peered all the way down to the far end. That door, the one I'd passed through from the rear parking area, was flung wide, now freely swinging in the night air. Perhaps too stunned to fear anything, I walked openly down the middle of the car wash, seeing no one. When I reached the large garage door at the rear and peered out through the filthy glass, I noted that the white Ford Taurus was gone as well. It didn't make any sense.

I glanced one last time into the long car wash, peered through the brushes and rollers, and called, "Carol Marie? Carol Marie, are you here? Are you all right?"

But even as I said it I knew she wasn't lying wounded, that the place was empty, and I turned to—

"Wait, don't leave. Not yet," beckoned a distant voice.

I leaned slightly against the large garge door, took a deep breath, as a faraway voice echoed through my head.

"Yes, just relax, that's good. Let your breathing deepen your hypnotic involvement. Breathing in . . . and out." After a moment, the soft voice called, *"Become completely absorbed in the experience of being in that car wash. Feel the throbbing on the back of your head . . . smell the odors of that musty old building. Replay the scene and look for things you saw or heard or smelled that weren't important then but are now."*

I shut my eyes. My hypnotically wise sister had long ago taught me that we take in much more than we actually realize. That we have a great deal of information stored in our minds that we simply fail to access. It was just a matter of opening up, unearthing things we know and letting them come to the surface.

"Exactly. So just think back over it, let it all unfold once again. You can slow it down and study things that you missed the first time. Let all of your senses contribute pieces of memory."

I let my breathing come slowly and rhythmically, and at the same time banished the pain from my head. Yes, that's right, I told myself. Back time up before the pain. Think back before you were struck. Let go of the pain and return to when your head didn't hurt.

It was as if I separated from the present. Using the skills Maddy had taught me, I left the present part of me standing there against the filthy garage door. I floated up. I floated away. Not too far away. And then I saw myself coming down Fullerton, driving my small red rental car.

"Was there anyone behind you?"

I was keeping a careful eye on Carol Marie up ahead in the white Taurus, so I didn't really notice anything else. All my attention was focused on her and what she was doing and where she was going. I noticed no other cars, nothing really until I turned the corner that the Octopus Car Wash sat on, then parked on the narrow street.

"And then?"

Two cars passed me. It was a narrow, quiet street, and I distinctly noted several vehicles.

"Visualize them. Experience that memory a little more intensely."

Not a car but a van popped to mind. That was the first vehicle. And there was a guy and a girl sitting up front. Next came . . . came . . .

"Came what?"

I saw the headlights. They were broad, set at a distance.

"So it was a large car?"

Yes, it was big. A big vehicle rolled into my memory, cruised the edge of it. I don't know why, but I just assumed it was an American car. It had that sort of a big Detroit look.

"Color?"

Dark.

"Dark brown?"

Maybe black. Maybe not. I couldn't tell. The light was faint, the image equally so. I strained to see the image in my mind, but I couldn't work miracles. I couldn't dredge up what wasn't there.

"That's okay, just go on. What next?"

A car door. As I slid open the gate of the car wash, as I spied Carol Marie's Taurus parked in the fenced area, I heard a car door shut. A gentle bang that stood out above the hum of the city.

"One door or two?"

It just went *thump*.

"Once?"

The sound bounced again into my head. Not *thump thump*. Just *thump*.

"So just one person got out."

Yes, that meant only one door had opened and closed. Which meant that whoever had followed me—undoubtedly all the way from the suburbs—was probably not in the van, but in the large dark sedan. And he got out and—

"He?"

Well, I guessed I'd noticed that, too. Of course. When the

dark brown or dark blue car had driven by I had seen a vague, very smoky shape behind the wheel. Nothing all that specific; it was just that the figure was broad, mannish-looking. Later, in the car wash, it was a man, so he had to have been the one in the car. And he'd followed me just as I'd followed Carol Marie, which meant undoubtedly that he'd been behind me all the way from the suburbs. From the mall or perhaps earlier.

"*Do you have any idea why?*"

It sprang into my head: because he was looking for the same thing I was.

"*Excellent. Can you describe him?*"

My memory bounded ahead. Sped up the story, skipped over the unimportant crud, and then slowed again. I was inside the Octopus Car Wash. He was outside. The first time I saw him he was little more than a threatening shape. Just an indiscernible figure lurking behind the murky glass. No. I couldn't see him then.

"*But later you did.*"

Yes, later. When he crept into the car wash. Through the door and inside. As he stalked me, who was stalking Carol Marie. I cowered behind the two metal barrels or drums or whatever you call those things, and I peered back. And through the cloudy light I saw a man who looked familiar.

"*Why?*"

I didn't know.

"*Hold the image of the man stalking the car wash. Describe his features. Pretend you're holding a photograph of him in your hands. Look carefully at it, study it. What do you see?*"

A man of medium height. Not a fat man. Not a skinny one either. So he was broad. Yes, a broad man of medium height. With dark hair. I could tell that because his hair blended in with the dark light. So it was probably someone with brown hair. And he was white. I could see his skin. His hair blended in with the darkness. The skin of his face stood out against it, glowed slightly in the darkness. I took a deep breath. That was the description that came rattling out.

"*Clothing?*"

It nearly disappeared into the darkness. But not quite. He moved into a small patch of light, and then the color brightened. Light brown. Next I eyed him as his right hand reached out, took hold of a pipe. I focused on the broad shoulders, noted how they dropped down, then how the arms got suddenly thinner.

"A short-sleeved shirt?"

A short-sleeved shirt, maybe a tan one. Light brown. Like the pants. The pants were tan or khaki, too. And then I saw his other arm rise and this black thing emerge. The gun.

"Alex, he looked familiar because he looked like someone you'd seen before, someone you'd met. Look at the man stalking the car wash. He looked like—"

Ray Preston. That was who he looked like.

"So what did Ray do next?"

No, it only looked like Ray. The shape, the features. But it was a cloudy picture. A blurred one, not at all in focus. I could only look at it and think that it might have been Ray. That this person resembled him. I could in no way, however, be sure it was Ray. It could just as easily have been some ordinary thug. Or a policeman.

"Why do you say that?"

I started trembling. Staring at the trance-frozen shape, a caffeinelike jolt suddenly ripped loose and started shooting through my body. I had to be careful of this man. He was dangerous. I knew he would do me harm. Physical harm. More important, he was a threat that wouldn't quit, that wouldn't cease. He'd pursue me because he wanted me to stay out of this. Some clairvoyant part of me knew that was what he would later say to me.

"Say what?"

Some time in the not very distant future this lurking threat of a man was going to come screaming after me.

"Screaming what?"

Oh, God. I knew, I knew, I knew that as long as I was poking around in all of Loretta's business, he would continue to pursue me. And—

"Slow down, Alex. We'll deal with that later. You have nothing to worry about now."

What? How fucking ridiculous. Of course I had something to worry about. My head began to ache in expectation. Throb. Oh, God. I was crouched behind those barrels, about to get clobbered. I was so stupid. So unsuspecting. They were behind there. The two of them.

"The two of who?"

Them! They came bursting out, right at me. I turned.

"And what did you see?"

Shit, it was a baseball bat. This guy with Carol Marie, the one who came leaping out along with her, was holding a god-damned baseball bat. I looked up. And, oh, shit. It really hurt. I saw it. Then I felt it. WHACK! I had my hand up to my head, and it smacked me on the knuckles, on my head. And I went tumbling over into darkness just as a gun was fired and someone screamed.

"Who screamed, Alex? Who?"

Carol Marie shouted out.

"Did she just yell or did she say something?"

Something. A word. I don't know. It burst over me, shot right above me like the bullet. It all passed over me as I dropped forward and tumbled into unconsciousness.

"But you heard it, Alex. Grab all that. Slow it down. Picture the bullet flying through the air so slowly that you can practically see it whiz by. And imagine that word passing by just as slowly, so slowly that you hear it loudly and clearly."

I was passing out. All I felt was the pain. I'd been hit. I was dropping to the ground and into a black hole, into a sea of warm, black water.

"And as you fell into that hole you heard Carol Marie scream a single word. Reach out and let yourself hear it again. She shouted—"

Carol Marie's shrill scream rose in my memory, calling, "Billy!"

Chapter 17

I retreated to my motel and slept with an ice pack that night. A big one. I gathered a full bucket of ice from the machine in the stairwell, then went to my room, locked and chained the door, and set one of the lounge chairs in front of it. Next I took one of the white towels, dumped a pile of ice into it, and made a large, lumpy, and frigid pillow onto which I placed my aching head. As I lay on my side, I reached up with my left hand, the one that had taken part of the blow, and nestled it into the folds, and then I didn't move for a long time. Later I got up, found the aspirin in my shaving kit, took three pills, and stripped and took a long hot shower. I wondered if I could have a concussion. My vision was fine, though. I had no urge to vomit. I had only some bruised fingers and a head that felt way too big for this world. So I crawled back into bed, laid my head on the nest of ice. And moved only once in the night, sometime around three when I got up and took more aspirin.

The next morning I awoke with a hangover of pain. I lay there for a long time, not sure I wanted to move, and then I got up, took more aspirin, and drank two glasses of water. After almost fifteen minutes in the shower, I decided to be butch about the whole thing and ignore the pain. I really didn't want to have to hunt out a doc-in-the-box, one of those quick medical-treatment places. Nor did I want to call my sister and report my night at the Octopus Car Wash.

Which was why I ignored her message. I'd either slept through the ringing or she called while I was showering, because I didn't notice the small flashing red light on my phone until I went to order room service. But I didn't want to call Maddy, not just yet. If we spoke now I was sure my sister would pick up on my grogginess and then she'd start zapping me with her usual string of penetrating questions, all very cool and X-raylike, until I'd told her each and every teeny detail. And I wasn't ready to do that. I wanted to give her answers; I didn't want to worry her. So I ordered eggs and bacon, toast and coffee instead. It was almost nine-thirty, and I could always tell Maddy that I hadn't received her message before going out.

I didn't feel half-bad when I left the motel almost two hours later. The pain was subsiding. My head ached, particularly when I touched the tender swell where I'd been whacked, and I could barely bend the middle finger on my left hand. But I was all right, and I felt well enough to be angry. And angry enough to want answers.

I drove directly to Loretta's. Barely noticing my surroundings, I drove down the broad four-lane road, turned into her subdivision, and pulled directly into the driveway. As I parked in front of the long, low house and shut my door, I looked up. Helen appeared in the large glass living-room window, hovered, and then disappeared. I thought she would go directly to the door, greet me there. She didn't, however, and I hit the button, heard the chimes announce my arrival in some musical dingdong sequence. No one came. I pressed again, and for a moment I wondered if Helen was choosing not to see me. When I pressed the button a third time and no one came, I began to boil. Finally I heard steps. I stared through the small glass panel in the door, hoped it was Loretta, but no such luck.

Helen's pinkish lipstick was fresh, her cheeks full of color, and her gray hair neatly brushed. So that was where she'd been, I realized, as she opened the door, smiled with formal stiffness. Powdering herself up.

"Good morning, Alex. How are you?" she asked in a polite and friendly manner that hadn't been evident before.

"May I come in?"

"Well, certainly."

Helen moved aside, and I stepped through the doorway and onto the slate stones that lined and defined the small entry. And then I halted and stood there by that planter. Beyond the little rim of green house plants spread a sea of white carpet. Yellow and blue couch. Mahogany coffee table with all the objets arranged just so. Nice framed pictures on a perfectly clean wall. My stomach rolled with a sense of doom. This was false perfection, this house, this room. A manufactured, dusted, and vacuumed perfection that would soon be most horribly destroyed along with the lives that inhabited it.

My head began to throb and I touched the bruise where I'd been walloped. I blinked. Little bloody-red blobs pushed at the edge of my vision. Just hold it back, I told myself. Keep yourself focused on the here and now.

I asked, "Is Loretta in? I need to talk to her."

"Why, no. She's at the library, but she should be back soon." Helen's false smile fell. "Why? What is it? Is there trouble?"

I had wanted to keep them separate, Helen and Loretta. There was something wrong between them, something twisted and warped, and I wanted to keep them in opposite corners in an attempt to sort out their muddy relationship. I hadn't wanted to trust Helen, either. That had been my knee-jerk reaction to her; I had quickly and conveniently cast her as the wicked stepmother. But maybe I had been wrong in trusting the simple Loretta. Perhaps I'd been mistaken in the belief that I'd get the straight, unfettered answer from her and not Helen, for Loretta had been obtuse, had sent me with a mysterious question to Carol Marie. And I suddenly wondered why Loretta hadn't just told me about Billy and if Carol Marie had lied to me. Billy's alcoholism might have been the reason he disappeared into the homeless masses, but people drink for a reason. So what was he trying to mask? What could he be escaping from?

I stood there in the entry of the home, Helen only inches from me, and I asked, "Can you tell me why Billy had to run away?"

In spite of the mask of blush and fresh lipstick, I could see her whiten. She glanced down, put a hand to her chin.

"Oh, God," muttered Helen.

Helen closed the door behind me, then silently started

across the sea of carpet, around a couple of upholstered chairs that looked as if they'd never been sat in, and into the back of the house. I followed her into the kitchen, and noted that the only things on the perfectly clean counter were a knife holder stocked with three or four knives, a ceramic canister that I knew from my previous visit held coffee, and a coffee maker, its small light glowing. Without a word, Helen ushered me once again to the dinette table that stood by the rear door, and I sat down, then watched as Helen opened one of the wooden cabinets, took out a mug, and poured coffee.

"Cream?" she asked.

"No, thanks."

She took another mug, poured herself a cup as well, did it all quite slowly as if she were trying to stall while she figured out not just what to say but how much. She put one mug in front of me, returned to the counter, opened a drawer, and took out a package of cigarettes and an ashtray. With a sigh, she sat down, coffee, cigarette, ashtray, and matches laid out before her like poker cards.

She indeed eyed me like a card shark, asking, "So what did she tell you?"

"Loretta? Nothing, just that her brother had to leave."

Helen scratched a match and brought it hissing and flaming up to the cigarette that was stuck to the pink lipstick rimming her mouth. She took a long, pensive drag, held it, then sent smoke spewing upward like a long, mournful thought.

"I've tried so hard to make things right, but we've had our share of problems," she began. "Particularly Billy. That poor child's been plagued all his life."

Helen waited, obviously wanting me to divulge what I knew. Or perhaps hoping that I would get the conversation going in a unexpected direction and steer her off course. But I let the huge hole of silence loom right in front of her and she finally walked into it.

"If only he were more like his twin sister, Carol Marie. She's so responsible. So resourceful. Not Billy, though. He's two hours younger, and oh, what a difference." She took another drag, stared out the window, then looked back at me and dug into the story. "He doesn't have the troubles that his big sister, Loretta, has. No. Loretta, she's different, what they call special. Truly so. Billy, though, just isn't responsible. He's always had trouble keeping a job. He never did go to college, you know, so he went to work for his father. We all thought that was a good idea, to get him involved in the family business, you see, but in the end I suppose it wasn't. He never became independent. Carol Marie, on the other hand, just went off on her own. She went to college, did beautifully, started a successful store. Maybe Paul, my husband, should have turned the business over to her. If he had, maybe it wouldn't have failed." She looked down, pitifully shook her head. "Maybe it's because they're not my real children, but I had no idea raising a family would be so hard."

Right then I knew what the family business had been, and I asked, "How long ago did the car wash close?"

"Let me see . . ."

Helen showed no surprise that I knew; she must have assumed that Loretta had told me about the building with the huge octopus above it. Instead, however, I'd discovered it furtively, finding the hulk of a once-large business deserted and crumbling, inhabited by rats and a derelict son.

Helen continued, saying, "Billy took over completely after his father died five years ago. He made a bit of a profit for a year or two, but then business began to go down, and then . . . then, well, there was the accident and we had no choice but to close it. Which was a shame. Paul had started it back in the fifties, and he practically lived there, building and expanding it. His first wife, Marge, did all the books, ran the cash register, and they even kept little Loretta down there in a crib. She grew up there, really. When she was about ten or so Paul let her go out there and help the guys at the end of the line—you know, dry off the cars. She really liked that, and I guess she was pretty good at it. That was, or course, before, when she still used to go out, when she'd leave the neighborhood. After Paul added some new and elaborate equipment, it was Loretta's idea to change the name and put the octopus on the roof."

I steered Helen back to Billy by saying, "This accident— what happened?"

"Oh, God." Helen puffed on her cigarette, rubbed the weathered skin of her neck. "Billy's a drinker. Ever since high school. Beer, then vodka. We tried to get him to stop. We watched him and then his father even tried to get him to go to Alcoholics Anonymous. But Billy wouldn't have anything to do with it. That was another reason Paul brought Billy to work for him—he wanted to keep an eye on him. None of it helped, though, and Billy's drinking just got worse and worse. I don't know how he was able to work, to go down to the car wash every day and keep it going. But somehow he did. I suppose he could have kept going, too, if it hadn't been for the driving. He had two accidents." She took another pensive drag, stared out at the backyard. "He's actually a very nice boy. Gentle, you know? I don't know why he drinks. His first accident was one winter and he just skidded across a road and ended up in a ditch. The second one, though, was in the middle of the day, broad daylight. He drifted out of his lane and smashed into another car. It was horrible. The driver of the other car, some poor old man, was in the hospital for a month. That's when Billy lost his license."

"When was that?"

"Not long after his father's stroke."

I was beginning to peel back the layers of unspoken truths, which were as thick as the layers of a huge, fat onion, and beginning to picture where this story could go and probably would.

"Neither of those is the accident you were referring to, is it?" I asked.

Helen shook her head. Looked into her lap. She dragged on the cigarette, stared out the window, then exhaled and took a sip of coffee.

"No," she said. "After he ran into the old man—Billy just passed out, you see, that's how the police found him—he lost his driver's license. Which was good, of course, but it meant it was very hard for him to get down to the car wash. He was living in an apartment not too far from here, and we worked it out that Carol Marie would drive him to work in the morning before the mall opened, and then I would go back in the evening and pick him up. I suppose he could have taken the bus or the train. That's what we should have insisted on. Maybe he would have learned something if we'd done it like that. But we didn't, and one night I went down there and Billy'd been drinking again. It was almost eight at night, and it was dark and chilly. The middle of October." Helen sighed, said, "He was drunk and insisted on driving my car. He's never much liked me, you know. He's always resented the fact that his real mother died and that I married his father. And he started yelling at me, told me if I didn't move over and let him drive, he was just going to throw me out. He would have, too. Would have left me down there to walk all by myself. Billy's an angry drunk. He went to grab me by the wrist, so I slid over. If he was going to drive, I thought it would be better, at least, to have me with him. I thought maybe I could . . . could . . ."

As Helen's voice trailed off into a pained memory, a tightening sense of dread began to grip my stomach. I pictured an angry Bill, drunk on beer or perhaps vodka shots, and I pictured his car driving down Fullerton, swerving and probably speeding.

Helen appeared frozen, and I jarred her by asking, "Did you make it to the freeway?"

"Yes."

"But you didn't make it home?"

"No."

"How far did you get?"

"Up to Northfield."

"Oh."

Just as I'd thought. Northfield, the small suburb where I'd recently been. Where I'd just delivered a photo of a dead little girl to a still-distraught father.

"Billy was driving much too fast," said Helen, her voice faint. "He was swerving in and around cars. We started arguing, and that's when he missed the turn. We were going up the Kennedy Expressway and he was supposed to go to the left up 90, then to 294, and so forth. But he swerved around a car and then couldn't get back over, so we had to go on Edens. We had a terrible fight. I wanted him to stop and let me drive. I was screaming. He was screaming. He said he was going to drive me all the way up to Milwaukee and dump me there. Dear God, I really thought he would, too. We were going so fast. But then he started laughing and swerved off at Northfield. He was going to cut across there, you see. Back toward where we lived. He was laughing so hard then, telling me how much he hated me, what a fool I was."

"And he ran a red light?"

Elbows on the table, Helen bowed her head into her hands. "Yes, and the other car was just pulling out from a little strip of shops on the left. Oh, that poor little girl. Her parents were divorced, and she had just spent the day visiting her daddy."

Helen told me the rest. She told me how Billy had been turned, looking at her, and yelling. Yelling as loudly as he could. And she had been staring at him. But then she looked ahead, down the road, realized that they were about to speed through a red light, and saw the car, that black one. But it was too late. Billy barely had time to hit the brakes, and they rammed it, broadsided it.

"Sometimes I pray I'll just forget that child's face," said Helen, choking back a sob. "Right before we hit, she was looking at me with these sweet eyes, sitting in the passenger's seat, wondering what this was all about, not realizing that she was about to be killed."

The other car had been crushed on the passenger side, continued Helen, killing the girl instantly, while the force of the impact had sent the driver, whom I knew to be Ray Preston, into a coma from which he hadn't emerged for three weeks. By that time, the mother had already seen to the child's burial.

"We were fine, Billy and I," mumbled Helen. "I guess somehow I'd at least gotten Billy to put on his shoulder harness. I don't remember. I had mine on, of course. There was that huge crash, metal screeching, glass flying. Then silence. Total silence. It seemed like ten or fifteen minutes later but it was probably only ten or fifteen seconds. Whatever. I got out, walked around the back of our car, went around and peered in. When I saw all the blood, the way that small girl was crushed by the door, I nearly collapsed on the hood of their car. We were right by the fire department, and I think the police were there in less than a minute. And by the time they arrived, Billy was revving the engine, trying to back up. He was crying, sobbing. I think he thought if he backed up, the door would pop out and that little girl would pop back to life."

But of course none of that occurred. In fact, from the intensity of the impact, I doubted that Billy would even have been able to untangle his car from theirs. It was clear, too, that the police recognized almost instantly that Billy was drunk. Nearly as quickly, they also discovered that he'd lost his license for driving under the influence. Which was why they arrested him and locked him up.

"What did they charge him with, manslaughter?"

She nodded, but Helen was never quite clear exactly what

charges had been pressed. I was completely aware, however, how severely the courts were now coming down on drunk driving. And rightly so, particularly on repeat offenders. There was no way Billy should have been out on the road, just as there was no way the bus driver who hit Maddy should have been behind the wheel. Two horrible and separate incidents with equally horrendous outcomes. At one time I'd loved wine, enjoyed a good gin and tonic, even a martini every now and then, but after my sister had been paralyzed, the pleasure of it all had been poisoned. I'd never been able to take a drink without imagining Maddy lying helpless on the sidewalk, and now I'd never be able to take a drink without picturing the body of a crushed little girl.

"I've blamed myself ever since," said Helen, turning to me, looking right into my eyes for the first time. "I should never have let Billy drive. I should have thrown the keys away, done something, anything. And I don't know why I did it, really, but I should never have posted his bail."

It all clicked. Like dominoes, the story was falling into line. I asked, "It never came to trial, did it?"

"No."

"He jumped bail?"

"Yes." Helen turned away, shook her head. "Loretta keeps saying that he's homeless. That's what she tells everyone. That's what she wants to believe. But that's not exactly right. Billy's homeless not because he doesn't have a place to live but . . . but because he's a fugitive from the law."

Chapter 18

I drifted out of that time, that story. I let go of the cup of coffee I had been clutching as I listened to Helen, and floated away like a balloon that had been released to the heavens. Escaped. It was sad, that story. Sure, even tragic. And it was all the more disturbing to me because, as they say, it hit so close to home. I understood Ray Preston's pain because my family had been wrapped in a similar nightmare. I wished every drunk driver would be chopped and mutilated and sent to hell.

I left Helen, not sure where I should go, what I should do next. I left her sitting at the dinette table. I wanted someone to give me some directions, some input, because right then and there I didn't want to go on. I wanted to go home, and that's what I did. When I no longer sensed my mesmerizing angel directing me on, when I could no longer even beckon her, I was sucked into the heavens, where I flew on, retreating to the present. Soon I realized I was no longer whooshing through the air, but was in fact lying down. Brushing away the trance like a heavy sleep, I rubbed my eyes, twisted and stretched, and then stared out the French doors straight in front of me. Maddy's island. Lake Michigan. Late afternoon. Like the lost Dorothy seeking Kansas, home was remarkably close, just the other side of the imagination.

I rolled my head to the left, saw my sister lying there motionless on the neighboring recliner. Had she employed the typical hypnotherapist trick, had she followed me into trance, been right there with me? Could she still be under or, I thought, tripping on the anxiety that used to beset me when I saw a therapist, had I totally bored Maddy?

I poked her with my worry, gently asking, "You're not asleep, are you?"

Her head moved slightly from side to side, and I was silent, lying there on my leather recliner, staring at my sister. I knew I believed in hypnosis, didn't know about ESP, but decided to give it a try. As hard as I could, I thought: Wake up! I silently chanted that over and over, my eyes focused on Maddy as I tried to beam that order over to her. And on the fourth or fifth time I saw her eyelids begin to flutter.

She turned toward me as if she were sighted, said, "Why?"

"Why what?"

"Why did you want me to wake up?"

"Oh." Could my sister and I be so tightly linked? "I just felt like we got disconnected there. I wasn't sure whether to go on or . . . or, I don't know. Did I lose you?"

"No, I was just digesting it all."

She rubbed her face, her mouth, like a queen bee who'd just gobbled up all that her drone—namely me—had brought back to the hive from the vast and distant fields. That was my job, I supposed, not just to bring back information from the outer world but to re-create the universe that lay beyond the limits of this island. I was to make Maddy feel not like a prisoner locked sightlessly in a wheelchair but like a wise and sage queen, someone with absolute and mystical powers. And I guessed it was working because I could sense what I'd just fetched for her was highly satisfying. Yes, studying that beautiful face and that long neck, I could tell there was something churning now deep inside her. Something formidable.

"What is it?" I asked. "And don't say 'Nothing.' "

Nothing meant there was something she didn't want to tell me. Nothing meant she knew something she didn't want me to find out. Nothing meant I was doomed to ignorant forages into the hypnotic past.

She smirked because I'd anticipated correctly, then said, "It all makes sense, doesn't it?"

"Don't answer my question with a question."

"But it makes sense. That's all I'm saying. Why Loretta came to see me, I mean. It just sews everything together. Loretta didn't come to see me because she was a friend of Ray's and he'd recommended me to her for her own personal problems. No, she was no friend of his. Not by any means. Her family had ruined him and his life. Her family had killed his only child. So it's just as I thought. Loretta came to me to confess this horrible thing. Loretta came to see me as a patient because she felt horribly guilty for what her brother had done to Ray."

But everybody knew what Billy had done, I thought. It was no secret. The police knew, all the neighbors knew, and it was probably in the papers.

I sat up, straddling the recliner, held my hands way in front of me, stretched, and said, "But didn't everyone know? What was there left to confess?"

"I suppose not much. Good point."

Maddy retreated into silence. She was very much into the belief that for every action there was a reaction. People do things for a reason, she had often told me. Or what they perceive as a logical reason. So what could Loretta's coming to Maddy actually have accomplished? What had Loretta known that no one else had?

I ventured, "I'd guess she wanted to tell you something that the police didn't know about." Then again, perhaps it was much simpler, so I said, "Or maybe she just wanted to help Ray. Maybe she thought if she told you how sorry Billy was or something like that you could then help Ray. Or maybe she just wanted forgiveness."

"No, I don't know about forgiveness." Maddy bit one of her thumbnails. "She wasn't involved in the accident, so there really was nothing for her to be forgiven for. But you're close."

"What do you mean?"

"I mean, I think you're partly right. Loretta came to see me, Ray Preston's therapist, because there was something she wanted to tell me. Something that she hoped I would in turn tell Ray."

So Maddy was to have been nothing more than a medium,

a vehicle for getting information to Ray Preston? I stared up at the ceiling that soared way above me, then turned, and my eye was caught by the Tiffany glass dome that capped the stairwell.

"But if Loretta knew something no one else did," I said, "why wouldn't she just go to the police? Or just tell Ray directly?"

"Because she was scared. Because she couldn't go against her family so openly." Maddy was nodding. "It makes sense. In therapy I learned one thing about Loretta—that she's very fearful of her family, that she needs their approval of her. At the same time she's such a moral person. She loves reading classical literature because she's fascinated by the dilemmas. And she's always tried to do what's right. So she might have been trying to do the right thing by getting some information to Ray via me without her family knowing about it."

"But what on earth could Loretta have known that no one else did, particularly then—what was it, a year or so after the accident?"

Maddy lay there, rolled her head away from me. I saw her bite her bottom lip, shake her head. Her handicaps had created any number of nearly insurmountable barriers, but to look at Maddy was to be deceived. She was so animated it was hard to believe she couldn't just jump up. She got around so well it was easy to forget she was blind. And she seemed so fucking well adjusted and happy about life it was nearly impossible to discern the pain she kept so well hidden.

"After my accident, I was so angry," she confessed. "At first I wasn't. I thought I could beat it. They told me I'd never walk again, but I was determined to prove them wrong. I was a survivor, I told myself. Someone who championed over the impossible, and I tried and I tried."

"I know. I was there. You were in physical therapy almost all day, every day."

"But they were right, you know. I kept hypnotizing myself, thinking I was going to perform a miracle, that somehow through hypnosis I could make myself heal. One day I put myself under, I lifted myself up on my bed, swung my legs around, and told myself I could walk. And I was sure I could. But as soon as I slipped off the bed, I just crumpled to the floor. I landed smack, face first on the linoleum, and I just cried and cried and cried until a couple of nurses came and hoisted me up like a wet rag and put me in bed. I wanted to die after that. Being blind was one thing; losing the use of my legs was more than I could bear. What good was I, what could I do with my life, who was going to love me?"

I sat up and reached out. At first she wouldn't take my hand. So I took her arm, brought it around, squeezed her hand between mine. And I wouldn't let go. This was something altogether rare, my sister opening up like this.

"I was so angry," she said, now tightly grasping my hand as well. "You've no idea how full of rage I was."

"No, I don't. You never let it show."

"Well, I was. Totally. And I hated myself. All I wanted was to rip out my eyes, chop off my legs. Then later I got mad at the doctors and of course I was furious at the bus driver himself. I had fantasies about taking that jerk and breaking him into a million pieces. I wanted to slice him open and punish him for what he'd done to me. And I wanted to go after the bus company, too, because it was their fault as well. They should never have let him drive."

"Of course not."

"I was so full of anger that I couldn't even begin to heal emotionally until I'd accomplished something like all that. And I did. I got my justice not by killing someone or blowing up the bus headquarters, but legally. I sued them head to toe and I was awarded all that money. Eight million dollars. All that wonderful money, which means nothing to me except wonderful and glorious revenge that I can count over and over again. Revenge that I keep reinvesting and turning into bigger and bigger revenge." She laughed. "You understand, don't you?"

"Of course."

"You don't think I'm crazy?"

"Maddy, I'm in awe of you."

"Oh, stop, Alex. None of that. You would have done better than I did in all this."

"Like hell."

"Like hell, nothing. You're stronger than you know. Trust me. I'm not only your sister, but an excellent shrink."

"Maddy, let's go away. Let's take a trip. Let me take you to Europe—what about Italy? Or Russia?" I added, "You have so much life left to live. You're so wonderful and so beautiful. You should see yourself."

"Believe me, I wish I could see myself. The last image I have of me is of some skinny, awkward teenager. Then my sight went."

"I mean it, Maddy, you're a very attractive woman. Do you remember Audrey Hepburn in *Breakfast at Tiffany's*? That's who you remind me of, her, Audrey Hepburn."

"Oh, stop."

"No, I'm serious. Picture her and envision yourself. You can be quite confident of that," I said. "So what do you say? Let's get away for a while. You need to get out of here and meet some new people."

"I'll think about it." She laughed, lifted my hand to her lips, kissed me on the back of my knuckles. "So I think she understood that as well."

"Who? What are you talking about?"

"Loretta, silly."

"Maddy, wait." It was hard to get Maddy onto the subject of herself, and I didn't want to get her off it so quickly. "What about St. Petersburg? It's beautiful and I haven't been there since I was a student."

"First things first," interrupted my sister. "So don't you see? Through all her reading Loretta understood the need for justice as a means of revenge."

"Wait," I said. "I'm a half step behind you."

"What I'm saying is that Loretta came to see me because she knew Ray Preston couldn't heal until justice was done."

"But Maddy . . ."

Had my sister been talking about her innermost thoughts not in order to shed light on herself but on Loretta? Of course, and Maddy had made her point, passed over my idea of a trip, and was now back to her client, whom she hoped I would better understand. Oh, shit.

"Don't you see, Alex? Loretta knew Billy had to be caught and put on trial. That's why she came specifically to me, to tell me, Ray Preston's therapist, where that child's killer was. That's what she wanted to do, reveal where Billy was hiding."

I gave up trying to steer the conversation, which Maddy so absolutely controlled, and I asked, "You mean she intended to tell you so that you could in turn tell Ray?"

"Exactly."

"But you couldn't have done that, Maddy. You said it your-

self, client confidentiality. There's no way you could have revealed what one client told you, particularly not to another
client."

"You know that, and I know that, but I don't think Loretta
did. And I think she wrote me because Billy had returned to
Chicago and resurfaced. He was hiding at the car wash and
Loretta had to tell someone."

"My God, you don't think she told Ray Preston, do you?"

"Quite possibly," replied Maddy.

Somehow, though, Ray Preston had known. Why else
would he have done what he did after that night at the car
wash, where else would all that rage have come from? And who
but Loretta would have told him?

"But maybe," I ventured, "Loretta told Ray thinking that
he'd only tell the police. Maybe she didn't expect that he'd go
after Billy himself. She didn't realize that until it was too late,
until it was—"

"Truly a matter of life and death." Maddy then said, "So
Billy was back in Chicago, Ray was hunting for him, and Loretta was afraid that her plan had backfired. Instead of bringing legal justice against Billy, she was afraid he'd be the victim
of bloody revenge. Which is why she wrote you."

I settled back on the recliner, all these ideas and possibili-
ties soaring through my mind. It was beginning to make sense,
to mesh together with what I knew was about to happen after
I left Helen's. Whom I was about to see. What I was about to
learn.

Chapter 19

I went to the library.

I left the rather pitiful Helen and her rather pitiful cigarette and definitely pitiful cup of coffee. Left them all at her
dinette table. I passed across the perfectly white carpet in the
living room, out the front door, into my rental car. And then I
headed down the snaky streets of the subdivision, out onto the
big concrete road, and to the library.

I found it less than half a mile from Loretta's house, a large
structure, a modern building of white stucco and few windows,
located just past her subdivision and on the other side of the
main road. It was an island surrounded by a sea of cars, just like
all the malls sprouting out here on the prairie. I imagined it was
as hard as a Pacific island for Loretta to reach, too. With her
fear of leaving the house, it must have been tremendously difficult for her to head off on foot, dive across all the roads, swim
among all these sharklike vehicles, and finally find refuge in the
stacks of books. But she did, apparently religiously so. Escape to
a library. Escape in a book. That was certainly how Loretta
explored the world beyond this prisonly suburb.

I parked and went up one flight, where I entered the library. Inside I passed the checkout line, paused on the deep-
blue carpeting, and looked around. Open stacks radiated out in

all directions, the magazines and audiovisual materials located
off to the left, the children's room off to the right. I heard
voices above, looked up, and saw first a broad skylight and then
a railing. So there was a second floor as well.

Loretta might not be here, I thought, as I headed toward
the magazines. On my drive over, I had kept an eye on the
sidewalks, hadn't seen her, but who knew what route she took
to and from the library. With any luck, though, she'd be here.
I'd find her and somehow get her to answer a couple of key
questions, and maybe this thing of car washes and car accidents
would all come together.

The magazine section was an open area, the racks of peri-
odicals facing out into a grouping of chairs and couches. There
were two older men and a young girl sitting around, but, no, I
realized, Loretta would never choose so open a space to sit, nor
would she choose so passing a thing as a magazine to read. If
she were anywhere, she'd be squirreled away in a carrel or a
corner or perhaps a private study room. And ten to one she'd
be in fiction.

I did only a brief check of the children's room, where a
librarian with a name tag that read PAMELA had twenty or so
kids engrossed in a story. Next a quick glance in the travel area,
where a handful of people were gathered. And then I headed
up the stairs toward the books that empowered the imagination. As I climbed toward the fiction department, I began to
sense it. I knew before I even saw her.

"Knew what?"

That she wasn't alone. That he was there. The floor was
blue. The walls a harsh, stark white. But I kept seeing, sensing,
feeling a light-brown color. I stopped halfway up, looked behind me, half expected to see someone back there, perhaps
even a ghostly creature. Instead the stairs beneath were empty.
I turned, continued my ascent, and reached a huge room with
stacks shooting off in every direction. She was up here, I knew,
and I started in one direction, came to a copy center, where a
young blond girl stood behind a counter making reproductions
for an older woman. I turned, started down that end of the
stacks. On a whim, I headed up one of the stacks, then stopped.
I looked behind me. I caught the last of it. Just a glimpse of a
leg. Brown pants. Quickly, I spun and headed to the end. Nothing. Only a teenaged boy seated at a carrel.

I went up to the kid, demanded, "Did you just see some guy wearing brown pants?"

He had a mouthful of braces and a face full of pimples; he looked at me, shrugged, said, "I guess."

"Where'd he go?"

The kid pointed toward the far wall. "That way, I think."

I trotted off. That way was back toward the copy center, but up ahead I could see only the older woman and the blond girl. As I rushed past the stacks, I glanced down one aisle. A man in dark brown pants and tan shirt was running, hurrying away. I skidded to a halt, charged after him. Just as quickly, he ducked to the left, disappeared. I broke into a full run, came to the end of the stacks, turned left, saw no one, then charged up another aisle. He was up ahead, glancing over his shoulder in fright, looking right at me. Running away from me.

"Snap that picture and hold it. Describe him."

Broad forehead. Long blondish-brown hair. Deep eyes. Skinny. And filthy. Face all smudged. Brown pants and shirt that were streaked with dirt. In an instant I saw the resemblance. Yes, this was definitely Loretta's brother.

He saw me and took the first right, darted down another stack of books. I came to the corner, charged after him. But the next corridor was empty, just a long, thin passage lined on either side with shelf after shelf of books. I spun around. Billy was rushing down the row behind me. I burst into a run, sailing through the quiet library. He glanced back, stared at me with wide, terrified eyes, and pushed himself on faster and farther. Jabbing one hand out, he smacked a row of books, pulled at them, and sent them sailing through the air and crashing to the floor. He did it again, sent a couple of dozen more books to the ground. When I reached the minefield of literature, I had to slow as I skipped and hobbled over the novels. Nevertheless, I landed on one, skidded, reached out and knocked another handful of books into the air.

When I reached the end of the stacks, I emerged into the large space at the top of the stairs and beneath the skylight. Billy was nowhere to be seen. He'd either headed down or perhaps, I thought, looking from side to side, he'd sought refuge in one of the back rooms. Or maybe he was hiding in a study carrel.

A man's voice rose sharply from the stairwell. I darted to

the edge, peered over the railing. Billy was flying down, two steps at a time, and a male librarian was calling after him, telling him to slow down. Billy paid no attention, of course, tearing off like the fugitive he was. I raced around to the top of the stairs, then down, past the librarian who yelled at me, past a couple of kids who stared at me. I came around the bottom of the staircase, darted toward the checkout line.

A figure stepped out in front of me, a hand like a traffic cop's held right up to me.

"Let him go," said Loretta.

I started to move to one side, to push past her, but she kept her hand held high. I began to say something, but didn't know quite what that would be.

The librarian, a man with glasses, in his late twenties, hurried up behind me, said, "What's going on? Was anything stolen? Should I call the police?"

Forcefully, Loretta said, "No."

I caught my breath, added, "It's all right. I . . . I just wanted to talk to that man. He did nothing wrong."

"But—"

"Everything's fine," I repeated to the librarian. Then to Loretta, I said, "Come on."

I took her by the elbow, leading her past several gawkers, past the checkout desk, and into the lobby where we could more easily talk. We passed the large staircase that descended to the parking lot, and crossed to a large window that overlooked the sea of cars. Just as we reached the glass, I spotted him out there, trotting between cars, making toward the edge of the lot, then disappearing into the trees of a neighboring lot.

"I know who that is," I said pointing to the figure.

"Oh."

"That's your brother, Billy, isn't it?"

She didn't reply, merely stood by my side, staring at the spot where he'd vanished.

"He's in trouble," I said. "And I need to talk to him."

Loretta still did not reply.

"Billy's not homeless. He ran away because he had to." I added, "He ran away because he killed someone, a little girl, and the police are now after him."

She spun, her eyes pinched with anger, and demanded, "Who told you that?"

"Helen."

Her voice was so low it was barely audible as she said, "Bitch."

This was going to take some careful negotiations, I realized. Loretta was undoubtedly as tough as she was stubborn. I had to choose my words carefully, take the proper tack, to try to get her to open up.

"Loretta," I began, "you wrote my sister, saying you needed help and that it was a matter of life and death. Your letter upset Maddy and worried her very much."

Loretta brushed back a bit of hair as she stared at the floor. Her face was reddening with shame. Good, I thought. Press on.

"That's why Maddy asked me to come down here; she wanted me to see if you were all right. But you're not. Something's wrong. I know that for sure, not only from what you told me but from some other things. The other night someone rammed my car and ran me off the road. Then last night someone hit me over the head." I bowed my head, showed her the bruise. "See? See where I was hit? I followed your sister down to the Octopus Car Wash and someone hit me with a piece of wood. I was knocked out completely."

Her eyes filled with worry, and she looked at my wound, half extended a hand, mumbled, "Oh. Oh, no."

"Yeah. I could have been killed, too, but I was lucky. I know I shouldn't have done that, followed Carol Marie, but how else was I supposed to find out what's going on if no one will tell me? Maddy would want me to try everything."

Loretta turned back to the window, stared out over the expanse of parked cars below.

I gave her my last pitch, gently saying, "If you're in trouble and you need something, Loretta, please let me help you. If you've changed your mind, though, and you don't want me around, I'll leave. I'll check out of my motel this afternoon and head back north. I won't bother you anymore, and I'll tell Maddy that you want to handle it on your own. It's your decision; just tell me what I should do."

She clasped her hands together. As she bowed her head, her flat, grayish hair fell over her face. Then she started shaking her head.

"Oh, God, I don't know. It's all so confusing," she whispered. "I don't know who to talk to."

"You can talk to me. Maddy can't be here, so she wants you to talk to me. I'll tell her everything you say and get her advice. Maybe later we can call her, too. Would you like that? Would you like to talk to Maddy?"

"Yes. I want to talk to Dr. Phillips. She's very smart, and I really need some help. You see, Billy's in . . . in . . ." She hesitated, turned away, then started over. "Billy's in so much trouble. Not just with the police, either. I'm afraid someone's going to kill him."

"Ray Preston?"

Loretta nodded her head.

"Loretta, do you think I could speak with him? With Billy, I mean?"

She nodded. "Yes. I guess so."

"Good. How can I find him?"

She looked back at me, her pale face expressionless. "Well, I know where he's having dinner."

Chapter 20

Loretta explained it all, gave me directions and a time, but she refused my offer to take her home. She said she wanted to spend more time at the library, but I didn't believe her. I suspected she either wanted to walk home—perhaps she feared traveling in my car—or didn't want Helen to see her with me. From her vague response, I sensed it was something like that. It occurred to me, too, that Loretta might be meeting someone else.

I returned to my motel room and wasted the rest of the afternoon reading the paper, starting a book, talking briefly on the phone with Maddy, who nothing short of interrogated me. She wanted names, descriptions, places. Reactions. She asked me if I thought Loretta was stable or in any way a danger to herself. I replied that Loretta was just as odd as ever but not likely to hurt herself, at least not as far as I could tell. It was the others—namely Billy and Ray—that I feared, for while I had nearly gathered all the pieces, I couldn't fit any of this together, couldn't assemble it into one cohesive picture. I wondered, too, what I had missed, what I had neglected to take notice of.

"You're doing an excellent job of reporting," chimed that bolstering voice, the one that seemed to come from behind me, just over my shoulder.

If nothing else, I had big eyes and a pretty good memory, and as I readied myself to leave at about five, I told myself to be sharp. Maddy was going to want a complete, detailed report on all this as well. And wasn't this, I thought as I brushed my hair, a hell of a lot better than my former career of technical writing? My last big project at work had been writing an installation manual for a desktop computer, which was about as dry as you could get.

Just before exiting my room, I hesitated. If nothing else, I was becoming paranoid, and I stopped by the window, lifted the curtain slightly, and peered out. My small red car was parked down below. Nothing wrong there. I scanned the rows of cars, noticed nothing really odd until I eyed the very last vehicle. A large auto, dark brown, it was unpleasantly familiar. Very much like the one that had rammed into me the other night after leaving Loretta's.

There was no other choice. I couldn't stay trapped in my room. As if I didn't suspect a thing, I stepped out onto the walkway that ran in front of all the rooms, locked my door, turned, and made for the open staircase. I purposely didn't look toward the end of the parking lot as I crossed to my car and started it up. I purposely moved slowly out of my space, as well, and drove to the front of the motel. This was like fishing, and I wanted to make sure I'd been caught.

I checked my rearview mirror. Nothing. No movement. Was I wrong, needlessly worried? I feared something, a murky figure, someone I'd seen before and who I was sure was now back there, lurking. There was no sign of any movement, though. Not until the very last moment, when I turned left in front of the main office. Just as I rounded the corner, I saw the prow of the large brown car begin to move like a huge shark coming to life.

I passed slowly beneath the portico in front of the office, bounced over a speed bump, continued straight, and turned not right onto the main road but left and back around the motel. I waited until the last moment, though, to make the turn. Waited until I was sure he was coming, for I wanted to be seen and tailed, at least for a short while. So as I saw that huge, formidable nose of a grille make the bend behind me, I passed around the far corner, down past another row of rooms. Pressing on the gas, I sped up. Raced on. Hurried down to the far end of the motel. There was another way out of there, a small service road. I'd seen it earlier. A single lane of pavement that led over a ditch, past some trees, into the rear of a gas station.

I glanced in my mirror. He saw me escaping, rushing out an unexpected route. In an instant his car was lunging forward, charging after me. I swerved right, steering into the service road that led to the gas station. As fast as I could, I drove around the back of the small, square building, dodging parked cars. I swerved around the front, where a truck and a sedan were parked at the gas pumps, steered around them and past a gawking worker, and then I looped the building. In seconds I emerged once again at the rear. And there was the huge brown car now zooming from the motel and down the narrow service road. I took direct and hasty aim, zeroing in on it with my small red car like some kamikaze doomed to death. I didn't slow, didn't jam on the brakes, and I saw the car barreling down on me, saw the figure behind the wheel growing more familiar with each moment.

I plunged the brakes down, just as he did, and we both skidded, stopping only a foot or two short of a head-on. I threw open my door, leaped out, ran around. By the time I'd reached the driver's side of the car, he had slammed his car into reverse and was readying an escape. I trotted alongside him as he started to roll.

"Stop, Ray!" I shouted at him.

He glared at me from his moving vehicle, his face flushed with anger. Sure, I might have caught him, but he wasn't trapped. And he had no intention of sticking around. I reached through his open window, grabbed him by the collar.

I yelled, "Listen, I know you've been following me. Now just shut off your fucking car!"

He punched away my hand, halted his vehicle, twisting the car key and cutting the engine. I looked through the window, scanned the seat beside Ray. Did he have a weapon? A towel was thrown on the big brown seat next to him. Anything could be hidden beneath that. Both his hands were on the wheel, though. I didn't think he'd harm me, not really, not yet. He had no real need to.

"Why have you been tailing me? What do you want, Ray?"

I asked. "Maybe I can just tell you and save us both a lot of hassle."

Ray Preston bowed his head onto the steering wheel, then pulled back, took a deep breath, looked at me. He was a handsome man, a youthful-appearing man, but he looked like shit. His eyes were red and lined with circles. Hair uncombed. Even his perfectly pressed clothes were creased with huge wrinkles. When had he last slept?

Finally Ray said, "He's back."

"Who?"

"Billy."

I didn't want to confirm or negate it, so I said, "I know about the accident. I'm sorry."

"Accident?" Ray glared up at me. "Accident my ass, the fucker was drunk! He didn't have a license. And he ran a red light and killed her. He's supposed to be in jail!"

"I know."

"He killed my daughter, my little girl!"

"I'm sorry."

From the driver's seat of his car, Ray studied me. "You know where he is, don't you?"

"No, I've no idea where he's staying," I replied, which was essentially the truth. "But I might be able to find out something. Then we can go to the police and—"

"The police are doing nothing. They let the whole thing drop. They don't give a shit about some drunken, homeless turd! I tried to tell them he was back, but they don't want to hear anything about it. They won't talk to me anymore."

I saw his hand move. His right hand. My heart tightened. Shit, was he reaching for a gun?

"There's just one thing I want to know," said Ray as he reached for the keys and brought his car to a roaring start. "Why the hell are you here?"

I didn't know quite what to say, where to start, how to lie, what he should or shouldn't know, and I mumbled, "Well . . ."

"I mean, why did your sister send you? To torment me?"

"Of course not. Don't be ridiculous. She wanted me to do some business down here for her. And she asked me to see you because she was worried about you. I know that much."

"Cut the shit," he demanded. "Just tell me one thing. What's the divine Dr. Madeline Phillips up to?"

His question so startled me that I was totally speechless. I stood staring at him, dumbfounded, and he jammed his car into reverse, backing away from his question as well as from one that he had just dumped upon me.

Specifically, was there still more that Maddy knew that I didn't?

Chapter 21

Billy was dining at a soup kitchen in the basement of an Evanston church. Once I'd made certain that Ray was no longer following me, I headed off, and the church wasn't that hard to find, an older stone building north of downtown and just a couple of blocks west of Sheridan. When I pulled up, I saw the line of homeless people—including a couple of women and a handful of children—trailing from a basement door and down about half a block. Suppertime. As I parked under the branches of an enormous maple tree, I scanned the large crowd of people and tried to figure out how Billy could have made it all the way over here by the dinner hour.

As I walked up the sidewalk, I approached the line from the rear. Old men with white hair. A young woman with a filthy and ragged dress. A handful of men who looked as if they might be Vietnam vets, or at least of that age group. It was a depressing and pitiful collection of people who'd fallen through the so-called safety net, landing in the hands of an obviously overburdened and overworked congregation. A few in line studied me as well, one man with a defiant gaze, another with a quick, shamed glance. I examined them all, looked for familiar clothing or that familiar brow, but didn't see Billy.

The line snaked up the side of the church, then turned and dipped down three or four steps and disappeared inside. I stretched my neck, stood on my toes, tried to see over the heads and into the dark chamber beyond. All I could make out inside was a thick crowd of people pushing anxiously toward one thing: food.

A soft voice behind me said, "Can I help you?"

She was a nicely dressed woman, blue pants, white blouse. Short silver hair, glasses. When I turned around and saw her I noted all that, understood at once that she wasn't one of them, the hungry. And when I saw the clipboard, I correctly assumed this older woman to be either staff or a volunteer.

"I'm looking for someone," I said.

"Well, as you can see, we have lots of visitors every day. And a fair number of people like you who come hoping to find someone." Her voice was soft and kind, her manner just shy of timid. "You're welcome to step in and take a look around."

"Maybe you can help me. Maybe you know. I'm looking for a man named William Long."

"Sorry, we don't have any idea who's here. We don't ask names and we don't ask questions. We open for the dinner hour, and anyone's who's hungry is welcome." She smiled. "But as I said, you're welcome to step in and take a look around. There's quite a crowd already. Perhaps your friend is here."

I followed her down the few steps, past the line, and past the cafeteria service tables, where sandwiches and soup and fruit were being offered. We entered a large room, walls a dull white, the windows few in number and placed high up, and the first thing that hit me was a thick, coarse odor that made me catch my breath. It was a heavy scent, oddly sweet yet definitely sour. When had any of these people last bathed? The place was nearly full, seventy-five, maybe a hundred people seated at the tables, and they should have been talking, even laughing. Instead they were concentrating on the food before them, and an odd pall of quiet hung over the room.

"There's coffee over here if you want any," said the woman, nodding off to one side. Then she patted me on the arm. "Good luck. I hope you find him."

"Thanks."

I started down one side, moving slowly along the wall, my

eyes searching for him. Each table had about eight people at it, and periodically someone looked up at me. Like the line outside, most of these were men; in fact I saw only a couple of women in here. I passed all the way down the room, swung around, went down the middle aisle. Never before had I seen such a collection of lost souls. Bearded men, raggedly shaven guys. Even a boy, a child really, who couldn't yet be sixteen. All of them, too, with hair tangled and matted. Each one of them had a story. Each of them had some hole of pain. I checked each face at each table, wondered from what parts of this great country they had come. But I didn't see him, not Loretta's brother, Billy.

Just when I was sure that I'd outwitted myself and was totally wrong, I turned, started down the last row of tables. A figure appeared that looked all too familiar. There were only three other guys seated at the table, and he was off to one end eating by himself. I wasn't sure at first, but then I saw the tan shirt, the pants. From the rear, it all looked like it might be him. I wasn't sure until I saw his profile. He looked like his two sisters. The broad forehead, the short nose.

I swung behind him, came up, and then sat down on the bench across from him saying, "Hello, Billy."

His face bearded, he looked up from a bowl of tomato soup, eyes perplexed.

"Remember me? We met last night at the car wash." I touched the spot where he'd clobbered me. "Don't worry. I'm all right. Actually we weren't introduced at the library this morning, either. I'm a friend of Loretta's. My name's Alex Phillips."

It took him a second, but when he recognized me, his eyes opened wide and he dropped his spoon. He put both his hands on the table and started to get up, but I grabbed his right arm and held on as tightly as I could. I looked to my left, saw the men at the other end of the table anxiously looking our way, wondering what was wrong, why I had come to corner one of them.

"It's all right," I said, my voice firm but low. "You don't have anything to worry about. I didn't come to hurt you. I only came because Loretta asked me to talk to you."

That kept him from bolting at least, and I sensed the immediate panic leaving his body. He remained on alert though, and he turned, searched the room, tried to ascertain if he was cornered.

"Don't worry. There aren't any police. No one's coming after you. I just want to talk."

I wasn't really sure if he heard me. His eyes just kept darting. Exit. Cafeteria line. Rear exit. Window.

"Really, Billy. It's all right. I'm alone. I came because Loretta's worried about you."

"What?" he said, turning to me, looking at me oddly, as if he'd heard me for the first time.

"I just want to talk."

He pulled on his beard, studied me, then said, "Does Carol Marie know you're here?"

"No."

"She's all right, isn't she? She hasn't been hurt, has she?" he asked, settling down on the bench.

"As far as I know, she's fine."

His voice was surprisingly gentle, surprisingly clear. Quite low in tone. After what Helen had told me of his drinking and rowdiness, I expected someone much rougher and coarser. A man given to harsh highs and lows. Billy was obviously well educated, though. That much was clear. If he bathed, shaved, and put on a pinstripe suit, he'd definitely pass for a corporate exec.

"Billy," I began, "you can't hide like this anymore. You have to stop. Would you like help?"

He looked at me like I was the world's biggest dumbshit. Shaking his head, he looked down into his soup, let go of his fear, and smiled. For a second I thought he was going to burst out laughing. Then he reached up and opened his collar and pushed down his filthy shirt until he exposed a six-inch scar, thick and coarse, that ran from under his neck and up toward his right shoulder.

"See this? Ray Preston did that. He jumped me from behind, nearly cut my head off. You know who Ray Preston is, don't you? The guy who owns the laundry?"

"My God."

It started to flow then, this other half of the story, the one that filled out the whole picture. I could sense his loneliness

almost immediately, for he seemed eager to divulge it all, to
have someone to listen to the great injustice of his life. To slap
someone with it.

"Didn't Loretta tell you? That's why I skipped bail; that's
why I had to go," he explained. "He did this to me, cut me
like this, about two months before the trial was scheduled.
I was at my mother's house, out on bail. I was just sitting in
the backyard, sitting there reading when all of a sudden he
comes flying out of the bushes with this huge knife. If Loretta
hadn't been there—she beat him off with a shovel—I'd be
dead."

"Did you report it to the police?"

"My mother called them, but they didn't care."

"What do you mean?"

"I mean some drunk bum like me wasn't their priority."

"But—"

"That was why I left." He picked up the spoon, began
rolling it in his hand. "I was just as afraid of the police as I was
of Ray Peterson, so I started running and I haven't stopped
since."

Billy shook his head, lowered the spoon into his bowl and
stirred the soup. I wanted to say he was paranoid. I wanted to
say he was totally wrong. But maybe he wasn't, not entirely so.
Certainly there were a number of biases against him. While
he'd done something horrible, killed an innocent child, couldn't
he be guaranteed not only a fair trial, but adequate protection
as well? Evidently not.

"So what are you going to do?" I asked. "Be a fugitive the
rest of your life?"

"What choice do I have?" He shrugged, looked up at me.
"Don't you understand what kind of person Ray Preston is? I
don't know if he was before, but he sure as hell is now. A killer,
I mean. And he's not going to stop until I'm dead. I'd never
make it to court. I swear, he'd kill me before that."

"What are you talking about? Why in hell wouldn't he want
this to go to trial?"

I didn't want to be so coarse and crude as to say so out loud,
but what judge and jury wouldn't want to grill Billy and find
him guilty as hell? It seemed all too simple. Ray Preston could
be virtually certain of that. As far as I understood, the legal

system had every right and reason to toss Billy in jail with the harshest of sentences.

Billy shook his head, looked down at his place. "It's just so complicated."

"Of course it is. But I'm sure you can be protected. And certainly you can get some good legal help. Carol Marie would do that for you, wouldn't she? Find you a good lawyer?"

Looking totally lost and defeated, he shrugged again. He took a noisy sip of coffee, put down his cup. He glanced at the main door again, perhaps to see that there still weren't any police.

"Loretta didn't tell you everything, did she?" he asked.

"What do you mean?"

He laughed. "That's why you don't get it." He looked up, leaned forward, lowered his voice, and divulged a secret that was burning inside him. "There's one more thing."

"Such as?"

"It wasn't me who ran the red light."

Oh, shit, I thought. What more could there be? How twisted could this thing get?

"What are you saying?"

"Yeah, I was drunk. Yeah, I had a bunch of beer down at the car wash. I was drinking with the guys and I had too much. Way too much." He took a deep sigh. "Oh, sure, it looked like it when the police arrived. They pulled me out from behind the wheel and smelled booze on my breath. And then they did one of those tests, you know, those breath things. And that was it, my fate was sealed. But I mean it wasn't fucking me who went ripping through that fucking red light."

"What?" I asked, wondering not only if I could believe Billy, but if I was finally getting the complete story.

"But there's no fucking way I can prove it," said Billy. "No one will believe a drunk like me."

I stared at the table. If it was in fact Ray Preston who'd run that light, it was clear why he wouldn't want this to come to trial. If the real truth came out, then Ray could be found responsible for the death of his own child.

"Do you get it?" asked Billy.

"Yeah, but out here Ray's hunting for you. He almost shot you the other night, didn't he?"

"Well, I'll tell you one thing. I'd rather be out here and free than locked up for something I didn't do." With that, Billy shrugged and stood, saying, "I don't mean to be rude, man, but I gotta get back in line or else I won't get any seconds. This'll probably be all I eat until tomorrow night."

Chapter 22

Billy took forever in line, so I left, thanking him for his time on my way out. As I emerged from the room that reeked of so much human neglect, then walked to my car, I wondered if Maddy, with all her millions, could find a wizard of a lawyer to prove Billy innocent. Then again, I didn't know how involved Maddy wanted to get, how far she wanted to take all this. Nor I, for that matter. Maddy had sent me down here to discover if Loretta had been in any mortal danger. I was sure I now understood the situation, that when Loretta had written of a life-and-death matter, she had been referring to Billy's dilemma. And with good reason, for I'd witnessed Ray Preston's fury and determination. If Ray did intend to kill Billy, then I was sure he would keep trying to find the means. And quite possibly succeed. No wonder both Billy and Loretta were worried. I found that I was, and I was sure Maddy would be as well. I didn't know what she'd choose next, however, whether to pull out of this mess entirely or to step further in and get really involved in the muck of it all. She was the boss, and I wondered if I'd be packing my bags and heading back to the island tomorrow.

I drove the few blocks into downtown Evanston and had a trendy pasta dish of chicken and red peppers that was nudged onto the wild side with a spicy apricot salsa. It was Italy meets Mexico and lives happily ever after in California, and while I enjoyed the dish I understood why plain old comfort food of mashed potatoes and meat loaf had made a comeback. When you twisted things too far, they became unappetizing, as had almost happened with that dish. At least that was my thinking as I sat there twirling some pasta onto my fork and wondering how far Ray would go to prevent the truth from coming out.

Sitting there in the chic restaurant that was so clean, so beautifully decorated with salmon-colored tables, turquoise walls, and black wall fixtures, I felt like a prince. Someone from the very upper class. Thank God, I thought, I had a roof over my head. And a shower. Food. Shoes. Then again, the distance from that church basement to this fashionable restaurant wasn't that far at all. Literally as well as figuratively.

My main goal had been achieved, I sensed, and as I ate, I started thinking about Maddy and what I would say to her. I thought of calling her right from there, from the pay phone I'd spotted back by the men's room, but the allure of my motel room was stronger. It was quieter there, our conversation would undoubtedly be lengthy, and so I finished up my meal and drove back to the distant 'burbs.

I was back in my room not quite an hour later. I kicked off my shoes, used the john, splashed my face with cold water. Settling onto the edge of the double bed, I was just reaching for the phone when there was a knock at the door. That had been the last thing I expected, and for a moment I didn't move, wondering if there was a mistake. I glanced at the door and was relieved to see that I had both locked and chained it. When again there was tapping, I got up and slipped around to the window. Could Ray Preston be out there, and just how close to the edge could he now be? When I lifted aside the curtain and peered out a crack, however, I was totally surprised. What could this be about?

When there was a third knock, I stepped over to the door and unlocked it. Carol Marie stood there, arms folded across her stomach. Face tight, mouth small. Her anger that clear and bold.

"Hi," I said.

"Why are you bothering my family?" she demanded, standing there on the motel walkway.

"I beg your pardon?"

"I hear you were not only at my stepmother's house today, but you saw Loretta at the library, and then you went and cornered Billy as well. He just called, all worried about me." Her scowl was painted on like thick makeup. "We don't want your help. Just leave us alone. Do you understand?"

I'd been worried about some imagined figure behind the door, someone with a gun who'd want to kill me. Instead I'd opened the door and found Carol Marie gunning for me. And I disliked it as much as if someone were shooting real bullets. The escapade at the Octopus Car Wash didn't help my attitude toward her, either.

"Hey, wait a minute, Carol Marie," I began, my defenses going up. "I'm not sure you—"

"You don't know anything, buddy. We just want you to go away. Got it? You don't know what this is all about."

I said, "I understand that Billy needs professional legal help and that Loretta needs professional psychological help."

She stared at me, eyes blazing. "Jesus Christ, where do you get off? And why have you been following me?"

"Like to the car wash, you mean?"

"Yeah, that's right. To the car wash. In case you haven't figured it out, trespassing is dangerous business. I'll tell you one more time, leave me and my family alone."

"Why?"

"Because it's none of your goddamned business, that's why, and because we don't want any help, particularly from you or your sister. Just tell Dr. Phillips to keep her nosy face out of this. She's never done us any good, that sister of yours. Not before, not now. Your snooping around has got Loretta nearly as upset as when she was seeing Dr. Phillips. Both of you just like to stir things up and get everything all messy, don't you?"

I was irritated before. Angry now. Carol Marie couldn't have done anything that would get me more quickly pissed off than attack my sister. I tried to hold my temper but it came steaming out around the edges.

"My sister did more for Loretta in a few short weeks than anyone had in years."

"Like hell. Loretta was a complete basket case whenever she saw Dr. Phillips. In fact, we were trying to stop Loretta from going."

This could get real nasty real quick, I realized as I stood in the doorway of my motel room. I took a deep breath, tried to calm myself. Don't do anything, I told myself, that you'll regret. Don't say anything. And then I went and said it all wrong anyway.

"I'm down here for one reason and one person only. That's Loretta," I said. "I don't think she wrote my sister because she was worried about Helen selling the house and then being kicked out on the street. There's something else."

"What are you talking about?"

"Loretta wrote that someone's life was in danger."

By the shocked expression on her face, I knew I couldn't have said anything worse. In one short sentence it was clear that I had betrayed Loretta and her desperate plea.

"Yeah, well . . . well," stammered Carol Marie, "half the time Loretta doesn't know the world's round. What did she do, write and say she was afraid to go outside because the mosquitoes were going to kill her? And then what did your sister do, tell her to get some insect repellent and charge her a hundred bucks?"

I said it pleasantly and calmly, voice low. "Go to hell, Carol Marie."

"No, asshole, you go to hell! And take your sister with you!" she snapped, losing it and losing all pretense at suburban pleasantries. "You just tell Dr. Phillips to stay out of this. Tell her to leave us alone. I know what's best for Loretta. She doesn't need any help, anyone prying around and upsetting her world. She's fine, you got it? Just fine. So tell that snoopy sister of yours to stay out of this."

I wanted to know how serious a warning this really was. How much of a threat we really were to Carol Marie.

And I pressed, "Stay out of this or what?"

"Or . . . or you're going to see what kind of trouble I can really make for you two." She furiously shook her head. "Jesus Christ, just leave us alone!"

With that, Carol Marie bolted her jaw shut, then turned and stormed off into the night like a thunderstorm racing across the plains.

Chapter 23

I never did get around to making that call to Maddy. About five minutes after Carol Marie left, I put my shoes back on, brushed my hair, grabbed my car keys, and headed out. As I drove from the lot, I checked my rearview mirror, hoping that I'd rid myself of Ray Preston, which it appeared I had.

When I turned into Loretta's subdivision, I found the broad, winding streets totally empty. There weren't even any parked cars, for it seemed all the residents had hidden away their vehicles in their attached garages. And when I glanced at the houses, I saw that most were already dark. It was just after ten. Soon the late news would be over, after which I was sure everyone would be in bed.

I was about a block, maybe less, from Loretta's when I saw it. The movement. There weren't any streetlights, but I was sure of it. Something up ahead slipping across the street. It caught my eye as if it were a deer slipping and bounding through the night. Crossing the road. Traversing civilization and disappearing into the woods. Only what I saw wasn't a graceful animal. It was a person who came into view and then disappeared within an instant. Someone, I was quite sure, whom I knew.

"Take another look. Let that image streak through your memory again. Be sure."

I parked beneath a tree, just a couple of houses short of Loretta's, bowed my head onto the steering wheel, and replayed it all. Let my memory rewind and run it a second time in slo-mo. And, yes, it was her. Loretta. I saw the legs, heavy and white. The arms, pale as well. And the clothing. The same loose dress as at the library. The one that hung like a bag, flapped as she moved. Without a doubt, it was Loretta. But what in the hell was she doing slipping into the woods where someone had so recently chased her? Why now, so late?

I sat in my car wondering if I was doing this all wrong. Then I climbed out, walked toward their house. I'd come because I was worried I'd landed Loretta in trouble. I feared that Carol Marie would have headed here directly, would have burst into the house and demanded to know just why Loretta had contacted Maddy. I could imagine Carol Marie bullying Loretta, pressing her until she revealed not only what she'd told Maddy but me as well. I'd thought of calling, but I doubted that I'd get through to Loretta; Helen or Carol Marie was sure to have screened out my call.

But Carol Marie's calling card, her white Ford, wasn't here, and the house was dark; only a single light burned somewhere inside, perhaps the one over the dinette table. I reached the edge of their lot, stood there and studied the long, low ranch house that seemed the epitome of suburban sleepiness. The right thing to do would be to turn around and head back to the motel, drop myself back on the bed, and call Maddy with a complete report. Actually, however, I'd come here for something else as well. Before I talked to Maddy tonight, I wanted to hear it from her, from Loretta: Did she really want Maddy and me to kindly, as Carol Marie said, butt out?

I stared at the point where Loretta had vanished, and my curiosity rose like a ghost, beckoning me across the street and toward the woods. Loretta was simple, perhaps. And definitely strange. But she was no dummy, not Loretta with her volumes of Shakespeare. So what could have lured her into those woods?

Looking one last time at the ranch house, I realized I'd been duped right from the start. Right from that first night when I'd arrived, stepped out of my car, and heard those screams clawing the night. Helen had said that Loretta had been attacked. But that wasn't the case. Certainly not. If it had been, Loretta would have definitely had a significant reaction to such a traumatic incident. Loretta, who was afraid to venture into the world. Instead, she'd just seemed . . . humble. No, guilty. That was it. No wonder they hadn't contacted the police and filed a report. No wonder Helen had been so eager for me to leave. No crime had been committed because Loretta hadn't been chased or attacked at all. She'd been out there in the woods meeting someone. Someone Helen hated intensely. Someone Helen was ready and willing, perhaps even eager, to see dead. But who could that be? Carol Marie?

I crossed a ditch and stepped into the woods. The path was once again fairly obvious, even in the night, in the dark, which was only a city grayness, not a country blackness. This time, however, I was quiet. I didn't call out, try to ascertain what was going on. I was only listening, trying to hear where Loretta might be. I came to a large oak, stopped. A voice. Two voices. I looked to my right. Was there an opening, a clearing over there? I started, hesitated. The depth of the night was playing tricks. The sound was coming from the other way, off to the left.

The path was like a creek of black water, and I silently trod along it and beneath the oaks and the huge pines that swayed overhead. A wind came up. There was a whirl and gush of leaves as the forest undulated erotically. I paused again, thought I heard Carol Marie's voice but couldn't be sure.

I heard the dry crinkling of leaves. An animal? No. There it was. Someone whispering. Oh, Jesus. I froze. It was coming from over there, I realized, just up a ways. I thought of announcing myself, but I hadn't learned anything from any of them by being direct and honest. So I pressed on, hoping to catch a snippet of conversation, a piece to the puzzle of this whole thing. An indication that would tell me what was really going on here. There was a small open area. I could see that. The trees gave way. The night pushed back. But through the dim light and the tangle of branches and leaves I couldn't see anyone standing there. I moved still closer. I heard whispering, hushed conversation. Whoever it was, I realized, was sitting down, perhaps perched on some logs or even the forest floor.

Then I saw Loretta's dress, the big baggy one.

It was flat on the ground, lying there empty, lifeless, formless. She'd stripped it off and thrown it aside among the leaves and dirt. My eyes darted from the abandoned clothing. I moved around a tree trunk, and some twenty feet away, Loretta's naked white body glowed like a fleshy moon. She was leaning forward, straddling another body. I nearly shouted out. That wasn't a dead body beneath her and this wasn't some kind of bizarre murder ritual, was it? No. I saw the person beneath her move. And I saw Loretta lift herself up slightly, then lower herself back down. And next I heard a moan. My stomach turned a second time. Oh, my God. Was it the two sisters, were they having sex, was that it, was that why Helen and Carol Marie hated each other?

No. I shifted around a tree just as another deep satisfied moan rose into the night. It was the groan of a man, and beneath Loretta I saw a pair of pants splayed open and pulled halfway down. I caught my breath. Loretta was totally naked, pinning someone beneath her and humping up and down. And now they were both doing it, thrusting and moaning as they fucked. I stepped around, and beneath Loretta I spied the familiar brown hair, the pressed shirt, the thick, smooth arms. I saw a corner of his face, now recognized the voice of Ray Preston.

"Oh, God."

Chapter 24

"Oh, God!" repeated Maddy, jerking me out of trance. "How could I have missed that?"

I'd been brought back much too quickly. Maddy hadn't even eased me out of it. No number routine. No reeling me back with coy words and gentle coaching. None of that stuff. Just pop. End of film, end of dream sequence. She'd heaved me out of that world and dumped me back into this one with one crude tug. I rubbed my eyes, stared upward from the recliner. Wooden ceiling. Boards. That was right. There were no pines and oaks swirling overhead like palm trees. No, this was a fixed wooden ceiling. Trance room. Maddy's house. Island. Forget then and there, Loretta and Chicago.

"How could I have been so goddamned stupid?" cursed Maddy. "I can't believe it!"

I could barely move, barely keep my eyes open. Maddy, meanwhile, was sitting up and dragging herself into her wheelchair. It seemed to take her no effort. With her thin, muscular arms, she was holding on to the arms of the chair, lifting her body from the black leather recliner. I watched her like a movie. The two of us here in the same room. But the two of us separate, not connected, not of the same dimension.

In an instant she was in her wheelchair, now positioning her lifeless legs, pinning them down, strapping them into place with Velcro ties. Then she was pulling out that wand, the fishing-rod gizmo she had rigged up to act as a cane. With a heave, she was off, rolling across the huge room, our trance room, that was meant to be a ballroom. A ceiling that soared some thirty feet. A room that was at least that wide, at least twice that long, where orchestras hauled by steamer from Chicago were supposed to play for the chewing-gum magnates and the department-store kings.

Lying on my side, I saw that Maddy was barreling over the planks, headed straight for the three huge leaded-glass windows at the far end. I was sure she would crash into one. But somehow she knew. Maybe via the wand/cane thing she could feel it, sense it. Or maybe my brilliant sister just knew how far she could go; maybe she'd developed batlike radar. Just at the last moment, just when I was set to force a shout, she clenched one wheel of the chair and went spinning around. With another heave, she was off, now zooming toward the Tiffany dome.

"Why didn't I get it?" said Maddy, continuing to berate herself. "I should have put it together. Ray and Loretta. I didn't even suspect that they might have been lovers."

I lay there like an invalid, and spoke with a faint voice. "They might not have been."

"What?"

"Just because they were having sex doesn't mean they were lovers." I added a brilliant and wise observation, saying, "Sex and love aren't the same, you know."

This was Maddy's form of pacing, this zooming back and forth. And it drove me crazy the way she ricocheted about like a pinball. She was now roaring toward the structure that held the stained-glass dome over the open stairwell. Did she sense it? Did she know how close she was? Oh, Maddy. I wanted to call out, but she hated that. Hated when I was, as she put it, overprotective. Still, she was about to crash, that much was clear. I couldn't just lie there.

I propped myself up, called out, "Maddy—"

"What?"

Proving me unnecessary, she braked, slowed herself, and coasted up to the wall, tagged it with her hand as if it were first base. Then she turned, and with another push sent herself wheeling into the middle of the room. My dear sister was stuck on high.

"I don't know," I mumbled, retreating and settling back into the recliner.

"No, maybe you're right. Maybe you've got something there. They might not have been lovers. But at the same time, it probably wasn't rape, either."

"She was on top. And if anything, she was holding him down."

Maddy braked to a complete stop, turned the chair toward me. "What do you mean, Alex? Bring back that scene. Slip into a light trance and let yourself see it again."

"Maddy, please," I chided, "I'm not a VCR."

"Of course you are." And as if by remote, she called, "Close your eyes, Breathe in. Out. Listen to me count: One. And two. And three."

I was that easy, that suggestible. That subservient. My eyes closed and I popped back to then and there, flipping realities as easily as flipping the channel. The woods. Okay. Just peer through the dark. Look past the bushes and trees. I saw what I needed, then opened my eyes and found myself back on the recliner in that room.

"Loretta wasn't just straddling him," I reported. "She was leaning forward. You know, reaching out, holding his arms to the ground."

"She had him pinned?"

"Exactly. He didn't really look like he wanted to go anywhere. I mean, he was obviously really into it, so to speak. But it was also obvious Loretta wasn't going to let him go anywhere, either."

"Do you have a problem with that, with aggressive women?"

"Oh, Christ, Maddy. Of course not. That's not the point."

"What is?" asked my shrinky sister. "I just want to make sure you don't have a bias in reporting what you saw."

"I don't. And now that I think about it, now that I look at it again, Loretta looked like she had a purpose."

"Go on."

"Oh, I don't know."

"Yes, you do."

"Well, she was staring down at him, for Christ's sake. You know, studying him, looking to make sure he was lost in it."

"What, the sex?"

"Yeah," I replied. "Like she wanted to make sure she had him completely."

Maddy muttered, "Control."

Somewhere behind me, I heard her, my sister, now rolling slowly across the room. Nothing quick. Not now. Maddy's anxious energy was zapped, overwhelmed by a wave of thought, deep and provocative. I could tell by the slow, unsteady pace of her chair.

"God, I wish I'd just had a couple more sessions with Loretta," said Maddy. "There was something more she wanted to tell me. And I'm sure this was part of it. I was just about to crack her wide open. It would have all come out."

"You're talking about her like she was a real nut." I laughed, couldn't help it. "Which I suppose she was."

Maddy ignored me, which made me feel like the stupid little brother. So naive. My sister just pushed on, approaching the French doors that opened onto the balcony and all of Lake Michigan.

My eyes settled shut. I was exhausted, couldn't move. I'd been used and abused, my memory taken and plundered. A part of me felt raped, actually. Like I'd been coerced against my will, been forced to hand over more than I wanted, gone farther than I could possibly go. I'd gone into my memory bank and not simply ransacked it, but wiped it clean. Well, maybe not clean. There was more there. More to tell. The rest of the story to finish. The remainder of that night. Oh, God, so much blood. It had been everywhere.

"Helen was probably killed about an hour after that," I said. "At least, I don't think she was dead then, you know, when I sneaked out into the woods."

"No, I don't think so, either."

I opened my eyes. Maddy had pulled up next to the screen door. Rather than going out, however, she was running her left hand up the screen. Did she know something I didn't? Had she possibly picked up on something that I'd said?

"Why do you say that?" I demanded.

"Nothing. Just a hunch."

"Yeah, right. Since when do you—"

"Control. I think that's what this is all about," said Maddy, not paying me the slightest bit of attention. "Loretta feared the world because she couldn't control it. That's why she wouldn't go any farther than the library. That's why she wouldn't go out into society. She didn't trust it, didn't feel protected."

Maddy was playing both hands over the screen now, slowly moving them up and down, palms against the mesh. As if she were gently massaging a lover. Rubbing. Caressing. And she talked on. Not to me. Perhaps to someone else. Some fantasy. But not me. I was gone. Not of importance right then.

"Something traumatic happened to Loretta," continued Maddy, sounding her thoughts and theories. "Not when she was a kid, but older. A teenager maybe. I don't think it was just the death of her mother. It was something harsher. And from then on, everything was changed. She never said so specifically, but I drew a chart of it all. Her life. When she stopped going out. And it wasn't long after her father married Helen and it wasn't long after they moved into that house. That's when it started. Or rather that's when it ended, her life, her dreams."

"So she came to you to tell you something about her family—what Billy had done, the car accident, I mean, and the little girl. Maybe even where Billy was. But all this other stuff came out?"

"Yes. It was all a matter of trust. Gaining her trust, earning it. And Loretta wasn't all that sure she wanted to betray her family. So she told me a lot about herself. I guess you could say, in our seven or eight sessions, Loretta and I were just getting to know one another." Her head turned toward the door and the lake; it almost appeared that she could see the water, its blueness, the tips of the whitecaps, and she added, "Loretta was just so bound up in shame and guilt."

An earlier thought returned. "You know, I wondered before if Loretta might have been raped. I mean, when she was young. What do you think?"

Maddy turned to me. Stared at me with her blind eyes. With those big sunglasses.

"It didn't occur to me back then when she was in therapy. But, yes, she very well could have been."

"And the poem."

" 'The Rape of Lucrece.' Of course. That would explain her fascination with it."

I closed my eyes. Let me hear her voice. Let her chant those lines again.

And mimicking Loretta, my voice taking on her sweet, deep tones, I recited:

"Poor hand, why quiver'st thou in this decree?
Honour thyself to rid me of this shame;
For if I die, my honour live in thee,
But if I live, thou liv'st in my defame."

Neither Maddy nor I said anything for a long time. We let the weight of Shakespeare meld with the possible, probable, tragedy of Loretta. We let all of it pin us down with horrible thoughts and endless speculation. Dear Lord, what, if anything, had happened to that poor woman in her youth and how was it twisted, even kneaded, into the present?

"It's no wonder Loretta wanted to kill herself," said Maddy.

"What do you mean?"

"Suicide is the ultimate and ultimately final act of control."

"But you yourself said you don't think she killed Helen."

"Yes, but by claiming to have done it, she's seizing control of the entire situation."

I closed my eyes. Rubbed my temples. I couldn't get up. That would mean moving into the present. Dumping the past. And part of me was still back there.

"Maddy, I feel all strung out. The physical part of me might be here, but I think my aura's still back there. You know, in those woods. In that night. In that time."

"Would you like to go back?"

"I have to."

"Why?"

"Helen's about to be killed."

"But you can't change that. What happened has happened. Helen is dead."

"Of course." Then why did I want to return to those few

hours when I was so brutally attacked and Helen so hideously butchered? "But I have to tell you about it. I have to let go of it. Get it out of me. There's something there."

"Very good."

I closed my eyes, and the next thing I knew I saw leaves and tree trunks and a naked, pasty-white body bucking and riding into delight.

Chapter 25

It wasn't a pretty sight, either, and I wasn't much of a voyeur. I'd seen enough to make my mind recoil, and so I kept my presence hidden, turned and more quietly than ever began to make my way through the bushes and trees, down the path, back to the road, out of there, away from them. Oh, shit. Loretta and Ray. How long had this been going on and how serious were they, this agoraphobic woman and this mournful, rageful dry cleaner? I heard them somewhere behind me. A groan of desire and lust and pleasure clawing into the heavens. Just wait, I thought, my feet quickly padding along, carrying me away. Just wait until Maddy hears about this.

"No shit, Sherlock."

The two of them, Loretta and Ray, had breached the hostile boundaries between their two families. Was it love that compelled them so? A sense of duty? Oh, God. This was just like a Shakespeare drama. No, a tragedy, because I sensed this was all about to come to a head. That nothing but pain and death would explode, soon splatter all of this with a shroud of blood.

Not far from me I heard something crack, perhaps the proverbial twig snapping beneath a foot. Another soul was out here, and I stopped, stood completely frozen except for my heart that thumped and swelled. Helen had been here before, knife in hand. Now I understood why. Helen hadn't come slashing out of the darkness because Loretta was being attacked. There had been no attack. Helen had come racing out of the dark, knife in hand, because she knew about Loretta and Ray. Hated it, the very thought of them together, having sex. Was revolted. And Helen had come chasing through the woods, ready to cut the whole thing to pieces. The Ray-Loretta thing.

So was that Helen now out here, lurking in the woods? A cool finger of fear zipped up my spine, tickled the back of my neck. I pressed myself up against a tree, hugged the coarse bark. Was she out there, that bitch of a stepmother? Loretta had saved me before, stopped Helen just before she attacked, but now I was on my own and defenseless. No weapon. No Loretta.

Or perhaps I was wrong. Perhaps there was no Helen out here. Maybe instead it was them, the odd lovers. I looked behind me, back where I'd seen Loretta and Ray going at it, doing it. Had they perhaps heard me? Had I disturbed, perhaps ended their feast of the body? Shit. If so, they could be coming after me. Or it very well might be just him. Ray. Which would be a hell of a lot worse than Helen.

There it was again. An abrupt noise. Something breaking, disturbing the soft silence of this forest of darkness. I spun to my right. I saw it. That figure, the shape that so closely resembled the one I'd seen over and over in my fearful dreams. A cloudlike form of someone whooshing through the woods. Oh, God. I saw it for just a moment. An indistinguishable form of flowing clothing. Tannish. Brownish. I couldn't really tell. But it was all too familiar, this unseen shape. Billy? Yes, perhaps.

Fearing for my life, I hunkered down, tore for the street where all of us and all of it would at least be out in the open. I came to a fork in the path, went to the left. Seconds later I burst into an opening where a picnic table sat next to a stone barbecue. That hadn't been here before. I spun, doubled back. The street. Where? Which way? A big round gush of wind billowed over the woods, swishing the leaves. I heard branches creaking, moaning as they tipped from side to side, and thought I heard a woman's deep, satisfied laugh.

Abruptly, I felt fingers and an arm dropping over my head

from behind. Wrapping around me. I shouted out, spun and twisted, battled away whoever it was. But there was no one there. Only a branch with little twiggy appendages and leaves. That was all it was. A ghostly branch that had dropped out of the sky and momentarily clung to me.

I started running. Had to get out of there. I came to the fork, turned the other way, the right way, and darted on. Yes, this was good. I could see things. Familiar shapes. The right blend of trees. Then an end. A gray opening. A hole in the woods. I was almost there.

I heard something pounding. Other steps. Somewhere behind me. As I ran, I glanced over my shoulder. An image appeared. That figure. Whether it was a man or a woman, I couldn't tell. But I could see it, that shape racing after me. I didn't waste a moment. Pressed on. And in seconds I'd reached the little hole. I burst through. Came speeding out of the woods, went bounding over the ditch, landed on the pavement. I took a few more steps, slowed. Stopped. I was breathing hard and heavy, and I tensed, expected to see that other person come zooming out after me. I waited, readied myself for the attack.

But all was oddly quiet. Unpleasantly still.

I glanced down at my rental car, which sat so quietly down the street. I should have gone straight to it. That would have been the wisest. Something horrible was brewing here. I should get away. Flee these sick people and this warped neighborhood. I should retreat to my motel, call Maddy.

But no. I had to find out.

Studying Loretta's house, I saw that another light was burning. I had to find out who was there, who was home. I crossed the street, approached the house, walking across the short grass. The front window was glowing brighter. I could see no sign of activity, however. I looked through the broad living-room window, a big picture-window affair, but there was no sign of Helen or Loretta.

"What about Carol Marie? Any sign of her car?"

I didn't even think, didn't even consider the possibility of that, of Carol Marie having arrived while I was off in the woods.

"Well, look now."

But I was focused on the house and I didn't even—

"When you were crossing the street, when you were on the grass,

was there anything on the periphery of your vision? Another car, per-
haps, parked down the road? Is there an image of anything like that
floating on the edge of your memory?"

With a shudder, I realized there was. Another vehicle.
When I had looked down toward my rental car, I saw but really
didn't pay any attention to it. Another auto, perhaps belonging
to a neighbor, perhaps not, parked on the outer edges of my
memory, right behind my rental. It was a sedan, maybe white,
maybe gray. Or silver.

"So she could have been there."

God, I had to be careful. I knew that. Felt that. I was
trembling as I approached the house, fearful of what I knew
was soon to come. I stepped onto the concrete sidewalk, neared
the front door. All was quiet, oddly still. I reached the door,
peered in through the little window. A light by the couch
was on.

"What about the floor? Is there anything unusual, particularly on
the carpet?"

I couldn't see much. I looked in, past the entry, toward the
kitchen. I could have knocked, but I didn't want to. But, no, I
couldn't see anything.

"Any blood?"

White carpet. Pale yellow walls. That yellow and blue
couch. All so clean. My curiosity gripped me. I didn't want to
knock, to announce myself. But I desperately wanted to find
out who was in there, back in the kitchen. If it was just Helen.
Or perhaps Carol Marie or even Billy. So, like a thief, I passed
around the front of the house, quickly made my way along the
bushes, past the far window, around the far edge of the dwell-
ing. I shouldn't do this, I thought. I should turn around. This
isn't right. I could be shot.

"Don't worry. There won't be any shooting."

Don't worry? What? I halted, stared through the night,
across the lawn and back at the woods. Were Loretta and Ray
still out there, still hidden in the trees, their bodies entangled?
Somehow I didn't think so. But if not, then had Loretta already
returned, somehow beat me to the house? And where would
Ray then be?

I crept on, touching the white siding, passing beneath a
bathroom window, a high window that opened out like an aw-
ning. Another window, also dark. Aside from me and the little

noise I was making, there was nothing but silence and stillness. I glanced over at the neighbor's house, some seventy feet away. If I were spotted, I'd be taken for a burglar. The police would be called, which actually wouldn't be so bad.

I came to the back corner of the house, looked around. The patio was empty, the backyard still with the night. I saw the yellowish glow of light flooding out the kitchen window. And something moving. A shadow. So someone was at home. It had to be Helen, didn't it? It had—

That charging sound. Oh, Jesus. I sensed the noise, the presence of someone else, but it was too late. Before I could spin around, before I could do anything to defend myself, something was thrown over my head. Oh, God. Dear God. A rope. A small rope. It was tossed over my head, then jerked back and I could feel its fibers burning and pulling, burrowing into me. I started twisting. I hit him. I reached back and smacked him on the head.

"Him?"

Short hair. Yes. I was sure of it. The hair of a man. But it was useless. He was strong. And the rope was cutting deeper and deeper into me, slicing off the air. I was gasping. Struggling for my breath. Falling. Thinking, wondering. Was this how I was to end? Because I was losing. I struck again. Saw a flash. An arm. A flash of brown shirt. He was winning, this man, this murderer. I was losing. I struggled and hit, but the night was becoming darker and darker, folding in on this, on me, because I could no longer breathe. Nothing. No air. And then, just as I was falling, I heard a scream. My own? No. Someone else's. A woman's scream.

And in an instant I was disposed of. Hurled into a black pool. Dipped into a muddy nothingness. Dropped on the ground and left for dead.

Chapter 26

I was gone for a long time after that. It was like I was hiding at the bottom of a black pool. Or maybe I wasn't hiding. Maybe I was stuck down there, unable to surface. Then, however, I heard that voice. And that's what pulled me up, brought me back alive. Eventually it did, anyway.

"And what is said?"

When I was coming back up, someone was talking. I heard the words. But I couldn't tell what they were. It didn't make any sense.

"But it does now. Let yourself hear those words."

No, it was all so mucky. So muddy. I think some part of me understood because I think that was what shocked me awake again. But exactly what was said, I couldn't discern.

"The voice says—'"

There on the bottom of that murky, black pool, I began to stir. It was like I was being talked at through water. Someone was saying something directly and clearly, and through the viscosity of the black water I was supposed to understand.

"Be there again. Be there with amazing hearing. One."

I felt the bottom of the pool, soft and smooth.

"And then you notice someone above. Two."

Yes, there was someone up there, right on the edge.

"And on the count of three you hear them say—"

I was struggling to see who it was. To see who was floating above me, trying to say something, talking. But I couldn't tell. Couldn't be certain. All I heard was that sentence, that heavy voice.

"And it says?"

God, I didn't know. Couldn't bring back the words.

Then suddenly it was like I was slapped. Or something exploded. Something went off and I was hoovered out of that darkness, sucked right off the bottom of the pool, and in a flash I was back on the surface. I opened my eyes. Looked up. Saw little bumps. Sprayed plaster. Off to my side, two armchairs, my jeans thrown on one of them. And there was my black nylon suitcase. The motel. I'd thought I was waking up back on Madeline's island, but I hadn't been. I was still there, down there in suburban Chicago. I was lying on the bed. What? Hadn't I just been at Loretta's? How had I gotten back here?

I swallowed, which proved to be incredibly painful. Something like a sore throat. More like a sprained muscle. I touched my neck and winced. The skin was tender, perhaps raw. I recalled the attack. The rope. I sat up. My head started spinning, so I didn't move. Just sat there. It hurt to breathe, to have anything going up and down my throat. I'd been attacked, nearly strangled to death. No wonder.

A few minutes later, I got up, went to the mirror. My eyes were all puffy. My dark hair matted and twisted. My shirt was slightly wet, too, for I could see the dampness on either shoulder. I pulled down my collar, saw the streak of red-raw skin, some little droplets of blood, and a black-and-blue mark that seemed to be budding and flowering as I watched. I reached for a washcloth, turned on the cold water, soaked the cloth, and pressed it against my neck. When I pulled it away, the washcloth was stained a bleeding red.

I cautiously opened the door, looked both ways, checked the parking lot. I saw a familiar car. My small red rental that was now oddly parked at an angle, half in one space, half in another. And then I headed for the ice machine. As I traipsed along, I wondered how I'd gotten back there, who'd delivered me to my bed and my car to its parking spot.

I returned to my room with a bucket of ice, settled a cold compress on my neck, winced in pain. And couldn't help but worry what was going on back at Loretta's house. I lay back on my bed, the ice pack on my throat, and realized that someone had gone to great lengths to get me out of the way. To remove me so I wouldn't be a complication. Something was going on back there. Certainly something dangerous. I found myself lying there, worrying about Loretta. She'd become involved in a series of circumstances from which she had no escape. Of that I was certain. And none of it was good. I thought of the night I'd been chased in my car, the time I'd been clubbed at the car wash. Now this, a strangulation, a near murder. My own near murder. I thought of Ray, Carol Marie, Billy. Loretta. And Helen.

I thought of calling the police. But what would I tell them? I didn't want to go into the attack, how I'd nearly been killed. That would stir up too much. Too much of nothing. Besides, it was Loretta I was worried about. She'd gotten involved in something and now she was in danger. I knew that then. I had to tell her . . .

"Very good, Alex. Just let it float to the surface."

I had to tell her to stay out of all this, whatever it was. I had to tell her she was in danger, that someone had tried to kill me for meddling and that she, too, was at risk.

"There it is, Alex. Excellent. That's exactly what you heard, isn't it?"

As I lay there, that frigid compress extinguishing the burns on my throat, I knew. I had to tell Loretta what I'd overheard when I was lying there half unconscious. How someone had blurted two words: "It's yours."

Chapter 27

I quickly sat up. I had to get back there, to Loretta's. For some reason I'd been spared; perhaps the whole idea was simply to get me out of the way. But that warning was echoing silently in my head. And that trance sense of mine was telling me something that I would find out all too soon: Something horrible had already happened at Loretta's. My heart began to race, to speed as if I knew someone was being killed right that moment. Murdered in a most gruesome fashion, over and over. In my mind's eye I saw blood being splattered and spewed, fountains of it. Jets of it. Spraying everywhere. All that furniture. That nice white carpeting. All of it covered under a red mist, no, a red snow of blood. Loretta, I thought, as I hurried to put my shoes on.

The phone rang. I jumped and caught it on the second ring.

"Hello?" I said.

For the longest while there was no reply. Only deep breathing. I could hear that, which was why I didn't hang up.

Finally, a voice said, "Alex?"

I held my breath. "Are you all right?"

"I . . . I guess so."

"But something's wrong, isn't it, Loretta?"

"Yes."

"Are you hurt?"

"No." Then Loretta asked, "How about you, Alex? Are you all right? I'm sorry about what happened. How's your neck? When did you wake up?"

Her voice was uneven. The words broken. I could only imagine what had happened at her house.

"I'm fine, Loretta," I said. "Are you alone? Would you like me to come over?"

"I'm the only one here now. Everyone else left."

"Then I'm going to come over. I'm leaving right now. Will you be all right until I get there?"

"Uh, sure."

"Should I call an ambulance?"

"Why, no. It's too late." She added, "Remember what I wrote Dr. Phillips? Remember? I told her it was a matter of life and death. I was right, too."

My stomach bunched up. Oh, God. I hung up, pulled on my shoes, tucked in my shirt, studied my neck in the mirror. I felt my pockets for my car keys, came up with nothing, then spotted them over by the TV, alongside my room key. And then I was flying out of there, down the stairs to my car, which was parked so haphazardly it seemed to take forever. I drove through Loretta's suburb as if I were being chased, racing around the bends, past the dark houses, toward the truth or what I'd be able to make of it. Too late. Loretta had said that, and I knew it was, too.

I pulled into the driveway. Just before I jumped out, I stopped, looked around. I'd been attacked here not so very long ago. I scanned the road, saw no other cars. I searched the lawns, spied no one else. Was I safe? I studied the house, saw the living room now blazing with light. I stepped out of my car, shut the door, hesitated as I checked the environs once again. And then I started moving. I think I knew then. I think I knew what I would see, what had happened. I had a huge vision of death, a wall of red that rose before me.

"Loretta?" I called as I approached the house.

There was no answer. I kept moving, came to the front door. I wiped my feet on the mat as I rang the doorbell. No answer. I rang again, those canned chimes dingdonging inside. I peered through the window in the door. Something was wrong. There was stuff on the walls. Something splattered. It looked like syrup.

I pulled open the screen, pushed open the door, called, "Loretta? Loretta, it's me, Alex."

No response. I stepped onto the slate entry. I knew someone was dead. I could smell it. So thick, so dirty. My stomach rolled. And I could see it, too. That stuff on the walls. On the carpeting. Droplets on the leaves of the plants that sat in the little dividers that separated the entry from the living room. Those weren't droplets of syrup. No, they were droplets of blood. Everywhere. On everything.

I panicked, was sure Loretta had been killed in the time it had taken me to get here, and I shouted, "Loretta!"

I took a couple of huge steps, froze right there on the edge of the white carpet. Helen. I gagged when I saw how she'd been hacked and knifed. Blood was pouring out of her chest, dribbling over the side of her body. I watched as the red liquid flowed down and over a footprint in the carpet. How the blood washed the track away. She was very dead. Horribly so. Oh, God. Had Loretta done this? I looked around at the yellow walls, the yellow and blue couch, the little coffee table that had been shoved or pushed out of the way. Everything splattered with blood.

The wind came up. I heard it gather outside, the trees bending and swooping, and then all of a sudden behind me there was a horrible explosion. A huge bang. I jumped, turned around, my feet sliding in some blood. It was the door. It had blown shut.

And really there wasn't much more. Not enough. I couldn't tell, didn't see. It was just so horrible and I was so afraid. If only I'd thought more clearly, looked more carefully at everything. All the evidence, the crime scene, where she was killed. Because then I heard the noise from the bedroom. I didn't know who or why or if I was to be killed next. I thought for an instant that it might be a trap, that I'd been lured here. Maybe sicko Loretta wanted me dead. Maybe to punish her shrink, Maddy. Dr. Phillips. I had to get out of there. Find some way to get the police. That was what I thought. But there was that sound coming from the bedroom and then, of course, I saw her. Loretta. Bursting out of the back. A mad tornado of energy. Streaking by the living room. Rushing into the kitchen.

"That's good, Alex. That's enough."

No, I hadn't done enough because I hadn't stopped any of it. Not one bit. Helen was dead.

"I'm going to bring you out of this. Three."

There was no escape. Not really. I couldn't get away.

"Two."

And there she was. Loretta, knife in—

"And one."

Chapter 28

I lay there in that magical, mystical recliner. Eyes open, head back. Looking up at the wooden ceiling. Then glancing out the French doors, into the dark night. Out at the black sky that I had somehow just flown through on my way back from Chicago. That bloody time with Loretta. I had just been there but that was over and now I was back here. In the flash of a second, in the diminishing count of *three, two, one,* I had flown through time and space and back to the island. Back to this recliner. Back to this room where one light was softly glowing behind me.

"Are you all right?" asked Maddy, her voice nearly a whisper.

"I guess."

"A little tired?"

"I guess."

It had been no fun, those other times, looking at the murder scene like that. Zooming in and focusing on all that blood; then pulling back, only to zoom in again. And again. Nor was it fun now. I hadn't just gone over what I'd found that night. I'd relived the whole event. Yet I felt empty, unsatisfied.

"I feel like a book on tape," I said. "You know, like I just told an entire story. Only I feel like I didn't come up with the

185

right ending. One that makes sense, I mean. Did I just waste an evening? I did, didn't I? We're not any closer to figuring this out, are we?"

"Oh, nonsense."

"Or should I ask, are you?"

When my sister didn't reply I glanced over, saw her reaching over to her wheelchair. Oh, God. I hoped she wasn't going to play another one of those wild pinball things, where she went blindly whizzing around this room. But she wasn't. Instead of hoisting herself into the seat, she reached over and pulled a cordless phone from its holster.

Maddy pressed a single button, and said, "Hello, Solange. An evening tray, if you would, please."

Evening tray? What the hell did that mean? I shook my head. Sometimes I was certain my sister enjoyed all this. I could never—and never would—say it to her face, but she seemed to get a kick out of it all. The royal cripple stuff. Evening tray? I'd always felt sorry for her. But maybe this was what she was meant for. This island. All that money. It was a role that she played beautifully. A life that she seemed to relish. I couldn't really imagine her as a mom, staying home, baking cookies in some suburb. That just wasn't Maddy; she'd never been that wholesome or down to earth. She always had been above the rest of us in some way, even as a kid. And as I lay there pondering all this, I knew she would have made her life unique even if she were sighted. Somehow. I couldn't imagine her as a lawyer or a corporate exec, either, even though she could easily be running a huge company. Maybe a doctor doing strange and wonderful things à la Mother Teresa with a dash of Dr. Albert What's-his-name. No, Maddy had never been meant to fit in. This was her path. Her place.

I got up and stretched and went over to the doors. I leaned against the screen and stared out into the night.

"What do you see?" asked Maddy from behind.

"The lake, but it's all dark."

"Anything on the water?"

I opened one of the screens, stepped out, and was embraced with the cool night air. Gentle billows of it. The trees in front rose in tall, broccolilike clumps. And from the beach down the hill I could hear the rhythmic slapping of waves. I took it all in, went to the railing, leaned on the wood. Off to the right, maybe ten miles away, I saw a mass of lights dazzling the dark waters.

"There's a boat," I said.

"Where?"

"Off to the west, coming from the south."

"From Chicago. It'll go up and around the top of Michigan, back the other side, then out the St. Lawrence and probably off to Europe," said Maddy. "Is it just a few lights or a long string of them?"

"A long string, from bow to stern. It must be a huge boat, too. God, wouldn't you love to be at that party?"

"I'm sure that's a freighter. Do the lights sort of gather at the stern, you know, like around a cabin?"

"Right."

"Then it's a freighter, probably carrying coal or grain."

I wanted to say, maybe so, maybe not, but I knew she was right. First of all, Maddy was always right; she read that much, studied that much, knew that much; so much that even the wildest-sounding bullshit she spouted always turned out to be, well, somehow the truth. Second, now that she'd said it, the long low shape of the ship did in fact look like a freighter. Besides, if I argued, she'd say something like, listen, do you hear any music? If that were a party boat, then you'd hear a band, because you could hear them, you know, all that raucous jazz and whatnot, for miles and miles across the water. Well, do you hear anything?

No, I didn't, I thought as I turned around, saw Maddy, lips pursed tightly together as she lifted herself into her wheelchair. I didn't move because I didn't want her to know I was observing. Nor did I move once she was settled and pushing on the wheels, struggling with the door, making her way out here onto the balcony. I only flinched once when one wheel got stuck on the threshold. When she reached my side, though, I was just leaning on the railing, looking down at the lawn, some seventy feet or so below.

"It's a long way down from up here," I said.

"Yes, it is. I hope the railing's safe."

"Me, too." I pulled back slightly. "When's Loretta coming tomorrow?"

"Midafternoon."

"Do you think this helped, my going through it all? Did you pick up anything?"

Maddy took my hand, said, "Oh, sure. Lots of stuff."

"Such as?"

A knock interrupted our conversation, and Maddy turned and through the screen door called, "Come on in, Solange."

The door beneath the Tiffany dome opened, and Solange emerged, her broad, attractive face void of expression. She carried a large silver tray, and I wondered why she hadn't taken the elevator and how, after she'd climbed all the way up here, she wasn't even breathing heavily.

"Just put it on the table. That'd be great." My sister added, "I think that'll be it for tonight."

"All right."

Which meant that Maddy wouldn't require any help getting ready for bed. I understood that. And now I understood what an evening tray was.

Nodding inside at the tray, Maddy said, "Alex, there's some coffee—decaf, of course. And some vin santo. It's a sweet dessert wine. It goes great with the biscotti. They're the good kind, made with lots of hazelnuts. You know what I mean? I don't like the real eggy biscotti. They taste too much like sweet Styrofoam."

An evening tray was obviously a code. It meant a tray with three things on it, coffee, wine, cookies. Nothing more, nothing less. An evening tray meant that Maddy wouldn't have to ask what was being served. And I guessed that the two coffee cups and the two small wineglasses each had a prearranged spot so Maddy wouldn't have to ask where everything was or go groping about. Everything in its place, which Maddy was certain to have memorized.

Maddy's housekeeper and companion silently retreated. Once Solange had closed the door, I turned back to the sky, stared at the millions and millions of stars.

"I hope I get to see the Northern Lights sometime," I said. "They should be spectacular this far north."

"You simply have to open yourself to seeing them, that's all," advised Maddy by my side, looking up as if she could see them but I, the sighted one, could not. "Just like you opened yourself to retelling the trip to Chicago. And just like I opened myself to hearing it all."

"Meaning?"

I watched her, sister of mine, open the door and head back inside. She went directly to the table between the two recliners, and there was only a moment of blind hesitation. But the thermal carafe of coffee was right where she knew it would be, and she took it, poured two cups without spilling a drop.

"Meaning," said Maddy, "you revealed a lot in trance, surely more than you realize."

"You know," I began, looking through the screen at her, "it's a good thing you stayed in the Midwest. At least you're still a little bit sane. If you'd moved out to California or the mesas of New Mexico, I think you would have gone over the edge and fallen way down into Groovy Canyon." I paused. "So, do tell. What jewels did I unearth but fail to notice?"

"Here."

Maddy held out a cup, and I dutifully stepped in, took it, and began sipping. I reached down and grabbed one of the biscotti, then strolled behind the recliners.

"Well," said Maddy, "just here, just now, you said a couple of things about the murder that you hadn't mentioned before. I'm not surprised the first didn't come up sooner because in the earlier trances we didn't start that early. At the motel, I mean. It was something Loretta said."

I stared at Maddy. Watched as she next poured us each a glass of the vin santo. Loretta, as far as I was concerned, hadn't said anything notable. Or so I thought as I dipped the hard cookie into my coffee and took a bite.

Maddy bowed her head. "Let me see. What were the words, how did you quote her? Oh, yes. You asked Loretta if she was alone, if she wanted you to come over, and she said she was there by herself. She said, 'Everyone else has left.' That, of course, means that more than one person had been there but had departed."

"Sure, but when? I mean, Loretta could have meant someone had left hours earlier. Then again, I could have made it up. I could have been imagining that."

"Doubtful. Here, try the wine. It's perfect for dipping biscotti." Maddy dunked one herself, then bit down with a crunch. "Besides, it fits in with what you said about the footprint."

"What footprint?" I asked, setting down my coffee and then picking up the small wineglass.

"You were talking about all the blood. How it was coming out of the body so quickly. You saw it flow across the carpet and swallow up a footprint. That's what you said."

I did? I started walking, pacing away from Maddy. Really? I'd said that? But even as I asked myself, I knew that Maddy was right. I could hear my own voice echoing that phrase, that statement. And then I could see it. As I walked, wine in one hand, the hard Italian cookie in the other, I could visualize that print. A track made in a few spots of blood that was then washed out by the deluge of red liquid. Something that was flooded over and out of existence so that the police never even knew it had been there. All that remained was an image in my memory.

Maddy said, "I want to ask her about that, see what she has to say about it."

"Loretta? But she's hardly talking. You don't think you'll open her up that quickly, do you?"

"I'm sure she'll let me hypnotize her, so I certainly hope she'll loosen up and relax. But that's not who I mean."

I was suddenly filled with dread. Another Maddy bomb. That was what she was dropping.

"What?" I cautiously asked as I stopped in the middle of the expansive room.

"I want to ask Carol Marie a few questions."

I knew what that meant. "Oh, shit, Maddy. You didn't."

"You mean invite her? Of course I did. I had to. I posted bail, of course, but Carol Marie wasn't about to let Loretta come here alone."

I stared at Maddy, who sat there in her wheelchair next to the recliners, and this throbbing sense of déjà vu whirled through me. I knew at once that Maddy could very well have a plan or some sort of scheme, one that I knew nothing of. Oh, God. And there was no way I was going to get it out of her, not yet, especially not tonight.

"I can't believe you did that, Maddy. I really can't," I said, a bolt of tension grabbing me by the neck. "This is something we should have discussed."

"Don't be silly. It's not that big of a deal."

"Of course it is."

"Well, you didn't honestly think that Loretta would travel by herself, did you?"

"I guess I didn't think about it." I paused, homing in on the crux of my anger. "What else do you have planned? Is there anything else you're scheming up?"

"Alex, stop," she nervously laughed as she wheeled herself to the French doors. "Really, you make me sound so devious."

"Sometimes you are."

"What does that mean?"

"It means that I think . . . I think you've become rather self-centered." Okay, I thought as I walked up behind her. Go ahead. Say what you've been thinking. She needs to hear this. "You have this island. You have this fabulous house. And you control it all. This is your little mini-empire. You make all the decisions as if there was no one else around." I hesitated, then added, "When I came here, I knew I'd be your employee but I thought we'd be working together. I thought it would be more of a joint effort."

"Are we having a fight?"

"Let's just say my pent-up frustrations are erupting, so I might as well get it all off my chest." I caught my breath, then said, "You've always been like this. Done things as you saw fit, I mean. As a kid you were like that. Only now, out here where you own everything, you're even more so. You have the money to back it up."

"Oh, stop," she sharply demanded over her shoulder. "That's such an ugly thing to say."

I pushed on. "Maddy, you need to get off the island every now and then. It'd do you a hell of a lot of good. It'd remind you that other people exist and that you can't always do things your way."

"I do just fine here, thank you."

I paced toward the Tiffany dome, suddenly seized by a realization that frightened as much as worried me. It was really quite clear, actually. I didn't know why I hadn't seen it earlier.

I turned, called to her as she sat motionless before the open doors, "You know, you've gotten to be an awful lot like her."

"Who?"

"Loretta."

Maddy braced herself on the sides of her chair, twisted around, and demanded, "What the hell does that mean?"

"Both of you have defined the limits of your world—the physical boundaries, I mean—and you won't go beyond them. Loretta wouldn't leave her yard except to go to the library, where she could escape into fiction. And you—you won't leave this island except via the dreamy state of hypnosis."

"That's not true!"

But I knew it was. Absolutely so. By the way she bit back, I could see I'd hit a sensitive nerve of truth.

I said, "Then how come every time I suggest taking a trip you ignore me or change the subject? We both think that something traumatic happened to Loretta when she was young and—"

"Alex, this is nonsense. Stop it."

"No, listen. Something probably happened to Loretta when she was young, a teenager or whatever. Something that was quite shocking to her. And after that she withdrew from the world because she felt so vulnerable. Kept withdrawing until she'd hardly go out because the world was this big huge place where anything could happen." I softened my tone, dared to venture, "And that's what's happening to you, Maddy. Something horrible struck you—literally—out there, and now you've retreated to this island. You say you triumphed over your tragedy because you sued and got all those millions. But you haven't triumphed, Maddy, you're just slowly being defeated. All those dollars have just let you build a glorious prison to keep—"

"What do you want me to say—you're right?" she snapped. "Don't you get it? I've been blind for almost thirty years and now I'm stuck in a fucking wheelchair, and since the world won't accommodate me, I've made my own world here. One where I know every nook and crevice, one that I can navigate relatively on my own. And one that won't hurt me. So technically, clinically, maybe I am agoraphobic. But how am I supposed not to be?"

"Maddy, I—"

"I mean, what good has the great wide world done for me?" She grabbed the wheels of her chair and spun herself in a flash. "I'm going out for some fresh air."

Well, I'd certainly stirred things up, that much was obvious, and as she went whooshing past me, I said, "Maddy, wait."

"I need to be alone."

"But it's late. And it's pitch-black out there."

"Alex, you don't understand, do you? My world's always pitch-black," she said, and laughed condescendingly as she reached the back wall, groped for the door that would lead to the rear of the attic and the elevator.

There was nothing I could say, of course, for I'd already said it all wrong and Maddy had stuffed it right back in my mouth. I stood there, my anger spent, my head now confused, and watched as my sister found the door and disappeared. I shook my head, knowing I had to let her go, couldn't go after her.

I went to the tray and poured myself some more wine, and from the back of the house I heard the hum of the elevator. Maddy would descend to the first floor, head outside, and then send herself around her island, whooshing and whizzing along, that wandish cane scraping in front of her. Well, maybe that's what she needed. A little night air. Space and freedom to ponder our heated conversation.

Perhaps I could have said it better, more simply, but I was right on this one, I knew as I sipped my wine, and she most certainly needed to hear it. Maybe this jolt would be enough to get her out of here, off the island and away from the house, after all this Loretta business was concluded. Still, I didn't feel particularly good about any of it. And stepping out onto the balcony and into the dark night, I didn't like the idea of her being out there. I knew it was supposed to be safe, this private island, but it was just so . . . so dark. And quiet, too.

I leaned on the railing, peered over and searched for my sister. Maybe it was my time in Chicago and Minneapolis. A holdover from the big cities. Maybe that was where this paranoid sense was coming from. Perhaps I was sensing something else. I didn't know. But it made me nervous, the idea of a woman, let alone a physically impaired woman, out at night, off in the woods, all by herself.

Chapter 29

An hour later I was lying in bed reading, and though I should have been way beyond tired, I was growing more and more awake with each moment. Maddy wasn't back. I'd been listening for the sound of her return, hoping to hear her in the entry downstairs or perhaps closing her bedroom door. But all was absolutely still. It was probably nothing. More than likely she was just off spinning along one of the many paths or perhaps perched on some lookout, her face pointed into the night breeze. But it made me nervous. Her being out there.

Then again, I thought as I folded shut my book, maybe Maddy had returned and I just hadn't heard her; my hearing was by no means as sharp as hers. I threw back the covers, jumped out, and went to the door in my underwear. Just as I was opening it, a large dark face appeared on the other side, and I jumped back a half step.

"Jesus, Alfred," I muttered.

"Get some clothes on."

"What?"

"Maddy called. There's someone on the island."

It took a moment for it to sink in. I didn't quite grasp his words, the meaning of what he was saying. Someone on the island? I stared into his large, stern face and was taken aback by the obvious tension I saw. Instinctively, my heart took off in a bolt.

"Where's my sister?" I demanded.

He nodded past me and toward the black night beyond the windows. "Out there."

Another figure was now entering the second-floor hall, and I saw Solange hurrying around the open staircase, a long knife in hand. Oh, shit. There wasn't a bunch of happy campers out in the woods. Nor a group of boaters who'd landed on the island and were partying madly on one of the far beaches. There was trouble, and my sister was apparently caught up in the midst of it.

I tore across the room and grabbed a pair of jeans, tugged them on, then pulled a blue T-shirt over my head. Slipping my bare feet into loafers, I was ready and dashed out of the room and into the hall. Not wasting a moment, Alfred led the way around the open stairs and down, with Solange and me right behind him.

"Did she call from her wheelchair or . . . or the boathouse or what?" I asked.

"Her wheelchair."

"When?"

"Not more than a minute or two ago."

"Are the dogs with her?" I asked, hoping for once that her humongous wolfhounds would do something more than kill deer.

"I don't know."

"What do you mean? What did she say?"

Racing after me and clutching the knife, Solange replied, "I answered the phone and—"

"I didn't even hear it," I said.

"At night it just rings in our room. And so I answered it, and it was Maddy. She was whispering, and she said to come quick. There was someone out there. She's just past the point. She . . . she . . ."

"What?" I pressed when we reached the main floor. "What happened? What did she say?"

"She said she flipped her chair."

"Oh, dear God."

"And then she hung up."

This went beyond my worst fear, with my sister not simply off on her own, quite possibly hurt, but also lying prey for some vandal or thief. Perhaps a group of them. I should never have said all that to Maddy, should never have gotten her so riled up by comparing her to Loretta. And in any case, I should have stopped her. I should never have let her go flying off so angrily.

Solange handed the knife to her husband, said, "I have to stay here in case she calls again."

"Right. Just lock the doors."

That was no easy feat in a house this size; I knew there were some twenty-five rooms, nearly a hundred windows, and God knew how many ground-floor doors. Solange was going to have to be quick about it, lock up the whole place and hope that whoever was out there besides Maddy wasn't going to try to breach the house.

"If you're not back in twenty minutes," continued Solange, "I'll call the police."

By then it would be too late, I thought. Twenty minutes would be an eternity, and then it would be another eternity before the police could travel the ten miles from the mainland. Either this was going to be no problem, or we were in deep, deep shit. In any case, if Maddy had been hurt when her chair overturned, we might need a helicopter to whisk her to a hospital in Petoskey. I thought of calling the mainland right now but resisted, not wanting to beckon help unnecessarily.

"What about flashlights?" I said.

"Here."

Solange hurried over to the front-hall closet, pulled out a small and a large one, handed them to Alfred and me. She then presented the long knife to Alfred, and then the two of us were off. We threw open the front door and bounded across the gray planks of the veranda, down the tall carriage steps, and along the dirt drive carriages had once used. Alfred paused briefly, checked to make sure Solange was bolting the door, and I raced off, the beam of the flashlight pointing the way, and me wondering how much time we had, what shape my sister was in, how dangerous a situation this really was. I was nervous as hell, hoped to God I was jumping to all sorts of needless conclusions, but this scared the hell out of me, this odd incident that just happened to fall on the eve of Loretta's arrival.

The house was on the southernmost tip of the island, and the spot where we'd hoped to find my sister was on the northern quarter of this thirty-one-acre drop of land. I circled the rear of the house, left the huge white structure behind me, and headed for the paved path that led along the eastern shore, past the dock and boathouse, then up and past the tall point and down to the glen. How long would it take to get there? Five minutes at a run? A little more? Maddy might have headed off this way. Perhaps not. Maybe she'd headed around in the other direction, had circled around.

Heavy steps and breathing were gaining on me, and Alfred wisely advised, "Cut your light."

Yes, we didn't want to be so obvious, so blatant, and I switched off my flashlight. Immediately the night pounced upon us, and for a moment I was as sightless as my sister. Then, however, my eyes swelled, sucked in all there was to see. Bushes, all black. Tree trunks, steely gray. A sky, blackish blue. I sensed, then saw, the oil-black ribbon of the path leading on and on, and my feet trod effortlessly and smoothly.

His body strong and thick, Alfred ran by my side. Our pace was nearly the same. That was why I heard it. That noise. Off to Alfred's left. At first I wasn't sure. It sounded like a branch snapping, a large step. I glanced over as I charged on. I saw something. A whoosh of a body. Oh, Jesus. Then something broke from the other side, from the right, bursting out of the bushes and grabbing me by the arm. I hollered out, tried to shake off the large creature that had taken my elbow and forearm in its mouth.

"No!" I shouted at Ollie, the Irish wolfhound whose huge head nearly rose to my chest.

Just as quickly there was not one, but two of them. Fran bounded into the path ahead, playfully half turned, half ran. So this was what it was like, I thought, to be a deer and be run down by these two. Nothing more than a playful kill.

Alfred's booming voice commanded: "Maddy! Find Maddy!"

For the first time I could see that the dogs had in fact been trained. And for the first time I could see their worth. With the mention of my sister's name, Ollie paid me no further attention. The two of them were off, loping onward. Alfred and I pushed our pace, tried to keep up with the dogs, for it was obvious not simply that they understood the command but that they already knew where to find my sister.

We soon passed the pier, its white planks stretching far out into the black waters, and my huffing lungs ached. Struggling to keep up with the dogs, Alfred and I ran on, passing the white clapboard boathouse that looked like a garage suspended over water. Leaving the small harbor behind us, we rounded a bend, then climbed the hill that led to the tall point, a spit of land that not only jutted out into the lake but was the tallest spot on the island. A gust of wind from the north hit us when we reached the top, and I looked off to my right. A handful of bushes swirled in the wind, a pine swayed gently, and then there was a drop-off, a sandy cliff that collapsed onto a shore of rock. I was relieved that the dogs were leaping onward down the hill.

But she had crashed at the very bottom. As I came over the crest of the point, I faintly saw her wheelchair way down there, some seventy-five below, at the base of a corner and upside down. My heart squeezed into a tight knot when I saw the wheels of the overturned chair spinning like pinwheels in the dim light. And I understood. Maddy had come over the top of the tall point, then raced downward, but had somehow forgotten or missed the turn, somehow not sensed its presence until it was too late.

The dogs started howling, and I shouted, "Maddy!"

I flew down the path, streaking way ahead of Alfred, fearing, remembering the time I'd been called to Chicago. The bus. Maddy in intensive care. How long it had taken me to get down to the city. The wheelchair I now saw at the bottom of the hill floated like some horrible mirage, a nightmarish vision. There was no sign of my sister.

I switched on my flashlight, and again yelled, "Maddy!"

Just shy of the wheelchair I saw Fran and Ollie bound into the bushes. Seconds behind the two dogs, I was running so fast that I couldn't stop myself. I tried to come to a halt, skidded off the path, my feet sliding out from underneath. I scrambled up, pushed into the bushes, saw the huge dogs standing over a body, pawing at it, almost mauling it. Oh, God. I recognized Maddy's clothing—the black pants, the deep red top.

"Maddy!"

Her words rose sharply and wonderfully as she ordered, "Get these goddamned things off me!"

I dove into the bushes. "Are you all right?"

"Get the dogs!"

I started yelling, then, as I neared, started shoving and kicking at them, anything to get them off my sister, who was lying in a small opening. And then came Alfred, pushing right behind me. He shouted something, his voice like a cannon, and Fran and Ollie scurried aside.

"What happened?" I demanded as I dropped to my knees.

I scanned her body with my flashlight, searched for blood. Her face was smudged with dirt.

Maddy said, "I'm fine."

"But what happened?"

"I dropped a wheel off the path and it sank in the sand. I flipped right over. Really, I'm okay." She pointed down the hill. "But there's someone here. One person. A man, I think. I was trying to get my chair up when I heard him. That's when I called."

"Did he come after you?" I asked.

"He saw my chair and then he heard me. He must have. It was as if he was stalking me or something. I think he knew it was me, Alex. I think he called my name. He said something—I couldn't recognize his voice—so I crawled over here to hide."

My sister, ever the survivor, I thought, and said, "What about your legs?"

"They're okay. I checked them."

I ran my flashlight down and did a quick scan to see that neither of her paralyzed and unfeeling legs was twisted or bloodied. At a glance, all seemed satisfactory, though I surmised it would be best to get a doctor over here in the morning.

Suddenly the buzz of a motor cut through the night, and Maddy exclaimed, "That's him!"

Alfred shouted, "Come on!"

"Yes, go!" said Maddy.

We were off, the two of us, cutting back through the bushes, onto the path. The dogs at first jumped around as if this were some sort of great game, but then Alfred shouted another command. In a flash, they were tearing toward the noise, which most definitely was a powerboat being revved up.

Alfred and I once again ran down the path and through the
dark woods. We came to a small bend where the pavement
curved alongside the rocky shore, and up ahead we could hear
the dogs barking furiously. The engine noise burst into full
power, sharply cutting the night, and just as we rushed around
the corner I could see the cool white lines of a boat blasting off
from the island. The dogs were up to their chests in the water,
barking with great fury, and Alfred and I slowed, for it was
clearly hopeless. I studied the boat, squinted, and knew that
Maddy had been right, for there was just one figure out there
in the speeding craft and it was indeed that of a man.

So he was gone, I thought, my eyes staring at the foaming
wake that melted into the gray waters. He'd been chased off the
island, but I couldn't help but feel a horrible question begin to
build in my gut, couldn't help but wonder, would he be back
and if so, when?

Chapter 30

Maddy's chair wasn't really damaged, just a bit dinged up, and by the time the three of us returned to the house it was after midnight. My sister kept insisting she was unhurt; I insisted more strongly that she let herself be checked. Which, in the end, she did. Maddy allowed Solange to help her bathe and examine her legs for bruises or anything more serious, and fortunately it proved Maddy escaped from it all pretty much unscathed. Meanwhile, Alfred made another check of the island, didn't return for an hour, and when he finally did, reported that whoever had visited us must have been your typical prowler, the kind that was easily scared away. Nevertheless, it all kept spinning around in my head and it must have been three or four before I finally dropped into a fitful sleep.

The following day I slept until late morning. The house was oddly quiet, and lunch wasn't served by Solange; rather, Maddy sent me back to the kitchen where I found a tray of sandwiches under a film of plastic wrap. Iced tea, too, of course, which I located in the refrigerator along with the proverbial pile of lemons that my sister required for tang. Maddy said only that Solange was out for a walk, and so I gathered the food,

201

headed from the kitchen and through the back hall and past
the elevator. Next came the pantry, a long room with double
sinks, an entire wall of dishes, then the dining room with that
huge table that seated sixteen. Stepping through a set of double
doors, I passed through the screen porch with wicker up the
wazoo, and finally outside.

We had a late lunch on the veranda, a long affair with all
those columns, and we barely talked, my sister and I. As for
myself, I was tired, and I just sat there staring at the cloudy sky
and the choppy lake. It wasn't simply the incident last night or
my lack of sleep. All the channeling in that regression yesterday, retelling it all in concentrated form, reliving all the highs
and lows, had sucked up tons of energy. It was hard bringing
that much past information up to the surface of the present,
and my mind felt used and exploited.

Maddy, wearing a brown top and plain khaki pants, was
equally withdrawn, pensively so. I glanced at her as she slowly
ate a tomato sandwich, her head turned toward the lake as if
she were looking off in deep thought. I wondered if she was
thinking about the prowler or if she'd already dismissed the
affair. I wanted to know, too, what she thought of my trance
back to Loretta and those Chicago days, what she had gleaned
and then mulled over in her sleep and during the long morning. It would only come out, I knew, in due time. Her time. And
I suspected that wouldn't be until Loretta arrived.

Loretta's plane to the airport on the mainland was late, and
it was almost six when we headed out, passing the attached
icehouse, a two-story chamber at the rear of the house that had
once been packed with lake ice and sawdust and was now full of
lawn tools and long bamboo fishing rods. Meeting someone at
the dock was a ritual on the island, one of the few things you
could really do on this isolated bit of land, even though I was
dreading meeting the two, Loretta and Carol Marie. I followed
my sister, half trotted as she rolled herself along the rolling
asphalt path, which continued up a small dune of a hill, past a
bunch of birches, then down again. Off to the left I saw a small
old barn, weathered and tumbling, where a handful of horses
had once been kept. And then a chicken coop, white with green
trim, that reeked of poultry, the aroma still fresh, even though
there hadn't been any birds there for at least forty years.

"You're slow," called Maddy from up ahead, her thin arms

grabbing at the wheels and propelling her along and down the slope.

"I don't have wheels for legs."

"Oh, you poor kid."

I didn't say it, but she was slower than usual today, too. I'm sure it was the accident she'd had last night; she didn't say so specifically, but it had to have scared the hell out of her, flipping like that. And now I saw her veer off the path, one wheel sinking into the sandy soil. It was an error she corrected immediately and with great force, steering the wheelchair back onto the path with a quick, almost panicky jerk.

"How long are they going to be here?" I asked as I caught up with her at the bottom of the slope.

"Maybe just overnight. Maybe for a couple of days. I don't know. Don't worry. It shouldn't be too long."

"You've neglected to tell me and I've neglected to ask: Do you have a plan?"

"Somewhat."

She was off in a burst, quite purposely running from me and my inquiries. Whatever her idea was in all this, however she wanted to proceed, I thought as I trotted after her, I hoped to hell it worked. I hoped to hell no one would get hurt. A fearful knot in my gut told me that was wishful thinking, however, for this was not only deep trouble, but a still-festering wound that we were poking around in. There was still plenty of blood to be spilled.

Maddy reached the top of another ridge, where she paused, turning the side of her face to the lake as if she were listening to the waves. I couldn't help but note the concern on her face.

She asked, "Alex, there's a boat out there, right?"

"What?"

"I hear something. A boat, not too big, with a whiny engine."

I quickly scanned the lake, which stretched out like a freshwater ocean stirred to whitecaps, and searched for the boat I'd seen last night. There was nothing, however, only an endless vista of water that today reflected the steely-gray clouds.

"I don't see anything," I said.

"Over there," she said, pointing to the southeast. "I hear something. Wait—maybe that's just our boat. Yes, that's right."

I followed Maddy's arm, searched the lake, and finally saw it, a long white fiberglass craft speeding toward the island. Now that I could see it, I could barely hear the hum of its engines as it bounced over the waves.

"There it is," I said. "It'll be here in another five minutes or so."

Maddy rolled on, and I hurried after her, down the path, through the woods, past a glade, finally reaching the small harbor with its long white pier. Here in this protected cove, shielded to the north by the tall point, everything was calmer, the arching strip of sand rarely disturbed by crashing waves. Not long ago Maddy had purchased a sailboat, a fairly sizable one, white with green stripes, but she had yet to use it, and I wondered if it was just for decoration, anchored out some thirty feet. Or perhaps it was just for guests, who admittedly were exceedingly rare, for I doubted that Maddy herself would use it; she'd grown shy of water since the accident. As we neared the pier, Maddy slowed, then stopped. She could run a wheel of her chair off the path with no repercussions, but the dock, I knew, scared the hell out of her.

"Would you push me?" she asked.

I took hold of the back of her chair, and said, "Sure, but you know, you swim really well. I don't think you have anything to worry about. Your arms are so strong."

"Perhaps. But when I turned over last night, it took me a while to get my legs unstrapped. I don't know how much time I'd have if I went off the dock. I'm just afraid of going right to the bottom with my chair."

I hadn't thought of that, but the mere suggestion made my stomach roll with dread. She might be right but I wasn't going to let on.

"I doubt it, Maddy. You're a real Houdini, and you know it."

"Well, let's hope I never have to test that theory."

The boat came in, this huge white speedthing with Alfred at the helm, and I wondered if Maddy knew how macho the vessel looked. A cigarette boat that looked phallic from its thick stern to its thrusting bow. I watched as Alfred steered it through the waters, cutting the engines as he entered the harbor.

"Do you see Loretta?" Maddy anxiously asked. "She's there, isn't she?"

At first I couldn't tell. At first there was only a black face at the wheel. But then the boat turned and spewed its wake in a different direction, and I saw two pale figures huddled on a seat at the very back. One was dressed in a blue blouse and slacks, the other in a drab, baggy dress that was flapping in the wind.

"She's there," I replied. "Carol Marie is, too."

"Good." Maddy lightly touched her head. "How's my hair?"

I peered over her shoulder as I pushed her along the slatted boards of the pier. That long neck. Beautiful face shaded with the large sunglasses. And the short brown hair that had the appropriate wave. A movie star. Maddy could have been that, too.

"You always look great."

"Oh, stop."

I pushed her almost to the end of the dock. It was perfect timing, the two of us out there as the boat cruised in. Alfred made another turn, slowed the boat, began to bring it closer. Stepping over to help dock the craft, I let go of Maddy's chair, and as soon as I did, I saw my sister's hands go down and lock the brakes on each wheel.

It was about then that I also noticed Carol Marie nudging Loretta, who in turn looked across the water at Maddy. Immediately, Loretta stood, came to the side of the boat, not sure whether or not to believe it. Then her mouth opened, shouted nothing but silence.

Now seeing her more closely, I couldn't believe it, and keeping my voice low, I said, "My God, Maddy, she looks terrible."

"Oh, dear. How?"

"Drawn."

More than that I couldn't say because the boat was pulling alongside the dock now and I didn't want to be overheard. But Loretta looked like hell. She'd been in jail since that night, of course, and her face was even whiter. Chalky. Her hair hung flat and straight, totally so, but it looked as if it had grayed considerably, if that was possible, in the few weeks since I'd last seen her. She'd lost weight, easily ten pounds, perhaps more, and I wondered if she'd been eating at all. That was the reason her face looked so drawn, and certainly why her dress hung more sacklike than ever.

I went up and caught the rope that Alfred tossed, then tied

up the bow of the boat. As I headed to the stern, I greeted the two sisters.

"Hi, Carol Marie." And then, "Hi, Loretta."

Loretta paid me no attention, and before I could tie up the rear of the boat, she was scrambling out. She eagerly jumped onto the dock, took a couple of quick steps, then froze, staring in disbelief.

Maddy said, "Hello, Loretta."

Loretta didn't reply, didn't move.

Maddy reached out, extending her hand. "I'm glad you're here. I understand things have been rough."

That beckoning was all it took. Loretta charged the last few steps, dropped to her knees, and placed her head in Maddy's lap. She took my sister's hand in two of hers, clutched it and kissed it.

With her other hand, Maddy stroked Loretta's hair, said "Oh, you poor dear. You poor, poor dear. I'm so sorry."

It took nothing more. Loretta's back heaved upward. Next fell. She started shaking, even bucking, and at first there was silence, then there were a series of long, hideous sobs. Painful, mournful cries that seemed to come from her gut, and I watched as Loretta's fingers dug into Maddy's numb, unfeeling legs.

"Don't worry," cooed Maddy, still stroking her. "Everything will be all right. You'll see. You're here now."

Carol Marie, Alfred, and I looked on as Maddy received Loretta like a princess receiving a serf. But there it was, I thought, the relationship between therapist and patient physically acted out. This devotion was why Loretta had made what was for her those long, dangerous trips all the way into downtown Chicago. And this salvation was why she had made the arduous trip here to Madeline's island. Yes, my sister was full of wisdom and insights that she could bestow upon a client like a blessing.

"Loretta," asked my sister, now sounding very much like Dr. Phillips, "would you like to go up to my house now?"

Loretta's head, still bowed in Maddy's lap, moved up and down, a nod that Maddy read by touch.

"Good. Would you mind pushing me? I had an accident, you know, which was why I had to leave the office. I'm sorry I couldn't see you anymore. And I'm very sorry I never had the chance to say good-bye. That made me very sad. Do you un-derstand?"

I stood on the dock, the boat just to my side. The wind came up, swirled around. Of course Loretta understood. But would she accept it, Maddy's apology? Seconds ticked by. A seagull soared effortlessly past.

Loretta lifted her head, uttered, "Yes."

"Good." Maddy turned her head in my direction, com-manded, "Alex, would you help Carol Marie with her bags? And Alfred, please put the boat away for the night. We'll see you all up at the house." Maddy flicked off the brakes on the wheelchair. "Let's go, Loretta. Come on, get up now. You'll push me, won't you?"

Eagerly, with even a hint of a smile, Loretta burst to her feet, ran behind the chair, then turned Maddy and started wheeling her down the dock. She didn't stop there, either. Not at the end of the pier where the black asphalt path began. Maddy, who so seldom allowed anyone to wheel her, let Loretta push her on up the slight hill, into the woods, and off toward the house. As they disappeared into the forest, I saw Maddy reach back with one hand, place it gently over Loretta's.

Then from behind me, Carol Marie, who was still standing in the back of the large white boat, said, "I still don't think this is a good idea, playing around with Loretta like this. But it was the only way." She lifted up a single nylon suitcase. "Here."

I stared at her, that prissy face that had appeared pleasant and even pretty in the shopping mall but now looked bland and almost ugly, and I didn't know what to say. I had countless questions for her, notwithstanding a good amount of ill will due to the acrimonious way she'd treated me down in Chicago.

I took her luggage, lifted it from the boat, rose above all my thoughts, and said, "I beg your pardon?"

"Your sister made me do this, bring Loretta up here."

"Oh." I could have guessed as much. "Is that the only way she'd agree to post bail?"

"Well, that, too." As she climbed from the boat and onto the dock, Carol Marie went on, saying, "Dr. Phillips volun-teered to post it because she said she had to see Loretta before-hand."

"Before what?"

"Before we enter her plea. I don't know why. Everyone

knows Loretta's insane. Of all people, Dr. Phillips should know that."

Which meant Maddy, of course, was to be a professional witness, testifying that Loretta was criminally insane. I suddenly understood and felt ill at heart. Could all of this and all of Loretta and her pain and tragedy be so easily and systematically—not to mention legally—dismissed?

As I unfastened the ropes that tethered the boat to the dock, I asked, "Is that the angle your lawyers are taking?"

"What other choice do we have? If we can prove that Loretta's crazy—which with your sister's help, shouldn't be hard—the sentence shouldn't be too harsh."

"But that's presuming Loretta killed Helen, which I don't think Maddy is quite ready to believe." I hesitated, then added, "And I'm not sure I am, either."

"Yes, well . . ." Carol Marie looked down at the dock, shook her head, moaned, and said, "I just don't know what to believe anymore. This whole thing's so confusing, so terrible. You're right. I can't imagine her hurting anyone. But if she is innocent, why does she keep saying she's not? It just doesn't make any sense."

There was a roar as Alfred fired up the mighty engines of the boat and began pulling away. I picked up the lone piece of luggage; then the two of us started walking down the dock. When we'd nearly reached the shore, I heard a short bark and looked off to my right. With both dogs leashed, Solange was making her way down the path from the tall point.

Yeah, right, I said to myself. Maddy had earlier said Solange was out for a stroll, but what was this, a day-long walk? Anything but, I thought, for Solange had just completed the outer path around the edge of the entire island. And with the dogs in tow, rather than a pleasant outing, it was obvious that Solange's duties for the day included patrolling for any would-be prowlers.

Chapter 31

I wanted to ask Maddy about Solange and her scouting, but there was no opportunity, for Loretta never left my sister's side. Maddy indulged her completely, too, first showing her her room—the one straight at the top of the stairs—then waiting while she washed, and finally making sure Loretta ate half a sandwich. I realized this was all part of the process of getting Loretta to relax, and it was well after eight before we were all led up to the third floor and into that room of trances. And it was distinctly odd to be up in that vaulting space and not to be in the recliner. Not getting ready for another blast-off. I didn't like it. Maddy settled into her chair and readied herself for another trance, while Loretta took my space, the other black leather lounge chair, and did likewise. Which is why I felt so out of place. Carol Marie and I were seated back about ten feet in two hard wooden chairs, and I couldn't relax. Couldn't get comfortable. Carol Marie and I were the observers. The sideline spectators.

As I studied Loretta, I could tell at once that Maddy had hypnotized her before and that it had been a positive experience. It was quite obvious, really. Loretta not only seemed eager, she seemed to know exactly what to do. She rolled her neck from side to side and got rid of the last kinks. She wiggled and straightened out her arms. Crossed her feet, then uncrossed them. Then crossed them again. Next smoothed out her large, billowy dress.

"Okay, Loretta, I want you to get comfortable. You've had a very long day, but now the sun's setting, the long trip is over, and you can relax. Just stretch out there and take a couple of nice deep breaths," began my sister. "Breathe in and out, and just imagine, Loretta, all the tension flowing from your body. You can let go of it now just like the sun is letting go of the day. You're here on my island and in my home, and everything is fine and safe. With each breath, with each gentle beat of your heart, you feel the tension slipping away."

I'd never done this before, witnessed a trance overtaking someone, yet I could sense that Loretta wanted this, wanted trance. Next to me Carol Marie shifted and fidgeted, obviously uncomfortable with it. I glanced at her, saw that she was focused on the phenomenon that was now licking at the edges of her older sister's psyche. Just wait, I thought.

"I want you to look straight up, Loretta. In the beam above you is a small nail with a red head. Look at that nail above you and focus totally on it."

This was new, a different method from the eye-rolling one Maddy used with me. To each his own. I glanced upward and saw what I'd never noticed before. A small nail with a red head. It was hammered into a beam about eight feet directly over the recliner.

"Focus on that, Loretta, and let your whole body relax. Your breathing is becoming slower and deeper as you feel this wonderful, warm sense of relaxation seeping into your body. You can feel it enter your feet and start upward. As you stare at that nail, this wonderful sense of relaxation is wrapping around your feet, your ankles, and now starting up your legs. It's a very warm, pleasant sensation, and now it's moving higher, up to your waist, into your chest, as if you were pulling a nice, secure blanket over you. Breathe in . . . breathe out, taking the rhythm and tone of my voice with you.

"As you stare up at the nail, you feel your eyes grow heavy. Go ahead, let them close. Let that warm relaxation move up your neck, across your face, and over your eyes. It feels good to relax like this. Just let the tension go. Let it fly out of your body.

You don't need it; you don't want it. Are your eyes closed now, Loretta?"

From behind I could see Loretta's head move up and down. Maddy, of course, could not. Which might have been part of her plan, her way of coaxing the silent Loretta into speech.

"Have they closed, Loretta? If you're nodding, I can't see you. Will you help me? I have no sight. If you've closed your eyes, it's all right to say yes."

Ten or fifteen seconds ticked by. Would Loretta bite?

"Loretta," said Maddy, "you don't have to worry. You're entering a state of hypnosis, but you don't have to say, and you won't say, anything that you don't want to. If you've closed your eyes, Loretta, it's perfectly safe and all right to say yes."

"Yes."

"Good. Breathe in . . . breathe out . . . Just let that warm, wonderful sense of relaxation seep across your shoulders, down your arms, into your hands." Maddy's voice continued, soft and smooth, yet firm. "All the tension is slipping from your body and all the fear is flying away as you fall deep, deep, deep into hypnosis. Imagine that you're lying on some grass. The sun is shining warmly upon you. You don't have a care in the world. You feel drowsy, maybe. All your muscles are relaxed and loose and you feel extremely comfortable. You're a very good hypnotic subject, Loretta, and you know how to go deep into hypnosis.

"Now I want you to imagine yourself standing up, Loretta. You get up from the grass and stand there. And before you are ten steps. At the bottom of the steps is a garden. When you reach the garden, you'll be in a deep trance. Take the first step. *One*. And breathe," chanted Maddy in a slow, deep voice. "Let the air come in, slip out. *Two*. You're walking down the steps, and with each step you take, you breathe in deeply and let it out. *Three*. The garden below is beautiful and you can't wait to get down there. *Four*. It's almost like you're floating down the steps. *Five*. Drifting deeper and deeper into a more pleasant state. *Six*. This is your private garden, Loretta. It's beautiful and filled with flowers. *Seven*. You're going down the steps, and you feel more and more safe. More and more sure about yourself. More and more relaxed." Maddy let a few long seconds slip by, then said with a measure of strong force, "*Eight*. You're only two steps from the bottom. You can smell the flowers now.

Breathe in. Smell them? Good. Of course you do. *Nine*. And just one more step and you'll be in a wonderful place. A safe place. A haven. Your haven. And *ten*. You're down in your own private garden, Loretta. Before you are some flowers. What color are they?"

"Red."

"And what kind are they?"

"Roses."

"Good."

If I wasn't hypnotized, if I wasn't right down there in that garden alongside Loretta, then I very nearly was, for the air smelled sweeter and the world felt less tense, even more colorful. I was truly mesmerized by Maddy's chorus, felt as if a trance had come over me as I watched my sister bewitch Loretta. Everything was gone. All that mattered, all that I could see and understand, was these two women, Maddy and Loretta, who lay before me.

"Loretta, I'd like to ask you some questions. Would that be okay?"

Loretta started once, stopped, started again, her voice slow and mumbled, and finally said, "What . . . what kind of questions?"

"I want to ask you questions that will help you and the people you love. Would that be all right?"

Not one to be tricked, in a deep, low voice, Loretta repeated, "What kind of questions?"

"Questions about the night Helen was murdered."

"You want to steal something from me, don't you?"

"No, I don't want to take anything that you don't want to give me, Loretta." Very softly, Maddy said, "I just want to ask you a few questions. Would that be all right?"

"Maybe."

"Helen was killed and—"

"Blood. Red blood like the roses in my garden."

"Yes, I understand she was stabbed. How did that make you feel, Loretta?"

"I'm glad she's dead."

"Did you stab her?" asked Maddy, directly.

"I hate Helen."

"Did you take the knife and stab Helen?"

Loretta twisted. Mumbled. Struggled with the words, finally said, "I told the police I did it."

"I see." Maddy twisted course, backed up a bit, and asked, "Before Helen was killed, you were in the woods. It was dark. It was night. Were you with anyone?"

"Ray."

"And what were you doing?"

"Fucking." Loretta giggled. "Oh, but don't think badly of me. I only did it for Billy."

"What do you mean?"

"I mean, sex calms people."

"And it made you calm?"

"No, it made him calm."

"Go on, Loretta. It's okay to reveal this. It will help me help Ray. He needs help, doesn't he?"

"His little girl was killed and Ray is very sad."

"I know. It's been terrible for him." Voice soothing, calm, Maddy asked, "Was that the first time you had sex with Ray?"

"No."

"When was the first time?"

"Um. Um. A couple of years ago."

Maddy asked, "Did he attack you? Did he make you have sex with him that first time?"

Loretta laughed. "No. I made him have sex with me. Maybe I raped him."

"How did you do that?"

"He was in the woods across the street. He was staring at the house, hunting for Billy. He wanted to hurt Billy. So I went out and crossed the yard. I went right up to him and talked to him. He didn't want me there, but then I got close. And I touched him there, you know. His weenie. I kept touching it through his pants." She giggled like a naughty girl. "And then it wasn't so weenie anymore. I unzipped him. And . . . and . . . then afterward he left."

"Did you have sex often after that?"

"Ah, pretty often. I had to protect Billy."

"What do you mean?"

"Like I said, sex calms people. So whenever Ray felt angry about what happened to his little girl, he came to see me. And then Ray went away."

"And then Billy was safe?"

"Exactly. Ray thought about me and sex and not about Billy."

Maddy said, "Did Helen know about this?"

"She was very, very angry when she found out. She went after Ray. She chased him in the woods."

"With a knife?"

"Yes. With a knife."

That, I thought, would have been when I'd first arrived. I'd heard the scream, gone running. I'd thought someone had been attacking Loretta, but that hadn't been the case. Ray and Loretta must have been in the woods, having sex. Helen must have spied them, and next she went after Ray, knife in hand. Which is why Helen hadn't reported it. She'd been the attacker.

"Tell me, Loretta, you were in the woods with Ray the night Helen was murdered."

"We were doing it because Ray was very upset. He'd heard Billy was back in town, so I took him in my arms, told him not to worry, but . . ."

"But?"

"But then we heard something. Ray got up. We saw him."

"Who?"

"Ray thought it was Billy."

"What did he do, Loretta?"

"Ray got very upset. He went after him. I tried to keep Ray, to hold him, but I couldn't."

Only it wasn't Billy out there in the woods. I knew the rest. Even as Loretta recounted it, I understood what had happened. Ray hadn't heard Billy, he'd heard me. Then he must have seen me creeping across the front yard, sneaking around Loretta's house. He must have thought this was his chance to get Billy, but he came charging after me instead. Jumped me. Nearly strangled me.

"But that wasn't Billy that Ray attacked, was it?" asked Maddy.

"At first I thought it was, too. I thought he was going after my brother. So I threw on my dress. I ran. But Ray was already there. By the time I reached the road, Ray had already jumped him by the house. He was killing him. And then I saw who it was."

"Alex?"

"Yes, your brother. I'm sorry, really I am. I thought it was my brother but it was yours. I did what I could, really I did!"

"I know," said Maddy. "And you did something wonderful. You probably saved his life."

"I'm sorry! I'm sorry!"

"No, Loretta. There's nothing to worry about. Alex is alive and fine. You did everything right. You saved him." Maddy gently said, "Tell me what happened next."

"Ray dropped him. Dropped Alex. He realized who it was. I thought Alex was dead. But he wasn't. Ray and I bent down, and Alex was breathing. Then I heard a scream. I looked up and saw someone standing there at the back of the house. She screamed."

"Helen?"

"Yes, it was Helen. She saw Ray."

"What happened next, Loretta?"

"Helen ran back into the house. I chased after her. I knew she was going to get the knife. I knew it. So I ran after her. I chased her around the back of the house. Across the patio. Through the back door. She was in the kitchen screaming she was going to kill him. 'I'm going to kill him! I'm going to kill him! I'm going to kill him!' "

"Why would she want to kill Ray?"

"I said, 'No!' " continued Loretta. "I said, 'No!' "

"And then what did you do?"

"I ran into the kitchen. We started fighting. Helen screamed and pushed me away. She shoved me against the counter. And then she ran into the living room. She was going to go out the front. I chased after her. She couldn't kill Ray. Ray was a sad man. She couldn't kill him. I wouldn't let her."

"You chased after her, and then what happened?"

"Oh, God!"

"It's all right, Loretta. It's over. You can tell me."

"I ran after her. She was rushing through the living room. I grabbed her by the sleeve. She pulled, and then she started to turn on me with the knife. So . . . so I pushed her! And then . . . then . . . "

Very calmly, Maddy said, "And then she fell?"

"Yes, Helen fell."

"Did she cut herself?"

"No."

"But something bad happened?"

"Yes. She hit the edge of the coffee table. Her head. It just cracked on it. Oh, God. Helen fell and hit her head!" Loretta started crying. "And she never woke up again."

"Where was the knife?"

Nothing.

"Loretta, where was the knife?"

"Over there, on the floor. By the chair."

"Did you pick it up and stab her?"

"No. I mean . . . I mean . . ."

"Was she dead?" asked Maddy. "Loretta, tell me, was Helen dead after she hit her head?"

"No!"

"You saw her lying there, and what did you do?"

Loretta was sobbing now. She'd raised herself forward in her chair. Still in a trance, she doubled over and buried her face in her hands.

"I didn't know what to do! I didn't!" she exclaimed. "There were two people. Alex and Helen. Both of them were like dead. What a mess! What trouble!"

"But neither of them was dead, were they? So tell me, Loretta, what did you do next?"

"At first I . . ."

"Go on."

Loretta shook her head furiously. "No!"

"What did you do next, Loretta?" pressed Maddy.

"I . . . I called . . ."

Bent over, her head pressed all the way against her knees, Loretta was sobbing so hard that we couldn't understand. She tried to say something, but it made no sense. No sense until another voice cut in and clarified it all.

Completing her older sister's words, Carol Marie, her voice low and rather numb, said, "She called me."

Chapter 32

A deathly silence descended over us all. Carol Marie just sat there, face blank, staring at Loretta, who was sitting in the recliner and still sobbing. And my sister, my Maddy, was sitting forward, reaching for her wheelchair, for the trance was broken, at least for now.

Finally, Carol Marie cleared her throat, and continued, saying, "I was at home. The phone rang. It was Loretta. She said something had happened to Helen. And . . . and she said there was someone outside who might hurt her."

As Maddy pulled herself into her chair, I looked over at her, tried to discern what she thought of all this. I was distracted, though, by a sudden noise from outside. Someone yelling. It was Alfred, his deep voice booming through the encroaching night. I turned to the French doors, feared what might be happening, and then heard the dogs start to bark loudly.

"What's that? What's going on?" said Loretta, raising her tear-streaked face.

Maddy quickly replied, "Nothing." She turned to Carol Marie. "Did Loretta say who it was?"

"Well—"

The phone on the side of Maddy's wheelchair began to

screech, shattering the already tense situation. Maddy, who never received calls up here, was clearly startled; her body jolted at the first ring, and then she quickly fumbled for the phone, snatching the receiver out of its holster.

"Yes?" she snapped.

I thought about last night and the noise we'd just heard outside, and I knew what this meant. I knew what was going on. I just didn't know how it was to be handled.

"I see," continued Maddy into the phone. "All right. Then you know what to do."

All three of us—Loretta, Carol Marie, and I—were staring at my sister, and as soon as she hung up, Loretta jumped to her feet.

"What's going on?" she demanded, and then hurried to the balcony doors. "What were those dogs barking at?"

Maddy turned her chair around, and said, "It's nothing for you to worry about, Loretta. I have several people working for me, and everything's under control."

"Is someone here?"

"Let's just finish up here and we'll go out and see, all right?"

Loretta, though, would not be so easily calmed. She rushed over to Maddy, stood right in front of her. I was behind my sister, and I studied Loretta's heated, blood-red face, which frightened me nearly as much as what might be going on outside.

"Is it him? Is he here?"

Carol Marie blurted, "Loretta, please . . ."

"Shut up!" Loretta leaned forward, pressed down on the arms of my sister's wheelchair. "Tell me, it's him, isn't it?"

A sharp gunblast from outside cracked the evening. Just a single shot that silenced us all, and for a long, awkward moment none of us moved.

"Oh, God, no," muttered Loretta. "They won't hurt him, will they? They won't shoot him?"

My sister, her voice strained, said, "It's all right. No one's going to be hurt."

I could see it all, the tension and the fear, about to burst within Loretta, and I stood and protectively approached my sister from behind. God knew what Loretta was capable of.

I said, "Loretta, why don't we—"

"No!" she shrieked.

She leaned forward and in one great heave shoved my sister's wheelchair backward. Maddy cried out as she was sent hurling and plowing into me. I tried to catch her, but the chair came with such force and speed that it hit my right foot and tipped. All at once I was lunging to the side, trying to catch my sister as she was dumped over. But it was to little avail, and the two of us fell in a tangled mess onto the floor.

As Loretta lunged for the door beneath the dome, Carol Marie screamed, "Loretta!"

Carol Marie tried to grab her as well, but Loretta elbowed her and sent her stumbling back.

"No, I won't let them hurt him!" shouted Loretta.

She threw open the door, bolted out and down the stairs. I scrambled to my feet, reached for my sister.

"Stop her, Alex!" she shouted. "I'm fine. Just stop her!"

I rushed across the room, through the doorway, and to the top of the circular stairwell. Loretta was almost down to the second floor, her huge dress billowing like a parachute as she charged downward. As if she were possessed, she screamed and shrieked as she ran, and I hung on to the oak banister, took the steps two at a time. I circled around, rushing after her, reaching the second floor just as she neared the first, then bounding down the last steps as she tore across the entry and out the front door. I was just seconds behind her, just a few mere steps, but when I hurled open the front screen door and then leaped out onto the veranda, there was nothing but the first darkness of the night. I jumped off the porch, onto the ground, hurried out to a clump of lilac bushes. Behind me I thought I heard a door. She wasn't sneaking back into the house, was she? No. There. Out in the woods. I could hear her now. Hear Loretta as she rushed into the forest and into the heart of the island.

Chapter 33

I charged forward and toward the old barn, passing from the lawn and into the woods. Then, however, everything was oddly and horribly still. I stopped, scanned the trees. The light was very faint, but up ahead I could make out the old barn and chicken coop, which stood in the middle of a clearing. If Loretta was out here I'd certainly be able to see her, but I couldn't, which meant only one thing. She'd tricked me; she must have somehow dashed back to the house.

I spun around and took off. As I ran up the old carriage drive and toward the looming white structure, a porch light went on and Maddy and Carol Marie emerged from the front door.

"Is that you, Alex?" demanded Maddy. "Where is she?"

"I don't know what in the hell happened," I began. "She just disappeared. She didn't come back in the house, did she?"

"No, she couldn't have. I'd have heard her."

"Oh, no," moaned Carol Marie. And then she stepped to the edge of the porch and shouted, "Loretta! Loretta, where are you?"

Another gun blast burst the night, this time followed by a

chorus of barking. It came from the harbor or perhaps the tall point.

"Dear Lord!" exclaimed Maddy.

She spun her chair as quickly and neatly as a tank, leaned over and lowered the wand thing down to the ground. Then with one big thrust she sent her wheelchair racing toward the rear of the porch and down the ramp. Carol Marie wasted no time in following, and then the three of us were rushing away from the house and down the path toward the harbor. I trotted alongside Maddy and, as we neared the grove of birches, noted that she wasn't going to make a corner. I leaned over, said nothing, jerked her back on course. Carol Marie jogged just behind us, her breathing growing more strained with each moment.

With the black sky spreading out above us, we followed the racket of the dogs. Minutes later we came over a small hill and reached the dock, where a light was burning from a single pole. Just twenty feet away, standing near some heavy brush, I saw Alfred and Solange struggling to hold the dogs, who were jumping and leaping as if they had a rabbit or fox cornered in the bushes.

"Maddy," I said, "they've got someone trapped in the woods."

"Oh, God."

With the dogs shattering the night with their hysterical barking, we raced along, and I came up behind Maddy's chair and started pushing. As we neared, I could see Fran and Ollie struggling to break loose and I could make out a revolver in Alfred's hand, which he had aimed carefully toward a large bush.

"Who fired?" demanded Maddy.

"I did, not to hurt, just to warn," replied Alfred.

"Good."

Carol Marie nervously asked, "It's not Loretta, is it?"

"No, it's a man," said Solange, struggling to hold one of the dogs. "I spotted him on the north part of the island and we chased him here. He has no weapon."

"I knew he'd come back," mused my sister. "Get the dogs away."

Alfred's voice blasted: "Back!"

Alfred and Solange struggled with the huge creatures, pulling and yanking them by the collars. When they were silenced and out of the way, Maddy started wheeling herself forward; I took a step after her, and she quickly held out a hand for me and everyone else to stay put. Rolling herself off the path, Maddy continued across the dirt and up to the edge of the thick bushes.

Into the mass of dark leaves, she called, "There's no need to worry; you won't be hurt. This is Maddy Phillips. Would you come out, please?"

From within the tangle of branches, there was faint movement, and Maddy bowed her head, concentrated on what she was sensing.

"You're perfectly safe," continued Maddy. "I can tell by your step that it's not Ray, which means it's probably you, Billy. Am I right?"

At once, Carol Marie gasped, "Oh, God!" She rushed forward, charged right up behind Maddy. "Billy? Billy, is that you? Are you all right?"

I saw a figure dart past a branch, heard quick steps, and the dogs went wild all over again. Solange and Alfred jerked on their collars, shouted at them, pulled them back under control.

A voice from the darkness shyly called, "Carol Marie?"

She demanded, "Billy, what the hell are you doing here?"

As he emerged from the brush, Carol Marie grabbed him, pulled him out, and gave him a hug. Just as quickly, she pushed him away and visually checked him.

"You're not hurt, are you?" she asked. "You're not shot or anything?"

"No, I'm . . . I'm fine."

From nearby, my sister said, "Hello, Billy. I'm Maddy Phillips. I really didn't expect you. What did you do, steal a boat? Maybe a car as well?"

"Something like that."

"You shouldn't be here. You're just complicating things." Carol Marie nervously asked, "But where's Loretta? She's somewhere out here."

Maddy said, "Alfred, Billy's fine with us."

"But—"

"No, he's fine, really. He won't cause any problems. We do need to find Loretta, though. Would you and Solange check back by the barn? Just be gentle. And please put away your pistol. She's very frightened already."

"We'll find her," confidently replied Solange.

Taking the dogs, the two of them hurried on, and I turned, studied Billy. He stood there in the dim light, looking tall and scruffy, his clothes filthy, his hair probably unwashed. I doubted if he'd bathed since I'd last seen him.

"We should scatter," suggested Carol Marie, obviously desperate. "We've got to find Loretta before anything happens."

"Absolutely," said my sister. "But first there's something I have to ask Billy."

"What?" shouted Carol Marie. "You can't be serious. Loretta's running around half out of her mind."

"There's something I don't quite understand. Something I need to know so I can help Loretta." She looked up at him, asked, "Billy, how much had you been drinking the night Ray Preston's daughter was killed?"

"I can't believe it!" said Carol Marie.

"Well, how much, Billy?" repeated Maddy.

He pulled away, stood there in the dark in those awful, reeking clothes. Khakis that were streaked with dirt. A tattered yellow shirt. I could almost see him trembling. Or was it merely his clothes flapping in the breeze?

"So you were pretty drunk, Billy, right?" pressed Maddy. "Aren't you getting tired of not telling what happened that night, Billy? Come on, now. We haven't much time. Helen's dead. It doesn't make any difference."

His anger burst, and he blurted, "Sure, I was shit-faced. I had a lot of beers. I don't know how many. I lost count."

"God, we can't get into this right now," said Carol Marie. "We have to find Loretta."

"Of course we do," agreed Maddy. "But for Loretta's sake there's something I have to find out."

Carol Marie shook her head. "Well, it wasn't what you think!"

"No, I suspect it wasn't," said Maddy. "Billy, the police found you behind the wheel of the car, didn't they? So was it you who ran the red light or not?"

"Go ahead, you might as well tell her, Billy," said Carol Marie. "It's about time someone knew the truth."

I noted how Billy looked at his sister. How their eyes met and held in the night. And then he broke his silence.

"I wasn't driving," he said flatly. "She picked me up. Helen did. She came down to work and I got in the passenger side."

"All right, so you got in the car," said Maddy. "I imagine that Helen was quite mad when you got in. She probably smelled the booze on your breath. And I'm sure she was mad because she was worried about the business. Did she start yelling at you?"

"Yes."

Carol Marie blurted, "But—"

"Don't worry, we'll find Loretta. For her sake, this is just as important," countered my sister. "Now Billy, what did you do?"

"I . . . I . . ."

"You said nothing? You sat there and let her yell at you?"

"Yes."

Carol Marie broke in, shouting, "That bitch was always riding Billy. Always telling him he was no good. Telling him he should be more like Daddy."

Maddy asked the stereotypical lead shrink question. The one that was like picking at a scab. The one that was really more antagonistic than it was sympathetic. Maddy the clinical psychologist asked the question that she'd probably asked a hundred people a thousand times.

She queried, "And how did that make you feel, Carol Marie?"

"Pissed as hell. Billy's my twin brother!"

"Yes, he is. And attacking him was almost like attacking you, wasn't it?"

"Well, of course."

"But I imagine you're a stronger sort than Billy. Maybe you have a little bit more armor."

Defensively, Carol Marie said, "Billy's an artist. Did you know that? He writes. He's a beautiful poet."

"I'm sure he is," Maddy said. "I imagine Helen went into a tirade. I imagine she was giving you a lecture, telling you that you were a no-good drunk. Or something like that."

Billy bowed his head, let the night breeze wash over him. "Something like 'You son-of-a-bitch! You lazy bastard!' And then she said something like it was obvious I wasn't her true son. I was too stupid for that."

"And she was yelling at you when she missed the turnoff, right? You went straight up Edens Expressway instead of turning on the Northwest. And that's how you ended up in Northfield?"

My stomach began to tighten, to fold in on itself. Billy had told me the truth earlier. He'd explained what had happened, only I'd jumped to the wrong conclusion. Back in that church basement he'd looked right at me and told me he hadn't been the one who'd gone racing through the red light. I'd thought Billy meant it had been Ray instead. But he'd really meant Helen had been driving, hadn't he?

Maddy said, "You see, Billy, Alex told me all about your conversation in Evanston. He told me all about a conversation he had with your stepmother, Helen, too. And there are a couple of things I don't quite understand."

Billy twisted away, walked a few steps up the path. He stood there, staring into the black woods, and his shoulders started to shake.

Right at Maddy's side, Carol Marie blurted, "Billy wasn't driving, for God's sake!"

"No, of course not." Maddy coaxed, "She was driving and yelling at him. It wasn't the other way around, as she claimed."

He stood there, nodding. "She missed the freeway turnoff because she was shouting and I had my eyes closed," Billy quietly confessed. "She was going on and on. She was hysterical."

"So you went straight up Edens, and she got off at the Northfield exit. You crossed back over the freeway and headed west, toward your home, and—"

"And she started yelling at me again. She said I was a slob and a bum. I started yelling back, you know," said Billy, his voice calm as he stood looking into the woods. "She was such a bitch. I always hated her. She never tried to be a mother, not a real one. She was too uptight. She was a cleaning lady, nothing more. I told her that, and that made her really explode. We were in the car, shouting at each other as loudly as we could. Turned toward each other, you know. Cursing and shouting. And then I looked up. There was this car pulling out. I screamed and Helen slammed on the brakes. But it was too late. We just went plowing right into that car, right into the side of it."

"But the police found you behind the wheel, right?" asked Maddy.

"Right."

I heard Maddy take a deep breath. I wondered if she were going into a light trance. Or perhaps she already had. Maybe she was under and she was pulling up all the bits and pieces I'd fed to her. Putting all the words and scenes back together. Making a picture out of it, one that she could study here and now.

"Helen told Alex," began my sister, "that the car had come from the left and that you'd hit on the passenger side. But then she said she ran around the back of her car, saw that little girl, and she—Helen, I mean—claimed that she was so upset that she collapsed on the hood of Ray Preston's car. Is that what happened?"

"We hit them, you see. There was that horrible crash. And then there was all this blood on our windshield. Helen got out immediately. She went around and then she started screaming. Something like 'Oh, my God! My God!' Then she told me to back up the car, someone was hurt. So I slid over."

"You did just like she said? You backed up a few feet?" asked Maddy.

"Maybe ten."

"The police must have arrived fairly soon?"

"Exactly."

"And they found you behind the steering wheel."

Billy nodded. "They realized I was drunk. Which is when they arrested me. Helen was over there crying and sobbing. She was hysterical."

Unable to hide her disgust, Carol Marie burst in, shouting, "She did nothing! Nothing! Helen should have told the police right then that she'd been driving, but she didn't. She was so scared! She wasn't any kind of mother—she let them blame the whole thing on him! She let them take him away!"

From her chair, Maddy said, "I'm sorry, Billy."

He bent his head, began lightly crying, said, "Even if she'd told the police, they probably wouldn't have believed it."

He was right, I knew. They'd found Billy behind the wheel, so even if Helen had told them the truth they would have thought this was a mother trying to protect her son. A son who'd already lost his license for driving under the influence.

Maddy said, "But in any case Helen said nothing. She let

them take you to jail. And she was going to let them put you on trial as well." Her voice gentle, Maddy asked, "Billy, will you tell me one more thing?"

He stood there but didn't speak.

Maddy continued. "Were you already at your stepmother's house that night? I mean, the night when Alex was attacked, were you already there? Had you come to visit Helen, perhaps?"

"No."

Maddy couldn't hide her surprise. "No? Then where were you?"

He slowly turned around. Slowly raised his head. Slowly looked at his twin sister.

He said, "I was at her house."

"Were you there when Loretta called?" asked Maddy.

"Yes."

"Then what did you do after the call?"

"Nothing."

"Weren't you worried about Helen? Weren't you worried that she might be hurt?"

"Hell, no." He admitted, "I was thinking how wonderful it would be if Helen were dead."

"But what about Carol Marie? What did she do?"

Billy didn't respond. Didn't say a word.

Maddy said, "Ah, I see. She got in her car and went right over there, didn't she? Maybe she made you stay at her house. Maybe Loretta had told her Ray was over at Helen's, so perhaps Carol Marie wouldn't even let you come."

But before Billy could respond, before Carol Marie could confirm or negate, a voice boomed through the night. We all spun, saw a figure hovering at the very end of the dock.

"No, don't listen to either one of them!" shouted Loretta across the water. "I was there, I know the truth!"

Chapter 34

Oh, God, I thought, staring out there at Loretta, whose straight hair and loose clothing were flapping in the wind. I had been right. She had circled around, somehow gotten back into the house and, quite obviously, the kitchen, for I could see a metal instrument glinting in her hand.

"Maddy, she's at the end of the dock," I said, my voice hushed, "and she has a knife."

A horrible memory collided with a horrible premonition, and my stomach shrank into a fist. I'd been able to stop her from committing suicide once before, but she'd been just steps away. Now, however, Loretta was out there, the other side of the path and all the way at the end of the dock, nearly fifty feet away.

Carol Marie broke into a desperate run, charging toward the pier, calling, "Loretta, please!"

"Stop!" screamed Loretta.

"But—"

"Stop!"

Carol Marie halted at the very end of the dock.

Loretta flatly shouted, "I killed Helen."

Maddy wheeled herself up behind Carol Marie, and with a

firm but gentle voice, said, "We need to talk about that, Loretta, but not just now. First, I want to tell you something. Shall we go back to the house? You'll come with me, won't you?"

"No."

"Well, then, I'll have to tell you right here," continued Maddy, undaunted. "Actually, it's something that my brother, Alex, pointed out. You see, you and I have something in common."

I couldn't help but be surprised. I didn't understand why Maddy would want to get into this now, but then again, I wasn't a shrink. I only hoped Maddy's tactic worked to defuse the situation.

"I didn't see it before, but I do now, and I think there's something quite similar about the two of us. Perhaps that's why we've always gotten along, why the chemistry was right between us," said Maddy, as she maneuvered her chair onto the boards of the pier. "I really haven't left this island since I bought it. It's easy for me to be here—safe, you know. It's important for me to have a place, a world, where I know nothing bad can happen, and that's what this place is for me. It's the same for you. That's why you didn't like to leave your house, right?"

One hand clenching the knife, with the other Loretta made a fist and nervously demanded, "Why do you want to talk about that now? It's not important."

"It certainly is," countered my sister. "You see, something bad happened to me—my accident—and something bad happened to you, Loretta." Maddy gently but bluntly asked, "Loretta, you were raped when you were quite young, weren't you?"

She twisted to the side a bit, stood looking over the black waters of the harbor. In that long moment of silence, Billy and I came up behind Carol Marie, but then Maddy motioned for us to be still.

Finally Loretta muttered, "Who told you that?"

"At the car wash?"

"Yes, that's where it happened. Who told you?"

"I just pieced it together. You and I talked in my office, remember? I enjoyed talking with you and learning about your life," said Maddy, who wheeled four or five feet down the pier before stopping again. "How old were you?"

"Th-thirteen. I was down helping a couple of the guys. We

were drying cars." She hesitated, then added, "Daddy was up in the office."

"I'm sorry. I'm so sorry. Is that why you've been afraid to go out? Were you afraid it might happen again if you left the house?"

"Sort of. I . . . I was the bad girl."

"Oh, no, Loretta, you did nothing—"

Carol Marie broke in, saying, "Go ahead, Loretta, tell her."

Loretta spun, her eyes burning, it seemed, all the way down that long pier.

"I know," continued Carol Marie. "I went to the lawyer's because I was worried about Helen selling the house and you getting thrown out. I wanted to see Daddy's will again. But when I went there, Daddy's lawyer was gone—he retired last year—and so this time they gave me his whole file. That's when I found it, our mother's death certificate."

Next to me, Billy said, "What the hell are you talking about?"

Carol Marie glanced at her twin brother, looked away, said, "Billy, she died from cancer three weeks before we were born."

"What? That's impossible."

"Don't you get it? Don't you understand, Billy? Loretta's fourteen years older than we are. She was raped, Billy, and she had two children. Twins."

"Dear Jesus," gasped Billy.

"She's our mother."

"Yes, of course," softly said Maddy, her hands trembling as she moved her chair onward. "And that was why you stayed home, wasn't it, Loretta?"

Loretta stood there, face blank, eyes hollow, at the very end of that long dock. "I had to take care of them. I had to always be there. I was their mother. My father and Helen pretended the babies were theirs. Daddy said that I was a bad girl, that it was my fault. He said I asked for it, being down there with those guys all the time. He said I was bad, which was why we had to move out of the city and up to the suburbs where no one knew us. I was bad and so they took away my babies. But I was always there, always home for them."

"Yes, and you were the best mother you could be. You gave up your life for them." Continuing to move on, Maddy asked,

"So, Carol Marie, were you at the lawyer's that day Helen was killed?"

Carol Marie hesitated, then admitted, "I'd already been talking with the lawyer, trying to find a way to prevent Helen from selling the house. But . . . but, yes, that was the day I went there. That was when I found the death certificate."

"And when you got that call from Loretta saying that Helen was unconscious, you came over. I imagine you were filled with rage."

"Helen was never a mother to me," she said, sounding worn out. "She denied me. And she denied me my real mother."

Billy muttered, "What . . . what are you saying, Carol Marie?"

"So you arrived at the house," pressed Maddy, "and there was Helen lying on the floor. Maybe Loretta was outside seeing if Alex was all right. Ray was already gone by then. He was scared and so he left. But that's when you saw the knife, the one Helen had taken from the kitchen. It was lying on the floor, and—"

Loretta shouted, "No! That's not what happened!"

"You stabbed her, didn't you, Carol Marie?" demanded Maddy, now halfway to Loretta. "And then you went outside. You had blood on your hands. Loretta was there, and she was the good mother. She washed you off with the hose, scrubbed away all the blood. You just stood there, told her—"

That phrase that had haunted me was now demystified, and I repeated, "She said, 'It's yours.' She was talking about the house. She'd killed Helen so that Loretta would have the house."

"Yes, so that her real mother wouldn't be forced out of the family home. And then you and Loretta took Alex back to the hotel. That would explain why his shirt was damp—from your washed hands—and that would explain why his car was so oddly parked. Loretta, who doesn't really drive, must have driven his car back to the motel. Then Loretta went home, became worried about who the police would suspect, so—"

"No! No, that's not what happened!" shouted Loretta, raising her knife. "Leave Carol Marie alone! She did nothing! I'm the bad girl!"

"Loretta, you're not bad and you never were!" shouted

Maddy, who wheeled herself forward with a forceful lunge. "Something terrible was done to you. You're a victim of a terrible incident. Just—"

"No! Now . . . now you stay back, you just stay away, or I'll do like Lucretia!"

"Dear God, no!" begged Billy.

Carol Marie started rushing down the dock, screaming, "Loretta, please!"

Loretta lifted the tip of the long knife to her throat, cried, "Stop! All of you just stay where you are!"

Maddy came to a quick halt, begged, "Loretta, just . . . just calm down. We'll get everything sorted out. Don't worry. Take a nice deep breath." Maddy breathed in and out, in and out.

"Just don't come any closer." Loretta lowered the knife, looked skyward at the endless night. "It's all so messed up."

I followed Loretta's upward gaze, then said, "Loretta, what do you see up there?"

"Just millions and millions of stars and a few—" She gasped. "Oh, wait. Yes, there's some red swirling up there. A little yellow. Are those the Northern Lights? Sort of undulating, you know?"

"That's them," said Maddy. "Are they pretty?"

"Oh, yes. Very." Her head tilted skyward, Loretta moved to the very end of the pier, then turned and looked past my sister and at Carol Marie and Billy. "I know I was a good sister to both of you, but all I ever, ever wanted was to be a good mother." And then to her children, she recited, " 'For if I die, my honour lives in thee, / But if I live, thou liv'st in my defame.' "

We all knew what those words signified, what was about to happen. What poor Loretta intended to do. In wicked slow motion, I saw her raise the knife over her own chest, then clutch it in both hands. I started running. Maddy, who was so afraid of that dock, was racing forward, propelling herself as fast as possible, no thought about jetting off into the water.

"No!" screamed Maddy.

But Loretta was just too far away. With one hard thrust, I saw her plunge the knife through her chest and into her body, spearing her heart of pain. Loretta didn't scream, didn't utter a sound as she pushed the blade as deeply as it would go. She gazed down at the handle sticking out of her body, looked up at her offspring, and then fell backward and off the dock. And like a bird who'd never left the nest, she tumbled through the air, crashing into the dark, chilly waters.

Epilogue

None of what happened that night will ever be pleasant to recall, and I hope one day to bury it all deep enough in my memory that nothing, not even hypnosis, will be able to unearth it. In the meantime, I keep reliving it, humming the sequence of events like a bad tune lodged in my head.

After Loretta crashed into the water, I lunged forward and grabbed the back of my sister's wheelchair before she, too, went tumbling off the pier. I then dove in and retrieved Loretta, but there really wasn't anything to be done, no way we could have saved her. The autopsy, which later found no water in her lungs, confirmed that Loretta had been dead by the time she fell into the harbor.

God, what a mess. It was such chaos and pandemonium, all of us yelling and crying, and my sister, who couldn't see how hopeless it was, screaming that I plug the knife hole and try mouth-to-mouth. Instead, as the blood dripped between the boards of the dock and into the lake, I just knelt by Loretta, watched as her body grew paler and paler yet.

The authorities—I guess it was the sheriff—arrived about an hour later. Questions galore, all that kind of stuff. It was suicide, though. All of us provided eyewitness testimony of that. But it was my sister who also informed the sheriff that he'd better arrest Carol Marie for the murder of Helen Long. That prompted a series of phone calls to Chicago, and when the police boat finally left the island that night, it carried not only the body of Loretta, but also her two children, both of them handcuffed, for it seemed that the inquiry to Chicago had turned up Billy's drunk-driving file as well. The last I heard, both brother and sister were still in jail, their independent cases pending. Ray Preston supposedly had some hot lawyers trying to prove Billy guilty of vehicular manslaughter. Who knew what would happen, what supposed truth they'd finally arrive at. I really didn't care. Or rather, I did care but I was doing my best not to.

I hadn't ever seen Maddy cry so hard or for so long, and in the days following Loretta's death my sister plunged into a sea of despair that she still hasn't shaken. Once again I suggested a trip, to which Maddy snapped, "Where, Chicago?" So, needless to say, we still haven't gone anywhere. I'm still working on it, though. Chicago, doubtful. New York, perhaps. Or maybe somewhere totally different, like Russia. Somewhere like St. Petersburg.

I don't know. Loretta and her tragedy are a hard one. I'd been raised on heroes like the Lone Ranger and Zorro and the fundamental belief that goodness always prevails. Nothing in my adult life, however, had ever been so clear-cut, so black-and-white, and over the past few years I'd also come to question which is more powerful, fate or willpower. I haven't reached a conclusion on that, but I've only recently learned that no matter how hard you try, there are some things you just can't fix, some things like Loretta and her life.